BEAUTIFUL COLLISION

BEAUTIFUL COLLISION

GRAFFITI HEARTS SERIES

TORI ALVAREZ

ETERNAL DAYDREAMER PUBLISHING

Beautiful Collision
Copyright ©2019 Tori Alvarez

Cover Design by Tori Alvarez & Maria Ann Green

Editing by Jenn Woodcock

Ebook ISBN 978-1-7343363-0-6

Published by Eternal Daydreamer Publishing
San Antonio, Texas.

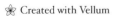 Created with Vellum

To my mom, I miss you every single day.
And to all the eternal dreamers out there.
Don't forget to work just as hard as you dream.

PROLOGUE

"I don't want to stay at Guela's again," I whine to my mother, refusing to get out of the car parked in front of my grandmother's house.

"This isn't a question, Toni. We are getting out, and you are spending the night here," my mother scolds me.

She exits the car, walking around and opening the door for me to get out. I still have my seatbelt on and sit stubbornly with my arms crossed at my chest. My mother is staring at me, waiting, but I refuse to budge.

"Get out of the damn car, Toni." My mother's patience is running thin.

"No!" I yell at her.

She bends down, reaching for the seatbelt button to release it. I squirm, trying to make it more difficult.

"I'm not staying here!" I begin yelling at the top of my lungs as only a six year old would.

She pulls me out of the car against my wishes, pushing me into my grandmother's arms. My grandmother clutches me tightly, probably scared I would try and run back into the car.

"*No me quiero quedar aquí,*" (I don't want to stay here) I begin to cry to my grandmother as I watch my mom drive away from me.

"*Vas estar bien aquí conmigo.*" (You are going to be all right here with me.) She continues to hug me tightly.

CHAPTER ONE

WHO IS SHE?

Toni

NOT FEELING like you belong to part of a community you have chosen to be a part of because you fear what could happen if the real you is discovered is the conundrum I have found myself in for the past three years. Avoiding as many campus parties I could has been my usual. Not saying I didn't go to any, but they were usually smaller parties I came across in my apartment complex. There was no use in attending if I wasn't hoping to befriend anyone. I kept to my side of town for nightlife or was busy working. But now, I'm being forced to stay away and "fit in" with the college crowd.

Walking into the fraternity house is like walking into a movie. You know, raging college parties, booze flowing, and people everywhere. I really thought movies exaggerated, but I guess not. I only came because my usual study partner convinced me. She wanted to pick me up, but I told her I would meet her. Now, I'm not sure I will find her.

My phone vibrates in my back pocket.

Running late, be there in 5

Text from Amy, my study partner. I walk through the house in search of the bar or keg to get a drink while I wait. There are enough Solo cups here to suggest a keg. A good beer would really be welcome since I live off the cheap shit.

"Hey! Can I get a beer?" I ask the guy next to the keg, unsure if he's manning it or if it's a free-for-all.

"For you, gorgeous, of course." He turns around and opens a large cooler and hands me a canned Dos XX. Good boy! "Sorry for the can, but no more bottles for us, because cleanup is a bitch—broken glass and all."

"Free beer. How could I complain?" I smile, knowing I could have him wrapped around my finger if I choose. "So what's in the keg?"

"The cheap shit. Good stuff is in the cooler." He winks. Yeah, I could have him, but this one is too easy.

"Then a bigger thank you is in order." I blow a kiss his way before turning around and walking away.

Vibration again.

Amy: *Where are you? I'm walking in.*

Me: *In the back, close to the keg*

"Toni!" I hear above the music.

I turn around to see Amy walking toward me. She gives me a brief hug before beginning again. "I desperately need a drink. Come with me."

"Go on, I just got this one. I'll wait for you here." I don't need to see Cutie manning the keg so soon. He will mistakenly think I want something with him.

"Okay. Don't move." She quickly walks away.

This college party is so different than the parties on my side of town. There, you better be bringing your own stuff to drink or else you will go thirsty—that is, unless someone takes pity on you, or a guy thinks he has a chance of getting down your pants. The difference between having money and poverty is astounding. I've had to learn these unspoken differences on my own. College was never in my sights growing up, but I've made it this far. My last year.

"He was really cute." Amy comes back, informing me of what I had already noticed. She looks at my drink. "Where did you get that?"

I see her Solo cup and keep my answer simple. "He gave it to me."

"Ah! So he likes you. You got the good beer." She smiles and I'm relieved. I guess this is common knowledge. "Come on. Let's go mingle. When his shift is over, he'll probably come looking for you."

"His shift?" I ask, confused.

"Yeah. You know. Different guys man the booze throughout the night, making sure people don't get too crazy and cutting you off if they think you've had too much already. When his is done, he will look for you." She bats her eyelashes dramatically and walks into a crowd.

I follow her, watching as she chats with different groups. She introduces me to people all while flirting along the way. I excuse myself to get another drink when the group of girls she is speaking with gets overwhelmingly annoying.

Back at the keg, a new guy is on beer duty. I watch a couple of girls hand him their cups for a refill. He looks at me, and I answer, "I'll take one, please." He pulls a cup from the stack, noticing I don't have one in hand.

"Just get here?"

"No, I had a Dos XX before," I answer honestly.

"Pete's a sucker for a beautiful girl." He laughs. "Too bad he can't see when the girl is out of his league." He hands me the beer. Just like I thought before. He would be too easy.

"Thanks." This one has the typical cocky-frat-guy attitude. I bet he would like me to flirt and beg for a good beer.
Not happening. I walk away smiling, venturing outside.

The climate outside is much calmer. People are standing
around or sitting in the few chairs, talking, conversations
flowing since the music from inside is muffled. I find an
empty chair away from others. It isn't the worst party ever,
but adjusting to this new life kind of sucks. Alex, my cousin,
has been after me to stay away from the neighborhood. If
he had his way I would leave and not turn back. Believe me,
I want to, but leaving the only life I've known has to be
done with finesse if I want to cover my past. I want out of
the hood, but I'm not quite ready to show myself to this
world.

"Toni, what are you doing out here by yourself?" Amy
asks, walking toward me.

"Just getting a breather. It was stuffy inside," I lie.
Keeping up my appearance is key. No one knows where I'm
from, and I intend to keep it that way.

She waves a Dos XX can in front of me. "Come on.
Tequila shots are calling our names." She grabs my hand,
pulling me up. The new beer guy wants down her pants, and
it looks like she may be easier than I thought.

"Free tequila? Why not." People like me don't pass up free
booze.

"Welcome back," Beer Guy welcomes us. He pulls small
cups out of a box and places them on the counter. He turns
around to the cooler the previous guy got the beer out of and,
magically, a bottle of tequila appears—and the good stuff, too.
"Lime and salt?"

"Of course," Amy chimes at the same time I say, "Nah."

Beer Guy raises an eyebrow at me, probably surprised
with my answer. "No lime?"

Shaking my head, I say, "Not necessary since you pulled

out the good stuff." The cheap stuff is what I can afford and purchase, so I really want to enjoy this shot.

"Impressed." His focus is directed to me now.

I see Amy from the corner of my eye, watching our interaction. The usual girl jealousy is beginning to rise. Quick to bring her back in the mix, I ask, "Where's Amy's salt and lime?" I make sure to use her name so, hopefully, he will remember it. I'm not interested, so there is no reason for Amy's feathers to ruffle.

Turning back to the cooler, he pulls out a plastic container of lime slices and grabs the salt shaker from the top of the keg. His attention is back to Amy as he's pouring.

"Ready, beautiful." He watches Amy. Did he forget her name already? Amy slowly licks the side of her hand before shaking salt on it and licking again. She's not playing hard to get.

We each grab a cup and tap them together. I watch as they throw their heads back, taking the shot in one swift motion. I pour mine back slower, appreciating the harsh but smooth taste. Amy quickly grabs her lime to cut the burn.

"You haven't finished it yet?" she asks, noticing my cup is still half full.

"No reason to slam. It's pretty smooth if you give it a chance."

"Huh. Not really a tequila girl, I guess," she states, confused at my answer.

"I'm probably the odd one out, not many people are." I try to keep her pacified. This is the reason I have avoided going out with study partners—especially girls. Girls tend to compete and get their panties in a wad. I don't need that shit in my life. I need to graduate and get the hell out of the hood.

"Another one, ladies?" Frat Guy asks. He's ready to get laid.

"No way. I won't be walking if I go in for another." Amy is

shaking her head dramatically. Weak, but probably a good idea to keep my wits.

"Thanks," she says to Mr. Cocky. "Come on, let's see who else is around." She grabs my hand to pull me behind her. I allow her to lead me, even though I find the action annoying.

SHE HAS BEEN BOUNCING from group to group, talking animatedly. I recognize very few people from classes or around campus. I'm not completely comfortable, but the buzz I have with the next couple of refills has relaxed me. As I'm walking to the bathroom, someone pulls my arm and yanks me into a dark hallway.

"What the hell?" I hit in the direction of whoever grabbed me.

"What are you doing here?" I turn around, recognizing the voice.

Garrett

I'VE DONE MY PART, making sure the underclassmen have taken care of the party duties. Busy for the past couple of hours, I have passed the torch. I have a few more hours to enjoy the night. The whiskey we have over ice in the back room will do the trick. Pouring it into a red Solo cup to camouflage it, I walk out.

"Partying. What does it look like?" I hear a girl exclaim angrily. Not sure if she will need a helping hand, I stop to listen.

"Why are you partying here?" I recognize a frat brother's voice.

"Why wouldn't I party here?" the girl retorts.

"You don't belong here." The anger in his voice is unmistakable.

"Why? Care to tell me why *I'M* not welcome but all these other drunk girls are?" She's not backing down. I peek around the corner to get a look at who Kevin is speaking to. Whomever she is, she's gorgeous. Long, dark-brown hair cascades down, helping to accentuate her thin, curvy figure. Her back is against the wall, and Kevin is inches from her. His jaw is ticking, and I hesitate whether to involve myself.

"Because... you know why," he states a bit more calmly. "How would you even know anyone who would be here?"

"Because I go here."

Kevin steps back, confused with her declaration. "Really?"

"Yes. Don't look so shocked. It's not like we have shared anything personal with each other. I didn't know you went here, either." She crosses her arms, which pushes her ample chest up. "Now, I'm going to the bathroom, and we can ignore each other. No one has to know we have met before."

"How about I give you something and you can walk out of here happy?" Kevin pulls a money clip from his pocket.

"Really? That's how you think this is going to work?" Her chin lifts a fraction.

"Isn't that how it works? I pay, and you give me what I want."

"Not this time. Not last time you asked. I don't want your fucking money." I'm extremely curious about what they are talking about. How does he know her? Tension is thick in the air.

"Are you sure?" His jaw tenses. She doesn't move. "Fine." Kevin gives in.

As Beauty is about to walk away, he grabs her arm to stop her. Standing behind her, he kisses her neck and whispers something I can't hear. She walks away without looking back. Good girl. He doesn't have her.

9

I count to ten before I come around the corner. Kevin is still standing where she walked away from him. He turns around, stunned to see me. "Hey." His nervousness is noticeable.

"Why are you hiding here? The girls are out there," I tease him, giving him a false sense of privacy.

"Yeah." He gives me a small smile. "Just needed a quick break. Come on, the least I can do is help you get laid after pulling a shift tonight."

I place my hand on his shoulder. "No need. One caught my eye earlier tonight." I pat his back firmly. He doesn't need to know how much earlier. "Take your breather." I walk away, hoping I can find the mystery girl.

Sipping from my cup, I walk through the crowd toward the closest bathroom. I stand around, watching as a few girls walk out. Wondering if she has left, I begin walking the party. Too many are already slurring and stumbling around. Not in the mood to deal with other people's drunken antics, I down the glass and head to the ice chest. I grab a beer before walking the party again.

After searching for several minutes, there is no sign of her. Giving up, I grab another beer and walk outside to find a very pleasant surprise. I make my way to the small group she is speaking with.

"How's the kick-off party?" I ask the group as I approach.

Everyone in the group, but her, turns to face me. She actually turns in the opposite direction.

"Booze, music, and friends. Nothing to complain about here," a bubbly girl responds happily, her eyes glazed and smile too big.

"Great. Glad you're enjoying yourself." I stand with the group. "How about you? Enjoying yourself?" I tap Beauty on the arm.

She turns to face me, her expression stoic. "It'll do. Excuse me." She turns away again and begins to walk away.

"Wait." Confused why she is ready to flee, I hold her elbow to slow her. We take a few steps away from the others. "What's the hurry? Did I say something wrong?"

"No. I was just getting ready to leave." Her voice is flat.

"Stay. Have a drink with me." I'm still holding her elbow, so I give it a small, encouraging squeeze. "I'm Garrett." I release her elbow and extend my hand to her.

She rewards me with a smile. She places her hand in mine. "Toni. Nice to meet you." I bring her hand up to my lips and kiss it. I wave my hand in the direction of a couple of empty patio chairs away from the crowd.

"Why don't you take a seat, darlin', and I will get us a couple of drinks."

"Trying to get me drunk?" She raises an eyebrow in question.

"No, just trying to get you to stay so I can talk to you," I blurt out too honestly. Her confident, no-nonsense attitude catches me off guard.

"I should probably be getting home."

"One drink?" One side of her lips pulls up slightly. I'm making progress. "One can't hurt. Sit. I'll be back." She moves slowly to the chair. I find an underclassman and bark orders for him to bring me a couple of the good beers.

"They'll be right up." I push the chair a little closer before taking a seat. "I got an underclassman to bring me a couple," I answer the question her face gave away. Wanting to know her story, I jump in. "You said you were about to leave. Did you come alone?"

Her lips pull into a brilliant smile. "I think that is a question no girl should ever answer if a guy asks." Her sarcasm is unmistakable. "I think that is Freshman Girl Going Out 101." A small laugh bubbles out of her full lips. "But since I think

you're harmless, I met a study partner here. She's over there."
She points to the group of people she was talking to.

"Well, didn't they teach you in Girl 101 to always let your
friends know when you're leaving—or leave together? Safety
in numbers and all." A sudden feeling of protectiveness overcomes me. Why would she chance going home alone after
drinking?

"Yes. They did. But I think I can handle myself." The
lightness she just possessed is gone.

"Got your beers," the underclassman interrupts. I grab
both cans. I place one down to pop the top of the other
before handing it to her.

"Cheers to strong women." I tip my can toward her.

"*That* I can drink to." The air lightens a bit again. "I'm
guessing you belong to this frat?"

"You would be correct. I'm a Kappa Tau. Being a senior
has its privileges."

"Like getting you beer at request." She bows slightly.

"Yes. I wanted to make sure I had a chance to talk to you
before you left. Didn't want you to jet while I was trekking
back and forth, getting our drinks."

"Smart. I may have." She shrugs her shoulders.

"I'm Garrett Anders. Can I get your number?"

"Toni Martinez. And that probably won't be a good idea."

"Boyfriend?" I inquire.

"No. No boyfriend to speak of. I'm just really busy trying
to finish my last year."

"You're killing me," I joke. "I don't think I've ever been
shot down this quickly. Not even a fake number to keep my
ego intact."

A sweet smile emerges again before she offers, "How
about a coffee sometime?"

"Tell me when and where." I pick up the scrap she just
threw my way, her disinterest challenging me.

"I have a break between morning classes on Monday. The Coffee House on Third Street. Nine thirty?"

Lucky me; I have a break then too. "I'll see you there."

She stands and extends her hand to me. "See you."

I grab her hand and bring it to my lips again.

CHAPTER TWO

IT'S ONLY COFFEE

Toni

GARRETT CAUGHT ME OFF GUARD, disarming my usual tactics to keep people at bay. He's a handsome guy, but the most memorable thing about him was his smile that disarms you, a small dimple appearing to plead for you to smile in return.

Walking away from people has never been a problem for me. I was never here to make friends. I am here to get that damn piece of paper that will get me a good-paying, honest job I can be proud of. And if I'm telling the truth, a guy with money wouldn't hurt, but I will never rely solely on him. I'm just not hooking up with some mooch who expects me to support him.

That is one thing I have never understood about Amelia, my best friend. Her boyfriend is a mooch. He's always asking her for money. I tell her to cut the fucker off, but she says she loves him. What the fuck ever. If my mother has taught me anything, it's to not trust men and their intentions. My mother has chased every guy she thought had money and could sweep her away on his white horse. They slum a bit on the wrong side of the tracks, but they always end up back in their cushy life. My mother would end up heartbroken until the next guy came around, making promises he never intended to keep.

She's a dumbass. I don't intend to ever become her. But I will allow myself to dream about Garrett just a bit more. I see my fair share of good-looking guys at the club, but there is something about him. He is gorgeous, but not into himself. His sandy, light-brown hair is a bit shaggy and out of control, and the lone dimple on his right cheek when he graces you with a true smile says *boy next door*. It makes me wonder what the boy next door is doing in a fraternity. He didn't give off the air of importance most of the frat guys emanate.

I lie in bed and let myself drift off to that dimple.

THE SECOND WEEK of classes has begun. I should have worked Saturday instead of going to the party. I'm exhausted from last night's shift, and the money could have been better. I need a good night to have a little cushion. Working all summer lets me relax during the school year, pulling shifts as needed.

I walk into my first class of the day. Professor Henderson is not all bad. Tough, but fair. I've had him for all my accounting courses. I should talk with him regarding any possible internships he may be aware of or connections I could use.

Many familiar faces fill the room, being together for many business classes together. Henry and Amy, my usual study partners, sit on either side of me.

"Well, hello, stranger. Didn't get much sleep?" He winks at me.

I woke up late this morning, so I skipped make-up and let my hair air dry. I roll my eyes at him. "I wish. I turned off the alarm instead of snoozing."

My life is split in two: the way I earn my money and college girl. I don't come from money. I come from the proverbial wrong side of the tracks, which means NO money or dirty money. My goal is to move as far away from that shithole as I can. But until then, I will make my money any way I can. I won't apologize for it, but it doesn't mean I want people knowing too much of my business. I always keep superficial "friends." I won't share much about myself, and I don't really care to know much about them, either.

Funny thing is, people are so egotistical. It's okay that I don't speak about myself, because it gives them more time to ramble on about their mundane lives. I've never really had much trouble with keeping a distance. I only socialize with people here occasionally. Saturday's frat party escapade was a first with Amy. I have never invited anyone to my place, because I don't need any unexpected visits.

"Yeah, okay." He winks at me playfully. I have never associated with him socially, so I can ignore his tease. "When do you all want to start planning study sessions?" he continues.

"Coffee after class today?" Amy jumps in.

"I can't today. I have plans. Next class?" I had been considering standing up Cute Frat Guy, but the temptation to see that dimple was overriding my usual reaction.

"Plans, huh? Do these plans involve the cute guy I saw you talking with Saturday night?" A smirk spreads across her face.

Not one to share my life, I shrug instead. They have no need to know who I will be meeting or what my plans are. Keeping my cards close to the chest has been a necessity to succeed.

My first glance into escaping the shithole, poverty-stricken life had been in eighth grade.

I HATE GETTING CALLED into the damn counselor's office. I can't think of what I could have possibly done this time. She begins, "Antonia (pronounced in Spanish), I don't know if we are going to be able to promote you to high school if we do not see improvement." I roll my eyes. This fuckin' lecture again. I slide a little lower in my seat. I get it at least once a year. My grades have taken a hit this year, and I probably miss more days than I should. My grandmother has her hands full, still working full time to support me and my cousins who live with her.

"Do you want to attend college?" she asks, like she really cares.

"What do you think? Do I look like your typical college-goer?" I roll my eyes at her idiotic question. She needs to head back to her part of town and leave me alone. My mom and her brother didn't even graduate from high school. My older cousins are in high school, but they aren't doing well.

"I don't know what the typical college-goer looks like, but it would be a shame if you didn't," she continued. "You have the brains. It surprises me to see such high standardized test scores with your lack of attendance and low grades. You are scoring this high on your own. I would love to see what you could do if you actually applied yourself."

Someone is seeing through my façade. I do the bare minimum to pass the classes but know I could do so much more. This book stuff is easy for me. I sit stunned, not speaking for a minute before I respond.

"The test is just easy," I answer, still unsure about her motives.

"It's not easy for everyone. Some students don't pass. They get retained because they can't pass this test. And you are scoring higher than the majority of this eighth grade class. I would really like to help you figure out what you want to do. What you would like to become."

. . .

THAT CONVERSATION STAYED WITH ME. It began to motivate me. I was born to a teen mom and raised by my grandmother. My mom's desperation to be rich clouded her good judgment —if she even had any. She hated this life, too, but went about it the wrong way. She was always the dirty secret "respectable" men came to for a good time.

Somehow, she never saw it, or if she did, she didn't care. I don't feel sorry for her. She was old enough to choose her life. I do, however, mourn my lost innocence. I was exposed to real world adult issues before I hit double digits. I knew what it was like to dwindle grocery items down at the check out lane because there wasn't enough money, shower quickly because the electricity had been shut off, rinse off in gas station bathrooms when the water was turned off, and visit the food bank when times got really bad.

I never shared any of this with my friends growing up. What could they have done? They lived in the same shithole part of town I did. It was just the way of life.

Class ends quickly, my mind still reeling from all the information he presented. These are the classes that actually challenge me.

HAVING to assimilate to a new culture, I quickly learned to people watch. Blending in was my ultimate goal, never wanting people to assume I wasn't one of them. Coffee shops, charging their insane amount for a damn cup of coffee, became my home to study how people interacted with each other. I fell victim to their yummy lattes my freshman year and had to cut back when I realized my money was dwindling faster than I expected.

If I tried to tell my hood friends about these people, they wouldn't believe me. It is odd how different things are in the same city when you venture outside the invisible walls. Everything we need is conveniently located in the bubble I grew up in. It makes you wonder if that's the point.

As I scan the crowd and eavesdrop on conversations, Garrett walks in, spotting me immediately.

"You ordered already, darlin'," he states the obvious as he sees the cup in front of me. "Can I get you anything else?" His eyebrows pull in.

"I'm good. Thank you." I don't want to feel obligated to stay longer if things go awry.

He orders at the counter and returns, sitting in the empty chair across from me. "How was your morning class? What class did you have?"

"As good as it gets for an accounting class."

"Yikes, that is a class I would never pass. Math has never been my friend. Is that your major?" These simple statements are part of the usual conversations between every college-going student looking to hook up, but somehow, he seems so much more interested.

"I guess you can say math is my best friend. It's always come easy for me. This past spring semester was the first time I encountered an accounting class that challenged me. And I can tell this one will too. It's actually kind of weird for me. I skated through the classes without much effort. I'm now working harder."

We both look up when we hear his name called. "Excuse me," he tells me as he stands. That's another first. I've never had anyone tell me 'excuse me' just to pick up their coffee. He returns with a cup and two plates. He places them on the table and walks to the self-serve counter, picking up a few things.

"Not sure what you liked, so I got a sweet and a savory." And with this simple statement, he graces me with the dimple. "Which would you like, or do you want to share?" He lifts a knife in his hand.

"Let's share," I offer, touched by the thoughtful gesture.

He starts cutting the butter croissant and scone in half. "Are you a math genius?"

"Huh?"

"You said math was your best friend and it was easy. So I'm guessing math genius."

He's brought the conversation back to me. He has not tried to overrun the conversation about himself. He was listening and picked up where we had left off. Wow. "I don't think I'm a math genius. Those guys are in the math department inventing new math. I just find this stuff pretty easy."

"So accounting is your major?" I nod in confirmation. "And this is your last year?" He picks up the scone and takes a bite, waiting for me to continue.

I'm now a little worried he will continue to ask questions about me and my life. Things I don't want to answer. Things I don't share. Things I need to stay in my past. I don't need people judging or pitying me because of where I came from.

"It is. And you? If math isn't your thing, what is?" I move the conversation away from me.

"Ag business. Animals are my friends." He takes a sip from his cup before continuing. "But I guess the animals—cows in particular—wouldn't think of me as a friend." His smile is huge as he winks at me.

"Why wouldn't they think of you as a friend? Ag. That's agriculture, right? Sounds animal-friendly to me." My brows pull together in question.

The laugh that escapes his lips is deep and full. I would never question its authenticity. "The cows would probably think I am betraying them since I raise them for slaughter." His lips pull down on one side. "My goal is to work at a beef producer ranch. Hope you're not a vegetarian." His tone is a bit more serious, wondering if he just offended me.

"I am." I drop my head.

"I'm sorry. I should have been more PC when speaking of my major. I never know if I will be offending someone." His tone is reserved.

I've just turned the tables on him. I begin laughing. "I'm not a vegetarian, but it was fun to see you stumble."

He lets out a long breath. "Ha. Ha. You got me. I forget not everyone wants to know where their food comes from. I usually leave out where I want to work. I hate it when protests erupt."

"Protests?"

"Yes. Sometimes, student organizations that are 'animal friendly'"—he air quotes with his fingers—"will gather around the ag buildings or the university land where we keep the livestock and protest. So, I have learned to keep my future line of work hidden."

Mr. Frat Boy keeps things hidden. Interesting.

Our conversation continues to flow easily, sharing tales of our classes and interests. It is nice and easy. Nothing forced. Time passes quickly, and we have to rush out to not be late to our next class.

I SCURRY INTO CLASS, which has already started, and sit in the back. This is not my usual area, feeling more comfortable in the middle. The students in the middle get to hide. This was something I had learned in middle school. Since I had the reputation, I was able to camouflage myself in this area. The front was filled with the 'good' students, and the back was designated for the 'bad' ones. Since I was already 'bad,' I decided I didn't need any more attention drawn to me.

I take out my notebook and pen as quietly as possible. I finally settle in, and it dawns on me: we didn't exchange numbers. This shouldn't bother me, but there is a nagging feeling of hurt. I don't typically date. I get my needs met when necessary without distraction or intrusion. Maybe I wasn't his type. Please, I can be any guy's type. I've become the master at morphing into whatever the situation calls for. How do you think I can still party in the hood and walk around college with no one the wiser? I let it go. No use in crying over spilled milk, especially when the milk was never mine. And I wouldn't want it to be.

Garrett

I CAN'T BELIEVE I let her leave before asking for her number or at least giving her mine. When we had realized the time, we both jumped and rushed in separate directions. I had enjoyed her company. She didn't know who I was. I didn't have to downplay my family's wealth for a possible vulture. That's the trouble with fraternities and sororities. Your family's name and influence is broadcasted for all. I learned early on that these girls are in it for a wealthy husband so they can be the next "*Housewife*." Not my type.

I walk into the frat house since it's my week to supervise study times for the underclassman and anyone close to probation. I sit on the couch, waiting for everyone to arrive, and begin to scroll my phone.

"Study duty, huh?" Kevin asks as he sits on the couch across from me.

"Yep. They have about 15 more minutes before they are late. I saw a couple already at the table. They are expecting brownie points, I guess." *Should I ask Kevin if he has Toni's number?* As heated as they were, he would have to have her number.

"I can stay and help you out. Who else is here?"

"Not sure. I didn't pay attention. I just looked at my duties." *Should I?*

"The party was good. There wasn't too much cleanup." He continues with small talk as I'm still pondering.

"It was."

"I saw you talking to some brunette outside. Hook up?"

"Nah. But I would like to see her again." I leave out our meeting today. "Do you know Toni?"

"Toni?" He's stalling.

"Yes. Toni Martinez," I push gently, not wanting to expose my knowledge. While I am curious about their history, I really don't need the visual.

"Toni. Oh, yeah, I do." He looks nervous. I'll cut to the chase and let him leave with his secrets. "Do you happen to have her number? I would like to give her a call."

"You didn't get her number?" His brows pinch inward.

"No. She left before I could ask." I hide our rushed departure today.

"Uh. I think so." He begins scrolling through his phone. I can't see what he is doing, but he is typing something. Then, my phone pings with an incoming message. I look at it, and a text from Kevin has a contact attachment. "I completely forgot I have to meet a study group. I need to go. I can't stay and help, after all."

I don't know their history, but this conversation has made him completely uncomfortable. It has piqued my curiosity, but I'm not sure I want to know more.

I look at the time to see how much time is left before demerits begin to flow for the guys who are late or don't show up.

WHEN TO TEXT? I lie in my bed, wondering what I should do. I won't call because she wouldn't know my number, so she probably wouldn't answer. Is it too soon? Fuck! Just man up and send a text. Why the hell do I have my panties in a wad? Shit.

Hello, beautiful.

I hit send. I wait. Will she respond or does she ignore anonymous texts? Will it be stalkerish if I wait too long to let her know it's me?

I really enjoyed our coffee this morning. Garrett

I begin making a sandwich for dinner as I wait for a response. Almost an hour passes before my phone pings.

Hello to you, too. I enjoyed the coffee, too. How did you manage to get my number?

I hadn't considered how she would feel about me getting her number without giving it to me. Will it bother her if I tell her it was Kevin? Will he tell her he gave it to me?

My frat brother, Kevin, saw me talking to you. I got it from him

I decide honesty will be the best path. I'd rather have shit blow up now than later if I'm caught in a stupid lie. Time passes. More time passes. No answer. I decide to leave it for now.

TONI

WHAT THE?? I stare at my phone. Kevin gave him my number? Why would he do that? People are going to find out. I knew running into Kevin at the party was going to come back and bite me in the ass. What's done is done. Fuck it.

I shut off my phone and turn the lights out.

CHAPTER THREE

REAL LIVES

Toni

I HAVE NEVER FELT guilty for anything I have had to do to survive the life I have been dealt. And I refuse to start now. No one will ever make me feel less. My freshman year roommate tried that. It did not go well for her.

"*SOMEONE PLEASE SHOOT ME. I am going to throw down,*" *I think to myself as my roommate walks in drunk, yet again. Second night of her and her damn friends being inconsiderate, coming in and taking over the room as if I'm not there. Food and loud talking all while ignoring the fact that I am lying in bed, reading.*

I tried to be polite and bring it to her attention the first time the following day. I asked nicely for her to keep her bitch friends at a distance, but she has done it again.

"I'm trying to read!" I yell at the girls, sitting up. They look at me,

roll their eyes, and laugh. Patience be damned. *"GET THE FUCK OUT OF MY FUCKING ROOM!" I decide being more direct is the only way to go.*

The laughter stops, but they continue to stare at me like I have a third head. "I'm waiting. Get the fuck out," I state matter of factly.

"Awe. Poor little girl has no friends and hates that others do. FYI. It's my room too, and I invited them here. They're staying," my room-mate finally states.

"I will throw each of these bitches out by their hair if you insist, but they will get out."

With alcohol-fueled bravado, she gets up and stands in the middle of the room. Poor little white girl. She may think she has no fear with the haze, but I am about to put her in her place. I stand slowly, biding my time, keeping myself in check. I can't do anything to jeopardize my scholarships. I need to let her know I can without actually landing myself with a ticket, in jail, or without money for school. I didn't like juvie, landing there once for breaking city curfew and tagging. "Sweetheart, I don't think you know who you are talking to. Let me give you some background." My voice is calm and steady, even though I am seething inside.

"Whatever." She rolls her eyes and begins to turn around.

I place my hand on her shoulder, squeezing firmly to stop her. "Again, you might want to listen." I pause, looking to her friends and back at her. "I grew up in a rougher place than this. A place you and your friends over there avoid like the plague. And let me guess, you have never thrown down in your life. So how about we try this again? Get your annoying ass friends and walk out to the common area or to one of their rooms. This year will go much better if you don't annoy me." My face is stern with the words just spoken. I cross my arms and hold my ground. Her eyes give her away. She is unsure if I'm telling the truth, but too chickenshit to test.

She swapped rooms with another girl a couple of days later. Better for me. The next roommate was quiet and all she did was study. Made for a very uneventful year, but it taught me I needed my own space.

Looking at my phone still off from last night, I decide to leave it that way. I'll check in with Guela later. I dress for class and begin my day.

Garrett

STILL NO TEXT FROM HER. If I'm going down, I might as well go down spectacularly.

Good morning! Coffee soon? Send.

If Kevin was that uncomfortable about giving me her number, is she too?

I get ready and head to campus. No reason to sit around and wait if I screwed the pooch on this one.

AS I'M in the student center, reading between classes, my phone begins ringing. Could it be? I pull the phone out of my pocket and glance at the screen. I swipe, answering.

"Hey, Mom. What's going on?" I thought it would be Toni.

"Hello, Son. Is that any way to greet your mom?" Her teasing tone is welcome.

"Of course not. Sorry. But really, what's the call for? You never call me during the day," I ask again because she always calls in the evenings when she knows I'm home and alone. She usually texts before to let me know she'll call. As she told me once before, she would rather live in blissful ignorance of my social life.

"Okay. You're right. But I needed to call while your dad is out working. There is so much to do around here, and he's being bullheaded about hiring more guys to help. If you aren't busy this weekend, I thought you could come down and help the guys."

"Of course I'll come home this weekend. What's happening at the ranch?"

"When they did a perimeter check of the land, there are several places where the fences need repairing. And your father refuses to hire more temporary guys to help until the work is done. You know him. Stuck in his ways." She sounds tired. I wonder if she has insisted on going out there to help.

"I'll be there Thursday night. I don't have classes on Friday, so I can spend three days out there."

My dad has the money. He just refuses to spend it. He wants to do it all himself. Looks like my weekend is planned. If Toni finally responds, I won't be able to see her.

A HOME-COOKED meal I did not mess up or burn is always welcome. I left right after my last class this afternoon, making it in time for dinner. My parents' ranch is a couple of hours from my place, too far to come and go easily.

"Last year, Son. Have you decided on grad school yet? Where are you thinking?" My dad may be posing this as a question, but we both know it's his way of saying I'm going and better decide where.

"Still weighing my options. I may just stay here. I know the school and most of the professors. It would make for an easy transition, and I know I will get accepted."

"When are you going to settle down, honey?" my mom asks, interrupting my father. It's her favorite question since I have never brought a girl home to meet her. "I see your pictures, so I know there are many girls around..." She lets this hang in the air. I know she stalks my social media to keep up with my life.

The girls around are super-fucking-ficial. It's all about what I have so they can eventually become a lady of leisure. This seems to be the goal of most girls I meet. How much do I currently have or what is my earning potential so I can support their dream of staying home and Botoxing for the rest of their lives. Don't get me wrong, I'm no hermit, and I do enjoy the company, I just don't keep them around.

"When I find one worthy enough," I answer honestly. Finding a woman isn't hard at all. Finding a woman who can stand on her own but let a man take care of her is a unicorn.

"You need to decide soon. No more dragging your feet. I expect applications to be sent out later this month," my father continues, coming back even after my mother's attempt to distract.

"Yes, sir," I agree, knowing this is not worth arguing over.

"Talk to Julio in the morning about the fences that need mending." Julio is my dad's ranch manager. He has been around for as long as I can remember. He didn't speak English when he began working at the ranch. We taught each other—me Spanish and him English. It was easier for me to work with the men, since most spoke Spanish. They did hard work out in the Texas heat, never complaining and always loyal.

I nod at him. "I'm heading up. See you in the morning. Good night." I walk over and kiss my mom's cheek.

I head up to the bedroom I have known my whole life. My parents wed and moved into my grandparents' home. It was easier for my father with the early mornings out in the field. My grandfather was able to expand his cattle ranch significantly when they found oil on his land. Now, we have the cattle and the oil. The oil is great for the security of the ranch, but it brings so much hardship when it comes to friends and potential women in my life. You never seem to know whether the relationships are based on me or the money.

———

MORNINGS on the ranch begin before the sun is up. As always, Mom has the coffee ready and jugs of cold water to take with us. I head to the stable, ready to saddle my horse, knowing I won't be able to ride for a while. I work quickly since taking the horse out is more time-consuming than jumping onto an ATV.

I ride out to join Julio and the guys, knowing the jobs on the ranch are never-ending. This isn't an easy life. It's not for everyone. In fact, it's not for most.

"Hola, Julio!" I yell as I approach. "*Como estas?*"

"Garrett," Julio responds, pronouncing my name with his thick accent. "Why you here and not in school?"

"*Estoy aqui para la fin de semana.*" (I'm here for the week-end) I respond in Spanish. These are our usual conversations, each of us trying to learn and practice each other's language. "*Que puedo hacer hoy?*" (What can I do today?)

"I have muchachos fixing the fence in the west side. Side closer to pond. Can you help them?"

"On my way." I loosen the reins and softly kick my horse on the side to take off in a gallop.

I find the guys already working on the fence. They brought one of the trucks filled with lumber. I jump down and wrap the horse reins around a tree nearby so she can stay in the shade.

"Hey, guero," Juan calls out, his version of white boy. "Get your lazy ass out of the shade and come help."

"*Ya voy, culero.*" The colorful Spanish language used is a gift from the guys.

Juan and two others are busy pulling planks from the truck. I haven't been this far on the property in quite some time. I scan the area, not realizing how worn the fence is. There are parts that could easily be pushed—the fastest way to lose cattle. *Shit, it's going to be a long, hard day.*

I pull another post from the truck and walk over to the section they are currently working on. They already have a stack of the old wood from the sections they have completed. We have a good 50 yards of repairs and mends. I walk the edge, inspecting what we can salvage by repairs and what truly needs replacing.

"How long has the fence been this bad?" I ask Juan while he is holding a board up for another to hammer in place.

"We just started riding out here a few weeks ago. Your dad asked me to check the perimeter. That's when I noticed the parts needing repair."

"The parts? How much?" Dad hasn't mentioned any of this to me. I should not have taken classes this summer so I could have stayed on the ranch to help.

"I don't know. But it is a lot. There are four sections he asked us to complete. The rest he said will wait until the cooler weather comes. It's fucking hot by 9:30."

Back at the truck, I pull out another tool belt, nails, and a couple more posts. "Hey," I call out to the guy who is watching Juan and the other guy work. "Come with me, and we'll work this section." No use in standing around. Working on two sections at a time will cut our time out here.

As I pull nails from the rotted wood, he holds boards so they don't fall, then holds again as new boards are hammered into place. The sun is beating down on us, the trees that could provide a nice escape from the torture not close enough. I take my hat off and rub my face and head with an old rag in my pocket. You don't usually hear men wanting a cold shower, but that's the only thing on my mind right now.

I'M IN BED, resting after another great homemade dinner, thinking of Toni. It's been three days and still no response from her. I'm not worried about staying at the ranch all weekend anymore. If I'm not spending time with her, all I would be doing is drinking at the frat house or clubbing. My phone pings with a text from Juan. *Come to our place. Bring beer.*

Looks like the guys are wanting to work in the hurt tomorrow. Might as well join them. I make my way down-stairs and pull a six-pack out of the drink fridge. No reason to mope around. I had coffee with her once.

TONI

AS I'M FINISHING the final touches of my make-up, my phone pings a text. I read what Sasha just sent.

We need you here now. 3 bachelor parties tonight

Almost done. Be there soon

A huge grin spreads across my face because this may be a good night after all. Bachelors and their friends love to throw money around.

I WALK in through the back, quickly stashing my stuff in my locker to hit the floor. There are girls running around in various states of undress, preparing for their numbers or relaxing a bit before walking the floor. I may admire how brazen these girls are, but dancing topless isn't for me. I'll stick to cocktail waitressing. The "private" rooms are gross. I'm not one for getting men off if they don't turn me on.

There is beauty in waitressing. I still make a good amount

of money because the men see me all night. The guys with money who strike my fancy are easy to pick up. I offer them me, and they offer me money. It's the perfect arrangement. They get to have a "side" chick who doesn't mind being on the side, and I get money and usually fantastic orgasms.

"Sasha!" I yell over the blaring music. She finishes at the terminal and comes to the side bar, handing me a tray.

"Could you take any longer, bitch? Look around. It's already a fucking mess."

"Calm the fuck down. You know they're happy. What side do you want me on?" I ask, ignoring her temper tantrum.

"Left side of stage. We'll have two parties on that side. Go make yourself a killing," she instructs with a smirk and a wink.

I grab my tray and signal to the other waitresses already on the floor. I approach the first bachelor party group. "Hey, fellas, what can I get ya?"

One guy raises his hand to me, motioning for me to approach. I walk around the group, watching him. The cockiness he exudes is dripping from the smirk he's wearing to his posture. "Hello, sexy. What do I call you?"

"Anything you want." I wink at him. The only part of this job I can't stand is giving out my name, not wanting to take on a fake "bimbo" name.

He tsks me while shaking his head. "Strike one. If I'm going to drop dime, I expect the service. And that means knowing who I'm calling to keep us happy." Fuck, he's a cocky son of a bitch. Not many of these come in. Men are usually happy to flirt, drink, and flash their money, not pull social rank.

I hold myself from rolling my eyes and place my most seductive mask in place to answer, "I'm Toni. I will keep you happy all night." This double innuendo always satisfies the most difficult man.

"Well, Toni, I'm going to need bottle service. A bottle of Belvedere and a couple of Buchanan's. The only mixer we need is Pellegrino and a side of limes." His all-business, demanding attitude is not one I've dealt with.

I smile sweetly. "Of course. Can I get a card to place the order?" He hands me an Amex Black. "I'll be back." I wink to lighten the encounter. I scan around to his friends, and they are all laughing and watching the show, oblivious to me and our conversation. I turn away to place their order and quickly stop at the group who just walked in, saying hello and that I would be right back shortly.

I place their order and walk back to the other group. As I approach, I see a familiar face. A smile instantly appears. I guess this night won't be as bad as I thought. "Hello, gentlemen. What can I get for y'all?"

"Hey, sweetness!" one responds, handing me a fifty. "This is just to get us started. I'm sure these clowns will be refilling often, and I don't want you to forget about us." he says, his good-natured smirk letting me know he's harmless.

I look over to the familiar face, Mark, as he watches our encounter. Mark is youngish, good-looking, willing to give an orgasm before engaging in his own, and quite generous with his money. He has been coming around for about a year. Dinners, a show, no-strings-attached sex, and some monetary relief or nice gifts has kept him around. It works for us.

"Okay, boys." I raise my voice above the music. "Let me have it. What will it be?" Each rattles off their drink of choice. My smile is genuine, knowing these guys are harmless and will tip well.

My order for the first table is ready at the bar, so I quickly place the second order before heading back to set them up.

I pick up one of the trays and wave over a couple of bouncers to help with the others. I place everything on their tables. I turn and look at the head guy. "What can I serve you?"

"Buchanan's over ice. Only a couple, please," he states flatly. I continue serving the others quickly so I can deliver my other party's drinks.

The evening continues to be busy. I stop by my second party often, always noticing when someone is running low.

Back at party one, I smile. "Gentlemen, the bottles are looking low. Is there anything else I can get you?" I had refilled different men a few times. Each time, they were polite but didn't really engage in conversation or flirtation.

"It's about time," the head guy replies sarcastically.

"I'm sorry. Did I miss you calling me?" I answer, confused by his statement. I have been attentive but didn't stick around since they did not seem interested in my company.

"No, but I notice the group over there has your full attention. I expected that you would have been solely catering our table. Instead, your attention to detail has been less than expected."

"I didn't know anything was needed. What can I get you to make your night more enjoyable?" I respond, surprised by his no fun attitude.

"Nothing now. We refilled our own drinks several times already. The check and a manager, now." I look at the men again, and each is ignoring the interaction, not one intervening.

At the bar, I call Sasha over. "The bachelor party with the bottle service is unhappy. They said I was not attentive enough." I roll my eyes. "The Amex cardholder has a stick up his ass."

"What the fuck? Does he not see the craziness in here tonight? I accommodated his last-minute request and he's still bitching? I'll handle it in a minute."

I pull his check and walk it to the table. "Here is the check, and my manager will be by in a second."

As I'm turning around to walk away, Head Guy states very loudly, "I asked for a manager, and I should not get this bill without speaking to them first." I turn back around and the man has stood up. "I realize you are uneducated and don't know the ways of the world, but if I'm dropping my money, I expect the service to be impeccable." He shoves the bill back at me. Another first.

I stand in a stupor for a moment, not knowing the correct response for his rudeness. I finally turn back around, but before I can, he grabs my shoulder to keep me in place. "You will go get your manager and be back with him."

"Get your fucking hands off her." I hear Mark's voice above the music, but before he can do anything else, a bouncer arrives and tells me to walk away.

I quickly head to the back, composing myself. Drunk guys being overly friendly I can handle. This—whatever this was—shook me. Uneducated. He believed I was beneath him. I have always known I was born at the bottom of the totem pole, and it has never bothered me—until tonight. Why tonight? I take a couple of minutes to shake off the feeling, straighten my back, get my chin up, and walk back out there. No one is going to make me feel less than. I don't care who they are.

I walk out and bump into Mark. "Are you alright?" he asks, hushed and hurried.

"I'm fine. I was pissed he thought he could put his hands on me. That's all. No reason to catch a case over a dumbass," I lie. My boldness is my saving grace. "Go back to your friends before someone notices us." I give him a soft shove away. No man is going to rescue me. I am my own knight in shining armor.

. . .

36

THE TABLES where the party was sitting are now empty and needing to be cleared. I walk to the bar to pick up a tray and rag. "Toni," Sasha stops me before I can walk away. "I handled it. It's not the best tip, but I did get something out of that asshole."

I nod my head slightly at her, not knowing why this feeling is lingering.

CHAPTER FOUR

HIDING

Garrett

WALKING INTO MY APARTMENT, I toss my overnight bag on the floor and fall into bed. I knew the weekend was going to be hard work, but damn, I'm exhausted. I pull my phone from my pocket and check messages. Still no text from her. I ponder whether I should send another text. I drop it on the bed, deciding against it. If she likes The Coffee House, maybe I can catch her tomorrow between classes again. It's harder to ignore me in person than over text.

I RUSH to The Coffee House after class, wanting to be the first one there if she shows. I find a table in a cozy corner not visible until you are in the café, playing it safe in case she decides to turn around if she sees me through the window. I scroll through the news apps while drinking my coffee, waiting. After sitting for about 15 minutes, I'm beginning to think this is a bunk mission. About to pick up my backpack, I hear the door open, and I see her walk through. Her long hair is pulled up in those crazy buns girls like to wear. She's more casual today than she was last week, jeans and a faded t-shirt. Knowing she dressed for me places a smile on my face.

I let her place her order then surprise her. "Hi, Toni." I raise my voice to ensure she hears me.

She pauses before turning around, her lips pulling into a forced smile. "Hi." She stands, unmoving.

"Come sit. I was about to grab another cup." The white lie slips past my lips. I stand to order another.

"That's okay. I was getting mine to go."

"Toni," the barista calls out, holding a ceramic saucer.

"To go?" I ask, looking at the mug.

"Was this to go?" the barista asks.

"Please. Have a seat," I say, nodding my head in the direction of the table.

She grabs the cup from the counter and sits at the table. As I place my order, I watch her from the corner of my eye. She looks uncomfortable, nothing like the girl from last week. How could she go from confident to unsure in a week? Kevin is the only explanation for this strange behavior.

"How was your weekend?" I ask to break the ice.

"Uneventful. No parties." Her eyes fall to the table. "And you? Another frat party?" she asks with a bite in her tone.

"Nah. I went home to help my parents. My dad needed help with some fence repairs." This is technically the truth.

"Wow." Her caramel-colored eyes come back to mine, wide with wonder. "You actually went home to help? Where's home?"

"Of course. How could I not help my dad?" This is what has impressed her. "My parents live in a small, no-name town south of here. You know, the one-light, blink-and-you-miss-it town." I wink, not wanting to give too much of my family away.

"Cute. Small-town boy. I would have never guessed." Her smile returns. What I wouldn't do to keep that smile on her face permanently.

"I guess you could call me that." Letting her believe this is easier.

"So, how was the manual labor?" She takes a sip of her coffee.

"Hard work as usual. Nothing like finishing a project well." I surprise myself, sounding a bit like my father. Biting the bullet, I decide to ask her about the radio silence after the text. "I hope I didn't cross any lines asking Kevin for your number. Since you didn't respond, I thought you may have been uncomfortable with my getting your number." Her eyes widen a bit.

"Uh...no. Uh..." She stumbles over her words. The confident woman falters a bit. "Sorry, no, not uncomfortable, just surprised. I didn't know anyone there, so it caught me off guard, that's all."

She straightens her back slightly and pushes her chin up a fraction. A pose meant to intimidate. She is trying to exude confidence, but I can tell she's uncomfortable. It's something in her eyes. Most wouldn't take the time to look hard enough, backing down from her stance. She has me hooked. I want to know what is making her tick.

"Kevin asked me about you last week. He saw us talking outside. When I found out he knew you, I took my chance asking for the number." I tell her the truth minus the interaction I saw of them earlier in the evening. As much as I want to know their history, I need her to trust me. I'll be shot down so fast if I push too hard.

. . .

TONI

I CAN RELAX EVER SO SLIGHTLY. I can't believe Kevin would ask about me and jeopardize outing himself and me in the process. I'm really regretting attending the party. Should I acknowledge this? I don't want to admit seeing him at the party. Our exchange was in private and not one to share.

"That's cool. Did he say anything else?" My curiosity is on overload, trying to figure out how much damage control I have to do.

"Nope. Just mentioned he saw me talking to you." He pauses, and when I stay silent, he asks, "So no parties for you? Get studying done instead?" He continues the conversation as if he didn't walk centimeters from a landmine which would have me sprinting from my seat in record time.

"Some studying. Mainly just bummed around."

He is veering this conversation too close for comfort. I'm not telling him I worked because the inevitable question of where I work would come up, and I'm not about to admit it to him or anyone else. If he's asking, Kevin has kept his mouth shut.

"Did you go out while you were at home? Meet up with any of your old friends?" I move the conversation back to him.

"Not really. Remember, small town. Not much to do out there. Hung out at the house." Gosh, he's cute, and this small-town-boy charm is somewhat addicting. It's quiet for a moment, and my phone vibrates. I glance to see an email come through.

Why am I getting the red notice email warning my grandmother's power is going to be shut off due to non-payment? My cousin is usually good about taking care of this bill—not always on time, but it gets paid. I'm not even going to bother calling him, because I'm too pissed to talk to him. This needs to be taken care of today before it closes.

"I'm so sorry, I've got to go." I pick up my coffee to pour into a to-go cup.

"Is everything okay, darlin'?" There's that word again. Each time I hear the word darlin' I swoon a little, and I'm not even the swooning type.

"Yes, sorry, I just have to take care of something." Not wanting to expose myself, I keep things vague.

"Anything I can help with?"

"No, I'm good. It just needs my attention now." He has followed me to the bar to get the to-go cup. He actually looks concerned.

"Can I call you later?"

"I would like that." My honest answer surprises me.

DRIVING to my grandmother's house, I am stewing. I have all her bills going to my email. This way, I can ensure everything gets taken care of. I love my cousins, but they still need reminding. My uncle and my mom are fucking leeches. Always with their hands out. Even with the miniscule amount my grandmother makes, they ask her to fix their problems. Alex and I have begun to take control of my grandmother's bills and money so she has what she needs.

Thankfully, this house has been in our family forever, so it's paid off. It's small and run down, just like all the other houses in this neighborhood. I would love to take her out of here, but I know she won't leave. She's still taking care of my uncle and cousins. I hate my cousins moving weed through her house, but since I don't live there anymore, I don't get a say.

My grandmother cleans houses. Uneducated, her options

for a career were very limited. She is on a tight budget, and she does not need any unexpected bills.

"Guela, I'm here!" I yell as I walk through the front door. I called her on the way to let her know we would be going to pay the electricity bill. "Let's get going and I will take you to a late lunch after." I don't want her to worry about this. Maybe a meal will ease her mind about the red notice.

"*Mija, no tienes clases?* It's fine. Alex is coming." (You don't have classes, dear?) She's walking out of her bedroom in the back. Our use of Spanglish is common, mixing Spanish and English in the same conversation and even the same sentences sometimes.

"I'm done for the day. Let's get going. I don't want to risk the power getting turned off. We don't know what time Alex will get here," I respond, wanting to take care of it now. Just then, my phone rings, and Alex's name appears.

"Hello?" I answer even though I know it's him. I'm still pissed.

"Toni. I'm sorry. I thought I would have it paid by now. I owe you." He apologizes, the sincerity in his voice apparent.

"What happened? You promised to take care of this for her."

"My dad. Need I say more? He got arrested again. Of course, he called Guela. She was going to put the house up to bail him out. You and I both know we can't trust my dad."

"What?" I ask confused. No one had told me anything about this. "When?"

"A few months ago. You were studying for exams. I didn't want to throw this at you. He got caught selling at a bar. You would think that pendejo would know better. I had to pony up eight grand and slow the business. I didn't want any attention turned to me and my brother. I'm still trying to catch up. If he fucks up, at least I'm only out money, and Guela isn't out a house."

"I'm sorry. Why didn't you tell me? I would have handled it. I could have worked extra nights at the club."

"Fuck that. That money is for you to live on during the year when you can't work as much. You know I got your back." I feel like the biggest shit. I should have called him and asked what was going on. Usually, he forgets, and that's why it's a few months behind. I should have had Alex's back the way he has had mine.

"I CAN'T LEAVE, Alex. What the fuck am I going to do in college? Really?" I roll my eyes and throw my head back into the old couch.

"Toni. You have to. Get the hell out of here. You are the only one that can. Don't give this up," Alex pleads with me. "Antonia," —*he pronounces my name in Spanish, knowing I hate it*—*"or Antonia..."*—*he says with a long 'o' and soft 'a'*—*"which do you want?"*

He pauses, watching me, waiting for another round of excuses why I can't leave. I take a deep breath, tears collecting in my eyes. "You and I both know that I will not fit in there." I want to go, but I'm terrified to admit it. There is so much I don't know about the world away from this side of town. This is our "Hotel California"; you can check out anytime you like, but you can never leave.

"You are strong. Be a chameleon. Be who they need you to be. Get the paper at the end of your four years and be done. You won't have to come back here unless you want to." He smirks. Everyone always talks about leaving, but rarely does anyone really succeed. "It's a full ride! Tuition, dorm, and books."

"Yeah, great, but what am I going to live on? I can't very well have no fucking money for four years."

"Work. You're a smart girl. I'm sure you can figure it out."

"And how am I to get to this job of mine from the dorms?" I need excuses to help me from accepting this as a thing that can come true.

"I'll get that for you. You will have a car—*more than likely a*

piece of shit, but it will run." The smile that appears on Alex's face is genuine.

"I can't accept that." Alex is three years older than me. He never graduated but has been on my ass to finish. His brother, Javie, graduated and is working at a tire shop. Alex has been floating from job to job. There is no way he can get me a car.

"You can. And this conversation is over." He stands up, comes over to me, and kisses my forehead. "You are the only one." He winks before turning around and walking out.

National Merit Scholar. That is what I have been called since our scores came in. The only one in my graduating class. I don't know if this says more about the education at a poor school or how smart I am. Because of this, my counselor made me apply to different universities. I filled out each application, wrote each essay, and gave them back to her.

"I'm at Guela's house now. I'll take her to get this paid and ensure the power stays on. We don't need another fee to get it turned on again. I want to take her to eat, and then we'll meet you back here. Okay?" My anger has evaporated and been replaced with guilt.

"Fine. Text when you're done eating."

I scan the room as I'm sitting down at a local hole-in-the-wall burger restaurant. So many familiar faces, older and worn down from the hard life they have lived. The same women since I was younger taking orders, another glaring reminder of the viciousness of poverty.

"Why didn't you tell me about Tio Alex, Guela?" I have been wondering why she never mentioned it.

"It was nothing you needed to worry about." She knows my frustration with him and my mom, so I guess it's her way of protecting her children. I don't understand how they could grow up to be such assholes when they had a mom who tried to do all she could for them. We grew up in the same shithole, but at least Alex, Javie, and I are trying to take care of Guela.

"Guela, you know I worry about you. Alex told me you were going to put the house up to bail him out. How could you do that? If he jumped, you are out a house." I am pleading with her to be smarter. She needs to learn when to cut them off.

"*Mija, es mi hijo. No tengo otra opción.*" (Sweetheart, he is my son. I don't have any other choice.) She has moved to Spanish. It is time for me to pull back. She is so protective of them, even if they are not in return.

"I know." I pause, giving just enough time to transition the conversation away so she can relax and enjoy herself. "What else is going on?"

"Have you talked to Javie? He is going to take classes to work on diesel engines." She smiles proudly.

"Really? Being in school this summer and working so much, I don't know anything." I'm flabbergasted by this bit of information and want to be proud, but I need to find out if this is true or if it's another one of his half-assed attempts at something. "That will be great for him. He enjoys what he does." I let my grandmother bask in this joy.

He may enjoy working on cars, but he is also in business with Alex. Their illegal dealings worry me, but they need the money to survive. Screw other's opinions of our family. I've heard every take on the evils of what they do. How they can get an "honest" job. How they are contributing to the downfall of our society. All those self-righteous people who look down on us can back up. Until they have spent a week in our lives, they have no right to judge how we survive.

"Yes, it will help him. Now for Alex to find something he

enjoys instead of jumping from job to job," she continues. The guys have hid their dealings from her, but I'm not sure if she is as clueless as we think. Alex helps her way too much, and this new situation with bailing his dad out without help from anyone...she has to know there is more to the story.

"He will," I add to her hope. "He's a very good guy." I'm not lying about this. He is loyal and trustworthy with the people he cares about. I wouldn't be where I'm at without his help.

DURING MY FIRST YEAR, he would come by, pick me up, feed me, and shove a few bucks in my purse while I wasn't looking. I knew at the time that he had begun dealing. I ignored it because it wasn't my business. Who am I to tell him he shouldn't? Living in the dorms my first year came in handy for his business, though. I learned who needed the connections and sent them his way. I felt better about the car he gave me since I was sending business his way. No reason for some college shithead to get the business when Alex needs it more.

Our lunch continued with more gossip from the hood: the latest drive by that happened a couple of weeks ago and the neighbor's granddaughter who is pregnant and still in middle school.

"DID YOU ENJOY LUNCH?" Alex asks Guela as we walk in.

"*Si, mijo*. I love spending time with my grandchildren. It was nice. *Has comido?* Do you need me to make you something?" (Have you eaten?) She responds, always thinking of taking care of others.

"*Está bien, Guela*. I'll grab something later," he tells her so that she doesn't head into the kitchen and begin working. "Go lie down and relax. I'm going to talk with Toni a bit."

I give her a hug and a kiss. "I'll tell you bye now in case you're asleep when I leave." I hug her a little tighter before letting go. We watch as she walks to the hall back to her room.

Alex takes a seat on the couch, kicking his feet up on the rickety coffee table. "So what did Guela tell you?"

"Nothing. I could tell I hit a nerve when I asked her how she could think of putting the house up, so I backed off. Changed the subject and didn't bring it up again."

"Sounds about right. She wondered how I was able to get him out without the house. I just told her I called in favors. She was insistent on putting up the house. My dad is a dumbass and has always been in and out, but this is the first time it's for something big. Unpaid tickets, fights in bars, public intoxication I can handle. I don't know what to do with this." His admission worries me. He could very well be in the same predicament if he was ever found out.

He continues, "Here's the cash to cover the bill. I should've told you what was going on, but I thought I would be on my feet already." Alex extends his money-filled hand to me.

"I can't take that. I'll pull a few extra shifts before the semester gets going. You just said it yourself, you aren't back on your feet, and if Guela needs anything, you will take care of her." The guilt for doubting him is eating at me.

"Please take it. Things are picking back up, but I don't want to rush things. I need to be careful. I got this covered." He is still holding his hand out to me.

"No. But I'll make you a deal. If I need anything, I WILL let you know. How's that? Better?" My offer is the best I can do, knowing we are both strapped.

"Fine, but you better let me know if anything comes up." I agree, knowing I would need to be desperate before asking. I have only come to him twice in the past 3 years for additional money. Both were toward the end of the semester when I was drowning in papers and studying, not bothering to pick up shifts at the club. He has also helped me by coming by the apartment with groceries. It may only be essentials, but staples in the fridge go a long way.

"I will." He nods at me, knowing if the time comes, I will call him. "I gotta go." As I get up, he follows me to the door, hugging me tightly.

"Take care."

"You know it. And let me know how things go with your dad."

Driving away from my grandmother's, away from the life I was born into and should be a part of, I can't help but feel a sense of relief. I breathe a little easier, knowing this doesn't have to be my destiny. The walls this neighborhood places to keep its inhabitants in are slowly crumbling for me.

CHAPTER FIVE

JUST ONE DATE...

Garrett

BACK AT THE FRAT HOUSE, babysitting the underclassmen during study time, I'm debating on texting her or not. My book is open in front of me, pleading with me to read, but all I can think about is whether texting her now is too soon. What was it that had her jetting so fast? I stick my phone back in my pocket and stare at my book.

My brain not registering the words I'm reading, I decide to walk around. She is absolutely captivating. Her beauty is unmistakable with her tan skin and dark eyes. It's those brown eyes that keep her secrets. I know she has some; I just don't know what they are. Enough daydreaming. I need to get back to work.

. . .

BACK AT MY PLACE, I scroll through a few texts from the day. A couple are from girls I dated for a bit. They are still hanging on after I called it quits. They loved to play it cool and "work" the house, seeing who would be best for their lifestyle. As soon as they found out who I was, they were like stink on shit. Thanks, but no thanks. I delete these without opening them. I scroll through again, hoping the one I want has texted. No such luck.

Everything turn out okay?

I decide to cannonball in. No use in pussyfooting around now.

I watch my phone, willing those stupid three dots to appear. After a few minutes of watching, I throw my phone on the bed to change. I can't let myself drown in thoughts of her when we haven't even had a real date yet. I don't know what it is about this girl that has me intrigued. The fact she is keeping a secret in knowing Kevin, her beauty, her aloofness to me, the fact that she hasn't thrown herself at me... Whatever it is, I figure I'm going to continue coming back for more.

Gym it is, to let out some of this frustration.

TONI

HE'S PERSISTENT, I gotta give him that. Most guys don't bother with the chase anymore. With so many girls willing to spread their legs in drunken nights out, the need to pursue girls is becoming obsolete. Am I jaded or is this really life? I can't tell anymore. Living in both worlds for the past three years has become second nature. My neighborhood girls don't mind a quick lay if it's going to get them something. No use in sleeping with anyone for free. You have to survive. The college-going, privileged girls fight for the guys' attention. They give it away for free if they perceive themselves to be the next "it" girl.

I know I have no right to speak. I have survived college with money from men. My justification? If I'm going to make it out, I need money to get me through it. Money makes the world go round.

All is well. Thanks for checking. I respond to his text. His charm, that dimple, and his willingness to keep trying is refreshing.

I'm glad. His response is short. No questioning what happened or quizzing me.

The phone rings as I'm staring at his response. Here comes the inquisition. I brace myself before I answer.

"Hey. What's up?" I answer.

"You know, normal Monday night. I just got back from the gym."

"That's dedication. Work all weekend AND go to the gym. Are you trying to impress me?" I tease him, but in actuality, I'm kind of annoyed. Trying too hard, dude.

The laugh I hear is loud and real. "Not really. It's just what I do."

"You're a gym rat?" Disappointment sets in fast. He's a pretty boy. Probably flexes in front of the mirror, too.

"Hardly." He continues laughing. Now I'm unsure whether he's just laughing or laughing at me.

"Care to explain?" Now I'm curious.

"Well, darlin', I'm in the city now. When I got bored growing up, I had plenty to do on the ranch to keep me busy. Like my dad said, 'No time for idle hands on the ranch.'"

Garrett

. . .

THE EXPLANATION just came tumbling out. This conversation is not going as I expected. How is it she continues to throw me off my game?

"Ranch?" I knew this is what she would catch. Am I going to have to end this before it has a chance to start?

"Yes, small town, remember? Not much out there to do except raise animals. And you need land for that." I try to downplay the ranch.

"Makes sense, I guess. I've never really thought about what there is to do in small towns since I'm a city girl." Her voice lowers with each passing word.

"No worries. How about you let me take you to dinner to make up for calling me a gym rat?" I am not above guilting her into letting me take her to dinner, especially since she didn't press on for more.

"Sure. When?"

I AM IN UNFAMILIAR TERRITORY. She wouldn't let me pick her up, insisting on meeting me at the restaurant, and to top it off, she picked a weekday dinner. She is keeping her distance. I can't help but wonder why. As I walk through the door, I see her. She has her back to me and is speaking with the hostess. I want so badly to wrap my arms around her and kiss the curve of her neck, but instead, I opt to place my hand on her lower back to let her know I'm here.

"Hello, darlin'."

The smile she graces me with is my new favorite. It reaches her eyes, and they sparkle. Her whole face is relaxed and unguarded for the first time since I've met her. "Hello yourself."

It dawns on me that she wears a smile as a mask, keeping people at bay. Rarely does it ever reach her eyes. My new goal is to have all her smiles with me be true so I can witness her eyes sparkling.

I place a bit of pressure on her back, pulling her closer to me, and I place a small kiss on her cheek. The flirtatious wink she gives me as I pull away could have been my undoing if the hostess hadn't gotten our attention to walk us to the table.

I chose a small Italian restaurant away from campus prying eyes or uncomfortable run-ins we most likely would have had any closer to campus. I know she'll jet faster than a bull out of the shoot if she gets spooked. Wanting to know the secrets she guards will take time, and I have to go about it with ease.

"Do you like wine?" I ask after we are seated. I'm not a big wine drinker, but if that's what she prefers, I'm game.

"If boxed wine counts, then sure." Her gaze drops to her menu.

"If it comes from grapes, then it counts. Want to share a bottle?"

The waitress comes up, asking for our drink order. "Start us with waters as we decide," I answer.

She watches the waitress walk away before she continues in a hushed voice, "It's so expensive. I'm a poor college student." Her smile says teasing, but her eyes speak the truth.

"It's on me. It's a date, remember. And we can always get the cheapest bottle. We are drinking it, not sip and spitting," I tease in return, hoping to get us back to the ease we had a couple of minutes ago.

"Are you sure? Not dutch?" Her eyes are still skeptical.

"Positive. Cheap red or white?"

"White."

"Just what I was thinking." Not much of a wine guy, I can stomach white. "How were your classes this week?" I change the subject before she has a chance to dwell.

"Fine, I guess. There is so much already. And you?" Her

answer is generic as she lowers her voice. Is it embarrassment for her?

"I feel ya. This last year will be no joke, that's for sure. I guess professors think we've had too much fun the last three years. They're cramming all the torture into the last year," I continue, trying to lighten the mood. I want her back with me.

"I guess you're right. I mentioned before that everything up until recently has come easy. Now, I have to actually put some effort into it. I guess that's what's throwing me off."

I want so badly to ask her something personal, but I know now is not the time. "What do you feel like eating?" I stay in the safe lane. I watch as she's browsing the menu.

"Spaghetti and meatballs sounds good." A small, fake smile appears.

"Hmmm..." I glance around the menu at the prices. I notice she has picked the cheapest item. Mention of the wine and now the cheapest item... She may not be exaggerating being a "poor college student." I decide to follow her lead and order the lasagna, which is only a dollar more than the spaghetti. No need to flaunt or make her uncomfortable. "The lasagna sounds good."

The waitress comes back with our waters, and we place our orders. I'm struggling to find conversation which doesn't spook her.

"Do you like working with your dad?" she asks, surprising me from my thoughts.

"Yes and no." I decide to open up just enough to build some trust. If this goes anywhere, she won't be able to say I lied. I just didn't share everything. "It's all I've ever known, so it's great. I enjoy being outdoors. I don't think I could be friends with an office—at least, not long-term. My dad is controlling, though. Everything is his way."

"So no office for you?" Her eyebrow raises in question.

"Not if I can help it."

"Well, an office is all I have in my future. I don't see an accountant working in the great outdoors. Where will I plug in my computer?" The lightness in her voice has returned.

"Very true. Are you planning on grad school?" I'm desperate to know anything personal about her.

"Probably. I'm looking into scholarships to continue on. There aren't as many for grad school as I'm used to. And you?"

"Also a probably. Looking at all my options." The waitress comes back with our wine and bread.

"Thank you," I tell the waitress as she begins walking away. "Tell me about you." I ask an open-ended question she has control over. She can share as much or little as she wants. I'm hoping this works and she doesn't shut down.

CHAPTER SIX

A FRIEND?

Toni

DINNER WASN'T what I expected. This was my first date. True date. And he didn't push too hard. When we left the restaurant, he walked me to my car and kissed my cheek, which was sweet. Men have always just been a means to an end for me. It's all about what I can get from them to continue on my journey away from the hood life I would lead if not in college. None have my trust, and I am not emotionally attached to any. "Mom" had a great way of teaching me this lesson early on. Seeing her so heartbroken each time another would leave her left me with massive trust issues. I know this, and I acknowledge it, but I won't apologize for it, either.

. . .

"Mom." I knock on her bedroom door softly. "Can I come in?" I always ask before walking into her room, because the couple of times I didn't ask came with a serious spanking.

"Leave me alone," she yells through the door through her sobs.

"I have a drink for you." I hold the beer tightly in my hand, wanting her to stop crying. I hate to be left again with my guela but I hate her crying in bed even more. I know once she starts drinking the beer, she will perk up, drop me off at Guela's, and be out with her friends. When I see her again, days later, everything will be back to normal.

"Come in." She sits up as I walk in and extends her hand to grab the beer.

"Get your things to go to Guela's." She wipes her eyes after taking a long swig.

I turn around and walk out.

WHAT SIX YEAR old should be burdened with taking care of their parent? None. But yet, that was my life. I never came home after that. That was when I moved into my grandmother's home permanently. Mom decided I was the reason men ran away from her. What man wanted to be burdened with a child that wasn't theirs. It wasn't me, though. Men continued to walk in and out of my mother's life, but she continued to blame one thing after another. She never saw she was her own problem.

WHICH BRINGS me back to Garrett. Last night was difficult. He was sweet and attentive and it would have been so easy to be pulled in by him. I want so desperately to fall into him and be damned with everything I have learned. But I can't. I know what can happen when you let your heart lead, and I'm not ready for that. I have to stay in control. If the hood is going to be my past, I can't let a guy derail me.

Why am I still seeing him when I close my eyes to let sleep find me? What is it about him? He's persistent but not pushy. He's a gentleman. Is that even possible? Do they still exist or did they ever exist? He let me lead the conversation. He asked about me but never pried. I was able to stay in safe lanes but came too close to the truth a few times. I admitted I was from town, but he didn't ask which high school I attended. If he had, I would have been in serious shit, because that would have given away where I'm from. I don't need him looking down on me or trying to save me.

My phone pings an incoming text. I pick it up to see a message from Garrett.

Goodnight beautiful! See u for coffee

I AGREED to meet him for coffee again. I don't know why I agreed. I should keep my distance, but I want to see him. Knowing I will see him tomorrow again, I drift off.

WALKING through the parking lot after class, I see a girl speaking on the phone, pacing. She spots me and quickly makes her way to me.

"I'm sorry to bother you. Do you think you could give me a jump?" She is a designer petite blonde, flawless makeup, a perfectly styled messy bun, and of course her Greek letter fitted tee.

I really don't have time for this, especially for the type of girl who turns down their nose to someone like me. Poor girl can't get her Mercedes to start. She can afford to call AAA.

The hesitation in answering gives her time to continue, "Please, I would really appreciate it."

She does not have the haughty look girls like her usually give. The one where they think the world owes them. She actually seems sincere.

"Uh, I guess so," stumbles out, surprised with the sincerity she seems to have. She smiles and hops around, walking past the Mercedes to the older truck on the other side of the aisle. An even bigger surprise. She jumps in, pulls the hood latch, and jumps back down.

"Where are you parked? I lucked out, because the space in front of me is open. I was keeping the space open so a car can get in to jump me." A small devilish grin forms, knowing college kids are vultures for open parking spaces. She opens the back door to the extended cab and pulls out jumper cables. I stand in the same spot, still stunned with the turn of events. I'm not an easy one to surprise. "Pull your car up."

Her statement pulls me out of my stupor. Luckily, I'm only a couple of rows down. I park and unlatch my hood before getting out. She has already placed the cables on her battery when I drive up. She lifts my hood and begins placing them on my car. She is doing this on her own, I think to myself. Usually, this type of girl is "helpless" and expects everything done for them.

"Okay, it's ready. Crank it." She turns to me and smiles. A genuine, appreciative smile. She jumps in her truck, and it starts. She revs the engine a couple of times before jumping back down. "My dad is not going to be happy." She smirks. "He hates that I drive this truck, but I can't part with it. For helping me, I owe you a coffee, lunch, drink..." She looks at me; I assume waiting for an answer.

"No worries. Glad I could help." I watch her take the cables off and roll them up.

"I insist. A couple of dumbasses couldn't stop for ten

minutes to help. If you follow me to drop off my truck, there is a great taco shack next door. I'll buy us a couple of tacos and beers for lunch." She waits on my answer. "Oh wait, are you done for the day?"

"I'm done, but I was heading to meet a friend for coffee," I reply so she does not feel the need to be around someone so opposite of her.

"Coffee?" Her smile widens. "Tacos and a couple of beers sound so much better right now."

Catching me off guard, I nod. "Great! Follow me."

I PARK at a small taco restaurant next door to an auto shop. I wait in my car as I watch her jump out of her truck, leaving it on and talking to the mechanic. I send a quick text to Garrett, explaining why I can't make it. She shakes the mechanic's hand and walks toward me.

I get out of the car as she approaches. Her smile is wider than before. "I can't believe I'm such a doof. Here, you have been helping me, and even followed me, and I haven't even introduced myself. I'm Lola."

Her energy and kindness are so unexpected; it hadn't occurred to me that we hadn't exchanged names. "Yeah, sorry." I shake my head slightly, not feeling like myself. "I'm Toni." I extend my hand to shake.

The taco joint is small, but the smell wafting through the place smells fantastic. I follow her as she walks to a table and sits down. She hands me a menu.

"I hope you're not on a diet, because these are the real deal. I try and stay away from this place because I swear I can eat my own weight in tortillas. But since I had to come to the auto shop my dad uses, well, I just had to walk in." A guilty smile reaches her eyes as they sparkle in mischief.

I'm not sure if I'm going to agree with this white girl's

61

opinion of the tortillas, but today has been a day of surprises. "Well, if the aroma of the food is any indication, you are right," I state politely.

A waitress walks up, and she jumps right in to order a couple of Dos XX for us. The waitress asks for IDs. "Shit, sorry, I didn't ask if you were of age."

I smile at her as I take my ID out of my wallet. "Here you go." I hand it to the waitress.

When the waitress walks away, I ask, "You really like this place?" Looking around, it has the vibe of a real taqueria you would find on my side of town, not here. I assumed a sorority girl wouldn't even look at a tortilla for fear of gaining weight just by the smell.

"YES!" she emphatically answers. "How could I not? Everything is delicious."

The waitress drops off our beers. She jumps in and orders some tacos before I have a chance. When the waitress walks away, we both take a swig of the cold goodness. "You mentioned your dad hates your truck? Why?" I was still curious why she would be driving the old truck.

Her eyes drop to the table, and she takes a deep breath. "It was my mom's truck. I can't let it go."

It is the start of an explanation. She looks around and back to me. "My mom passed away my senior year. I've just been floating around since."

Her honesty in that one sentence is raw with emotion. "I'm so sorry. If you love it, then it's a keeper." Not knowing what we could talk about, "Are those your Greek letters?" falls out of my mouth. Ugh, now I'll have to listen to sorority stories.

"Yes." Her answer is flat. "But I'm not really active in their activities. First clean shirt I found this morning. What are you studying?" She changes directions again.

"Accounting and business. One more year left. You?"

"Media and marketing. But I really don't have a clue." She shrugs.

The conversation flows throughout lunch about superficial things. Music, movies, and school keep us in a safe zone. Lunch ends and I wonder how she will get back to her place. We walk outside toward my car.

"It was nice meeting you. Take my number in case you need anything. I owe you."

"Not necessary. Glad I could help."

"Just punch my number in your phone and call me. Lunch was fun." She stands, waiting for me to comply. I do as she asks. "Thank you. Now, I'm heading next door to see if my truck is ready. Text me later." She smiles before turning around and walking to the auto shop.

I'M BEGINNING to regret saying yes to this party tonight. Garrett guilted me into it since I canceled our coffee date, and when I called Lola to tag along, she somehow had me agree to meeting here. I have never shared my place with anyone. This was always my secret sanctuary. A place I had all to myself.

I'm just finishing up when I hear a knock at the door. One last glance in the mirror before I take the few steps to the door. My hand is frozen on the handle as I scan my apartment—the one room. Shame begins to fill me. This is a foreign feeling. I have never had to worry about what others thought, because I did things on my terms. This is the first time I am allowing someone to walk slightly into my life.

"Come on. Open the door. I can hear you," Lola speaks through the door.

Her demand spurs my hand to turn the handle. I open the

door slightly, thinking about just walking out and not inviting her in.

"It's about time." Her smile is crooked as she rolls her eyes at me. Her relaxed nature is a change from most girls. "Are you going to invite me in, or should I just invite myself? You know I'm really good at inviting myself to things, right?"

"Fine, come in." I open the door wider and step to the side. She walks past me, holding a bag.

"Eats and drinks before we go." She places the bag on the small coffee table. "Food is always a good idea before a night of drinking. And it's going to be keg beer. Thought we could have some good stuff before we go." She pulls out a six-pack of Stellas.

"Thanks." Her thoughtfulness surprises me. I should now just expect the unexpected from her.

I sit beside her on the couch, grabbing a beer while she pulls containers out of a to-go bag from a cheap TexMex restaurant. She opens up boxes of quesadillas and flautas while placing different salsas and queso in front of us.

"Dig in. I bought so much. I couldn't decide what I wanted and didn't know what you liked."

"Thanks. I haven't had anything since lunch, so this is a great idea." I grab a flauta and dip it in queso.

"You've got it made. An apartment to yourself. Do you get lonely?" she asks between bites.

"Not at all. It's my little piece of the world away from the craziness of others. I was in the dorms my first year, and it nearly killed me." I shrug. She is only seeing the positive of my crappy studio, not the size or the second-hand furniture.

"Yeah, the dorms aren't ideal. I didn't mind it, but I also dreaded being by myself that first year. It gave me too much time to think of my mom. I needed to be around people."

"That must have been a hard year," I respond, sympathetic to how she must have felt. "I don't know how I would manage without my grandmother."

"Where's your mom?"

I slipped and may have opened a can of worms. She doesn't miss a beat. "She's around, but we have never had the typical mother/daughter relationship. My grandmother raised me," I try explaining without giving up too much.

"That's really sweet of your grandmother to step up like that. To have such a close relationship with a grandparent. Many times they just come around on birthdays and holidays. People you are supposed to be close to but only see a couple times a year."

"She's the best." I think of how hard my grandmother worked to ensure my cousins and I had everything we needed since our parents were assholes who only thought of themselves. "When do you want to get there?" I move our conversation away from me.

"No rush, really. It will be going for a while. Thanks for inviting me. I was thinking about going, but I really didn't want to head over by myself."

"If you are part of a sorority, why would you need to go by yourself?" I ask, confused, remembering her Greek letter shirt the day we met.

"I don't want to be active. My dad pays my dues, but they are not really my kind of friends. They can be so vapid. How many times can we shop and discuss money and guys with money? It's really a bore."

"Then why be a part of it?" I'm utterly confused by her admission.

"My mom. I'm a legacy. My mom was president way back when, and it's an automatic admission for me. I want to like it by the stories my mom told me, but times have changed." She pauses, taking a bite, and I let the information settle. "I just got back this year from my year off. I don't plan on participating in their activities. Just the minimum so I can keep the letters for my mom. Maybe it will change if and when I have a daughter." She looks past me with a sadness in her eyes.

"Sometimes, the shoe just doesn't fit no matter how hard we try to squeeze it on." A genuine smile creeps on her face as she looks back at me and takes a long swig from her beer. "So a year off? What did you do?" I'm curious how someone can afford to do that.

"Yep. I know I'm lucky because not all people could do that. I won't forget the experience. I took classes in Italy. I still think of it as a year off, because I did not take a full load."

We get out of the Uber she insisted on getting us for the night so that we were both free to drink. That is an expense I rarely splurge on.

I can't help but begin to notice the 'nose stuck in the air' attitude many of the girls walking around have. Last time, I was taking in everything, and I didn't pay attention to individuals. These privileged girls are carrying around expensive designer bags and tossing them around as if they got them at the local thrift store. I wouldn't even do that with my thrift store finds. When gems are found, you have to take care of them, because you don't know when another lucky find will happen. Another large disparity between them and me.

Knowing what to expect, I'm not as shocked or disgusted. I've had a few years to build my tolerance for the snobs. I don't want to be one, but I do want to have their money. Their kind of money will let me take care of myself and my grandmother. Give her peace of mind.

I watch as people are entering and the excitement in seeing each other is put on display. We have passed a couple of people who Lola has quickly greeted and made introductions, but there is a coolness in her greeting. Not recognizing anyone yet, I follow along to gauge the crowd and place. I still wonder more about her. It's obvious she comes from money, but her nonchalant attitude about it is not something I have run into yet.

I fear the run-in with Kevin that is bound to happen, but it is unavoidable if I keep saying yes to Garrett. My brain tells me to say no to both Lola and Garrett, but their charm catches me off guard, and I am agreeing to things I usually have no problem staying away from.

I can't stop myself from scanning the room for any problems which could arise. This behavior has been ingrained in me by my cousins. Growing up in the ghetto, you never knew when trouble was coming, so no matter how wasted you were, you'd better keep one eye out to save yourself.

Garrett is also the other reason I keep scanning the room. There is no shortage of girls here, all dressed to perfection, so I don't understand the reason he keeps up his pursuit of me. I mean, yes, I know I have the goods, but I'm not blind to know others have them too.

"Ha, found the bar!" Lola breaks me from my thoughts. "It's crap beer, but it'll do." She smiles at me as she scoots her way past a few people to get our drinks. I follow her lead.

"There are more people here than the last time." I casually mention my observation.

"Yeah, that's expected. We are only a few weeks into the semester. If you came the first weekend, not enough people knew about it yet." That is something I would never have known on my own since these things are not my norm.

The guy behind the bar is about to hand us two Solo cups when I hear, "Get those ladies a can, please." That voice. What is it about him?

I turn around to see Garrett strolling confidently toward the back of the bar. His attire is in contrast to most of the frat guys. He is wearing a snug-fitting t-shirt with jeans and boots. His hair is tucked away under a backwards baseball cap. He isn't dressed to impress like all the others. The underclassman, I'm assuming, passes the Solo cups to a couple of people on the side of us and turns away toward the ice chest.

Garrett comes to stand right in front of me and takes my hand, pulling it up toward his mouth. He places a gentle kiss on the back of my hand. "I'm glad you came." He lets it go and extends his hand to Lola. She takes his hand as he shakes. "I'm Garrett, pleased to meet you." He gives her one of those dazzling smiles that accentuates the dimple, and I feel a pull of jealousy that she is the recipient. Such an unfamiliar feeling.

"Lola." They pull their hands apart just as the underclassman places two canned beers in front of us.

Garrett's eyes are back on me as he begins, "Give me about thirty more minutes, darlin', then I'm all yours. Gotta finish up my duty and pass the baton off." He watches me, waiting for my answer.

"Okay," is all I can muster.

He brushes the back of his hand lightly on the side of my cheek. His large, rough hand sends a tingle down my spine. "I'll find you in a bit," he says as he walks away.

"Boy oh boy, does he have it bad," Lola says as she lets out a low whistle.

I turn my head to her and away from Garrett's departure. "Huh?" I'm truly confused by her statement.

"You have that boy so wrapped around your finger." She grabs her beer and begins walking.

"No I don't. We've only been on one date." Guys—especially guys this age—are after one thing and one thing only. "I'm sure he's just working really hard on getting down my pants," I respond, unwilling to accept her analysis.

"If that's what you think." She rolls her eyes and laughs at me.

What would she know? She just met him. And me. She is probably one of those girls who believes in love at first sight and mushy feelings. I know it is just a matter of time before the "real" guy shows up and the "love" he declared has faded away to his next conquest or back to the unsuspecting wife at home raising his damn kids.

We are standing around, talking to a group of Lola's friends who don't seem too bad, when I hear, *"Garrett, I haven't heard from you."* I turn to see a girl as she wraps her fingers around Garrett's arm. I step behind a guy in the group, hiding so Garrett doesn't see me, wanting to witness yet another reason men should not be trusted. She continues, *"Not one single text. I didn't even see you on campus last week."* A seductive pout appears.

"I've been busy. Working at my parents' ranch and classes have filled my time." Yup, here we go. No mention of this stupid cat-and-mouse game he thinks he is playing with me. Little does he know, I'm wise to guys' ways.

"You were at the ranch? I would love to see it." Why would she want to see a family ranch? She does not look the type to rough it.

"Yeah, it's beautiful out there. But as beautiful as it is, it's a shit-load of work." There he goes, bragging about his helping Daddy on the farm. That's his pickup line.

The giggle that escapes her lips is like nails on a chalk-board. I can't stand when women do that. So not necessary. I should know; I seduce them all. *"That's what you have employees for."*

"Darlin', we may have employees, but I will always be the one working the ranch. I need to be out there, making sure all is well." What does he mean he has employees? *"I need to get back to*

duty." And just like that, he walks away, leaving her staring at the nice ass which fills a pair of jeans perfectly.

Garrett

I'M glad I was able to guilt another date out of her for canceling coffee with me, but I'm annoyed we are hosting another party. I originally had the last duty slot but was able to switch at the last minute so I could enjoy the party with her. She texted me, saying she was bringing a friend, which I wasn't thrilled about, but at least she has someone with her while I'm still working.

I'm walking around, trying to find David so I can pass my party responsibility to him. I enter the private back room and find him pouring a glass of whiskey.

"Hope you haven't had too many of those, man. It's your turn." I jest with him, but I really hope I don't have to pull another shift. These parties are getting fucking old. They may be a blast for the guests, but duty sucks.

"Nah man. Just my second. Not looking forward to this. I'm done with parties for a while."

"Me too. If votes come up for another, we gotta veto the shit out of it."

David laughs as he clinks his glass to my can. I quickly give him the rundown while taking a couple of shots before leaving to find Toni.

"HEY THERE!" I see Toni from behind and, having dosed myself in liquid courage, I wrap an arm around her waist and kiss the top of her head. I needed to feel her. She has kept things so cool with me; I had to do something to pacify this ache I have for her.

"Hi," she responds coolly. She quickly glances at me, and her body tenses as she pulls her body away just enough for me to feel the difference. "I need to use the ladies' room." She pulls away completely, walking away.

I smile at the group, hiding my confusion, as Lola comes up and takes my arm. "She looks up at me and whispers, "Something happened. Don't know what, but all of a sudden, she wanted to leave. I talked her into staying. Just so you know." She squeezes my arm before letting go and falling back into conversation with the others.

"I'll be back," I tell Lola before walking toward the restrooms.

MAKING my way to the restrooms, another past fling, Julie, comes up to me. "Hey, Garrett!" These girls are trying to wear me down. They think if they keep pestering me, maybe I'll change my mind about dating them. One date is usually enough to figure out how shallow they are. This one took a little longer.

"Hey." I keep it simple because she's a needy one.

"Dance with me." She reaches for my hand and gently tugs me toward her.

I pull my hand back a bit. "I'm tired tonight. I just pulled duty, and I'm looking for a friend."

"What friend? I can help." She holds my hand a little tighter.

"I don't need help. Thanks. I need to go."

She comes up close, pressing her body flush to me. "Forget the friend. Let's get out of here. We can head to your place." Her suggestive tone is not to be missed.

I hate this part. I don't like being a dick to girls. I'm not an asshole, but damn, some of them are pushy and won't take no for an answer. This one is definitely hard to shake. She was able to cover her shallowness for a few months. I step back, placing space between us. "Not a good idea. I'm not taking you home with me."

She steps closer, speaking in a hushed tone. "Why can't we try again? You didn't even give us a chance."

"Like I said, not a good idea." What does she want me to tell her? *I don't want to date you because you have nothing to offer.* This has taken too long, and I don't want to miss Toni. I scan my surroundings, being near the restrooms, and I find her behind me, close enough to hear the conversation that just took place. Raising my brows at her for a little help, she smiles at me.

"You can't even look at me when I'm talking to you?" Julie is still speaking in a hushed tone, not wanting others to know I am turning her down.

I look back at Julie, then to Toni, and mouth to her, "Well?"

Toni strolls up, her shoulders pushed back just enough to dominate. The confidence she exudes is the sexiest thing I've seen. "Gonna keep me waiting any longer?"

"No. Let me get you a drink." I place my hand on her lower back before turning to Julie. "Have a good night. My friend found me."

Julie rolls her eyes at me, mumbling, "Whatever," as she walks away.

BACK OUTSIDE, sitting on a couple of chairs with fresh drinks in hand, we can finally talk without the blaring music. "Thanks. I needed saving."

"Ah, I think you could have managed yourself just fine. You seem to be Mr. Popular tonight."

"Mr. Popular?" I ask, confused.

"I saw you with another girl earlier tonight. She also seemed insistent on picking you up." Her voice has gone flat.

"So you noticed me, huh?" I tease her. Was that the reason she was going to leave? Did she think I was going to be with another girl when I invited her to come?

"It was hard not to. You were standing a couple of people away from me." The nonchalant tone bugs me because I can't read what's happening.

"I politely turned her down also. The second one was a bit more persistent." She is watching me, and I don't know where or how to change the conversation. "Did you want to go find Lola and the rest of your friends?"

"Those are her friends, not mine. I don't know anyone here. I could leave now and no one would be the wiser." She shrugs.

"I would be. I don't want you to leave." I grab her hand resting on the armrest, giving it a squeeze.

"Yeah, well, maybe you would notice."

"Hey, guys! Come on over and jump in the beer pong game we have going," Lola says, full of drunken cheer.

I look at Toni for direction. "You in?"

"Let's go kick some ass," she responds.

THE NIGHT PROGRESSES into a drunken frenzy of beer pong and tequila shots. Not what I had planned for getting to know her, but at least she didn't leave before *that kiss*.

CHAPTER SEVEN

WANTING

Toni

RESTLESS SLEEP due to everything we drank last night is keeping me in bed well past my usual time. I thought I would head to the library this morning to get ahead on reading and projects, but here I continue to lie, thinking about that kiss.

That kiss.

"I've got to go. I want to get to the library and get some work done tomorrow." I pull Garrett away from the beer pong tables where the tournament Lola helped coordinate is still going strong.

"You can't go. We are in the winning bracket," he whines.

"Yes, yes I have to. And I don't think Lola is going anywhere soon, so I'll need to find a ride." I don't want to spend the money on an Uber, but it is looking more and more like I would have to.

"Okay, okay." He wraps an arm around my waist and turns to the table. "We're out," he says, finishing with a fake salute.

He is looking at his phone as he walks me to the front of the house. "An Uber will be here in about five minutes."

I turn and look at him, confused. "You didn't have to. Thank you."

"Of course I did. I invited you, and I am in no shape to drive you home. This is the most gentlemanly thing I could come up with to get you home safe."

Adding this to the considerate things he does, I reach up and place my hand on his cheek. The scruffy five o'clock shadow gives his All-American look a rugged feel. I can see desire in his eyes, but he is keeping his cool. I am the one in control. I tip-toe up as I place my hand on the back of his neck to pull him down. When our lips meet, I feel a tingle travel all the way down to my toes.

I AM WELL aware of what a good kiss feels like, but last night with Garrett was different. I wanted to melt into him. He lips were firm but soft at the same time, inviting me in. His body strong against mine but not obscene. That's what had me. He was in control the whole time, but didn't push too fast. The kiss...that kiss...stayed a kiss which held a promise for so much more. He didn't act like some guy who just wanted to hit it and quit it. When the Uber arrived, it took everything in me not to invite him home. I have never had a problem with that because I never invite guys to my place. But last night... Last night, I needed him. Pulling away to get in the car was a chore.

I don't know what is happening. Why am I reacting to him this way? How has he made me lose my senses? This is the most unnerving thing I have been through since I began this adventure to escape my past.

Thoughts of him continue to swirl. Not accomplishing anything today is not an option. After another hour of letting myself dream of having another life, I get up and head to the library. I need to pick up another shift tonight if I'm going to make it through the year.

DRIVING into the parking lot of the club is a relief with the amount of cars already there. Looks like I'm in for a good night.

Sasha is behind the bar again, managing her controlled chaos. Anyone just walking in may think there is no real reason for what is going on, but Sasha has everyone and everything timed to perfection. There are always enough dancers walking the floor, entertaining, pause-times between dances, and all her cocktail waitresses are sectioned to ensure everyone is tended to for more sales and bigger tips. She is a genius in this business and the reason I only waitress exclusively here and don't moonlight at different places depending on the nights. Many girls do. The more experience and clout gets you the bigger nights. I was able to get the bigger nights right off the bat thanks again to Alex. He called in a favor to Sasha. She brings in most of his referrals, and he trusts the people she sends his way.

I quickly introduce myself to a couple of my tables, explaining I am taking over. I always give them the option of closing out and tipping the previous girl. I learned this unspoken code through Sasha. It helps you avoid the cattiness of the women.

The night is progressing nicely as I'm trying to ignore the exhaustion setting in from last night's drinks and partying. As I'm picking up a tray of drinks to deliver, Sasha stops me and hands me a Red Bull. "Drink up, princess. Tonight is not even halfway over." She laughs at my startled expression. She has never needed to correct me in any way. I am always a professional when it comes to waiting tables, because I know it's easy to fall from grace if you don't get the job done right.

Never bite the hand that feeds you. I guess I wasn't hiding it as well as I thought. I open it and chug. No time to waste.

"HEY, GORGEOUS," Mark calls to me as I walk by a table to deliver drinks. He's back, so my worries of not making enough for the year have just evaporated.

"Give me a sec, honey." I turn around to give him a wink. The night is looking up.

Back at his table, I am instantly more alert. I scan his table of two other men dressed upscale-casual. Being with Mark the past year has given me a better insight into wealth. He has guided me through events, shows, and fancy dinners. It may not be politically correct to say, but it is very *Pretty Woman*ish. He will come into town for business for a couple of weeks to a month at a time. When he's here, I get nice meals, some fancy clothes, and extra money. This help keeps me afloat and able to splurge a bit.

"Well hello, good looking." I never greet him with his first name in front of clients, colleagues, or friends. Ours is a relationship no one knows about. "What can I get y'all?"

"He is not the best looking one here at the table," the man to his right chimes in. "How about you bring that nice ass this way, and I'll let you know what we want."

He is right. Mark isn't the most attractive one at the table. Mark is a normal, good-looking guy, but he is nice and takes care of me. Mr. Cocky is a true specimen. He looks taller than most with broad shoulders, chiseled facial features, and the clearest blue eyes. I would let him play his game here. I always do.

"Well okay, confident sexy pants," I greet him as I walk the couple of steps in his direction. "What can I get for your table?" I lean in slightly, placing my cleavage in his direct line of vision. Just like I thought, his look leaves my eyes and travels down, holding there for a few brief moments before he brings his gaze back up.

"Three Blantons, neat."

Just as I'm about to turn away, fingers graze the side of my mid-thigh and slowly make their way up just under my skirt. He's a bold son of a bitch. "Be right back!" I smile and step away.

Men trying to cop a feel at a strip club is not a new thing. It makes me uncomfortable happening in front of Mark, but I guess he knows who he works with.

The night progresses smoothly. The Red Bull from earlier had its desired effect, and last call is minutes away. My bed is calling my name already. Checking all my tables for any last-minute orders and closing customers out is going smoothly. I'm at the computer, running some cards, when a warm body comes up flush on my backside. I turn quickly, ready to slap the offender. The good-looking guy at Mark's table leans closer, whispering in my ear, "I need to see you again." He places a small kiss to my earlobe and shoves a napkin in my hand before walking away.

While the banter we shared throughout the night was flirty and fun, I tried to keep it to a minimum. I still felt off doing this in front of Mark. If I think about it, Mark sees me with other tables and could assume so much more if he wanted. In this, I am choosy. Taking men home from the club is not good business—especially if they are repeat customers. The fantasy is gone once they fuck you.

I shake off the surprise and continue closing the evening down. Once all my tables have cleared and I clean out my section, I pick up my purse from the back, having a bouncer walk me to my car.

Driving home, I think of him. Charlie and a phone number were scribbled on the napkin. I ponder if this is something I would consider. I can't say I'm a saint, never taking men home from the club. There have been a few, like a super-hot guy I swear must have been a model, and a couple of older men who like to take care of women. But like I said, the fantasy is gone. One hot guy was as stupid as stupid comes, and he was more concerned with his orgasm than mine. The older men were fine for a minute, but they had lives to attend to.

Mark is the only one who I have enjoyed even when I looked behind the curtain. He's attentive, caring, generous, cultured, and smart. He runs some app company, so he is constantly traveling. He doesn't live here but keeps an apartment. I have been introduced to dinners at upscale restaurants I had never heard of—despite growing up in this city—and theater shows. I may not have a typical relationship with Mark, but it works for now.

Garrett

I CAN'T BELIEVE I let her leave. Wanting to take her to my place and show her just how good I could make her feel was all I wanted to do. But I didn't. I'm letting her call the pace. She's skittish, and I don't want to push too hard and have her spook. Right now, she's holding all the cards. I look around the small café students crowd to study. The never-ending coffee and reasonably priced snacks go a long way to keep the place busy all hours of the day.

I have a couple of the new kids with me. I was tired of the walls in the frat house, so I suggested we move mandatory study hour here. I'll probably have some explaining to do later, but I could not sit still anymore. At least here I have some distraction with the comings and goings of campus. It has nothing to do with the possibility of catching a glimpse of her. I'm not sure if this place is her thing, but it is worth it to find out.

"What are you doing here?" Lola's voice breaks my focus on the front door.

"Mandatory study." I wave my hand in the freshmen's direction.

"Isn't that supposed to be done at the house?" Her brows furrow in. "They never let us leave the house during study hour."

"Yeah, well...I was tired of the house. I needed a change of scenery." I try and sound as nonchalant as possible.

Her laugh comes fast and loud. "Whatever, my friend. You're looking for Toni." Her laughter is contagious.

"Nah," I try and deny.

"Yup. You got it bad, just like I told her." She nods her head, confirming her own observation.

"You told her?" Nervousness of her not giving me a chance if she thinks I'm a dimwit falling all over myself overcomes me.

"Sure did. At the party. As soon as I met you, I knew." She winks at me. "As you walked away, I saw her staring at that nice ass of yours. Thought I would help her out. If she knew you were in deep too, she wouldn't be so hesitant."

"Huh?" I raise my index finger, asking her to pause. "No leaving this table, guys," I direct the freshmen before getting up and pulling Lola with me to a corner. "I repeat, huh? She's in deep?"

"I've got a great sense about these things. My mom was a true romantic. We would people watch, and she was so good about picking up people's body language and mannerisms. I learned. You both have it bad, but y'all are trying your damndest to hide it. At least, that is what I think."

She has it bad? Could she really? "When did you tell her?"

I need to know if I'm going to have to do any damage control because this one thinks she's cupid.

"Like I said, as soon as I met you." She looks at me like I have a third eye.

"When I was still working my shift?"

"Uh, yeah." Her eyes roll.

No damage control. Everything happened after.

"Thank you." I really did mean it. But the thought of her thinking of me is causing my jeans to get tight.

COFFEE TOMORROW? I text her and wait. Several minutes pass by. I put my phone down and attempt to, at least, model good study behavior.

CHAPTER EIGHT

WHAT'S NORMAL?

Toni

As MUCH AS it may not be a good idea, I type the word "yes" and hit send. I read his text and was planning on ignoring it. If I didn't answer, eventually he would get the hint. But I couldn't.

I can't even think about what I'm doing right now. Mark is in town. I'm meeting him tomorrow night. I can't "date" and be a ... what do I call myself? Is call girl still a thing? But call girl isn't right. Men do not call me up and I head out. I choose when and if I want to. Prostitute? Not right either. We don't always have sex. Sugar daddy? I guess that is the closest. But aren't sugar daddies for girls with daddy issues? I don't really have daddy issues. The majority of the men are scum, and I am not in denial about it.

. . .

"*OH, TONI! I'M IN LOVE!*" *My mom is gushing over her newest boyfriend. I let her, because nothing I say will change her mind. She never learns. At least I'm getting a good lunch out of him.*

"Great, Mom." *I try and hide the annoyance in my voice. It's only the first time this year she has said this and it is summer.*

"*I've told him all about you. We are looking for a house to rent. You can move in with us this school year.*" *Her smile would be contagious if I believed her.*

"Are you looking in the neighborhood?" *I'm skeptical, but it would be nice to have a bit more room. Guela's house is small, and my uncle just moved in again. The small, three-bedroom is already tight with my cousins, Alex and Javie, my grandmother, and me. My uncle is taking over the living room, and I hate it when his friends come over.*

"Of course not!" *Her eyes widen in horror. My mom will do anything to leave our neighborhood.* "We are looking in Ingleside."

"Ugh, Mom. I don't want to change schools again." *I roll my neck, knowing this conversation is heading into an argument.*

"*There are better schools in Ingleside. We will finally be out of the ghetto.*"

"Really? And what happens when he dumps you?" *The words tumble out. I haven't lived with my mom for a while. Years of pent-up anger are unleashed in those seven words.*

"*If that is what you think, stay at Guela's. You'll probably drive him away with your selfish attitude.*" *She stands quickly, knocking the table, causing her drink to fall.*

Frustration and guilt hit me fast and hard. Knowing things always end badly, I know I'm right, but I didn't have to be a bitch about it. I watch the tears come as she turns away and walks out the door, leaving me with the check and without a ride.

I wave the waitress down to ask for the check. Knowing I do not have enough to cover what we ordered, I'm about to ask about doing dishes.

"*Want me to cancel the order?*" *a middle-aged woman asks me from behind.*

I turn and nod. I'm guessing it is a manager. I get up and make my way to the closest bus stop.

UGH! What has he done to me? These questions were never an issue to me before. I do what I do to make money. Men are a distraction. A distraction I don't need. I just need to finish and get in the real world. A world where I'm not hiding anymore. A world where I can be anybody. I've learned the language, mannerisms, and I sure as hell know I have the brains. The cattiness of college is what I can't wait to leave behind.

I SCAN THE COFFEE HOUSE, walking in. Not seeing Garrett anywhere, I begin to order.

I place my order, and the barista asks, "Name for the order?"

This is a change. They usually just call out the type of drink from the counter. "Toni."

"Okay. Thanks!" She smiles brightly at me.

I hand over my card to pay, knowing how much it is even if she didn't say the amount. I order the same thing every time.

"No need. Your order has been taken care of already."

"By who?" I ask, confused.

"I got it." I'm startled from behind as Garrett whispers in my ear. The chills he sends down my arm as I feel his breath so close has my body humming.

I step to the side, placing a bit more space in between us. "Thank you, but I can get my own coffee."

"I'm sure you can, darlin', but let me." He grabs my hand and places a slow kiss on the top. He pulls my hand away from his lips and winks. "There are people behind us waiting. Let's find a place to sit."

Luckily, we find a small corner table away from the traffic. "How did you manage to swing this?" I can't help but smile at his effort to continue impressing me.

"Credit card over the phone. I called it in on my way to class. Since you were nice enough to give me another chance, I wanted to make sure I made an impression." His dimple is on full display with his flirty, shit-eating grin. I feel my cheeks heat up with thoughts of me licking that dimple. "So I guess it worked."

Just as I'm going to deny, our order is called. "Hold that thought, sexy." I watch him move through the tight space to the counter. He is not the type of guy I would have given a second glance to before. A rugged, good-looking, boy next door. He doesn't scream for attention. His casual dress and carefree sense is refreshing.

"Penny for your thoughts." He brings back two cups of coffee and a couple of plates with scones. "Blueberry or cranberry-almond?" He is sliding the plates back and forth in front of me.

"Blueberry. Thank you."

"Thoughts?" he asks again.

"Honestly?" I ask.

"Of course." He doesn't hesitate.

"You."

"Hmm... Sounds good, I think. What about me?" His brows raise in question.

"You aren't what I thought. Most guys are..."—I pause, not knowing how to explain without coming off like a bitch— "into themselves and getting what they want. You have been nothing but thoughtful and nice."

"I'm glad you think so. I guess I can thank Mama for that."

"Helping Dad at home and thanking Mama for manners. You are a different breed." I giggle, teasing him a bit.

"You saw it the other night. I dated the girl you saved me from for a couple of months. I broke it off nicely. But being nice doesn't seem to get the job done. I have told her several times since the break 'no,' but she keeps coming back for more. Am I supposed to be a dick?" His shoulders shrug.

Garrett

I CAN'T BELIEVE that came out. She unnerves me. Compose yourself. Grow a damn pair.

"What does your week look like?" I ask, curious if I can see her again this week.

"Same as always. Classes, studying, wor—"

Her eyes widen just a fraction as she doesn't finish the last word. I'm guessing she was going to say work. It didn't look like she wanted to let that slip. Another money-hungry female not wanting to admit they have to work?

"Me too." I decide not to pursue what she was going to say. "Free night?" It will be a damn shame if she is after the money, too.

"Uh...sure. How about Thursday?" She may not have looked like she wanted to agree, but since she did, I'm taking it.

"So tell me, what would you like to do?"

"Hey, guys! I'm so happy to see a couple of friendly faces." Lola grabs a chair and plops herself down at our table. "What's up?"

"We were just discussing plans to get together on Thursday," Toni pipes up.

"Fun! Let's all go bowling. We can get a few people

86

together. We can do Glow Bowl." Lola is clapping her hands like a five year old and hopping in her seat.

"Glow Bowl?" I ask. I was hoping for just the two of us, but maybe this will help take some of the pressure off.

"Yes. The Lane Bowling has games that begin at like nine-ish, and they have black lights and fun music."

"I've never been bowling, but I'll give it a try." Toni's words are hesitant.

"We're in," I chime in for her. I grab her hand on the table and give it a reassuring squeeze. She looks up at me, and her lips turn up just a fraction.

An order is called from the counter. "Gotta go. I'll text you later for specifics. Toodles." She waves her fingers back and forth, bouncing toward the counter.

Toni and I sit for a bit in silence, taking drinks, and I watch her nibble a piece of scone.

"I'm not the best bowler, but I can help you out." She looks up at me, emotionless.

"I'm sure I can figure it out. How hard can it be? Send the ball down the lane and hit the pins." Her words and the confusion swirling behind her eyes are clashing.

"I have no doubt. But just in case, I'm here." I grab a scone and take a large bite. I place it back down and grab the bottom of her chair. I pull it closer to me. The internal struggle I'm watching is too much. All I want to do is wrap a protective arm around her and keep everything at bay. I rest my arm on the back of her chair and graze my fingers up and down her arm.

"No frat duties this week?" Her body leans a bit toward me.

"Nope. We voted on a party hiatus. They are too much damn work."

"You just realized this? But don't y'all have them all the time?"

"We do. But I guess I didn't mind working before because I was partying, too. But when you just want to spend time with a certain someone, the duty shifts suck." Again, information vomit. Another admission I was not ready to share.

She comes in slowly. Not knowing what she plans, I stay still, not wanting to misread this. Her lips lightly graze mine.

"Favorite song of all time?" she asks out of nowhere.

Our coffee date is saved with confessions of favorites.

TONI

I AM GOING BOWLING. This is another activity the poor folk don't do. I have never stepped into a bowling alley. All I know about bowling is what I've seen on movies or TV. Does it sound cheesy as hell? Fuck yes. Am I curious? Yes.

And what was I thinking kissing him? Even if it was sweet. His affirmation of wanting to spend time with me stirred something I have never felt before. I didn't think about it. It just happened. But when it finally clicked what I did, I needed to change the mood quick.

I've learned during my time here that 'favorites' talk can last a bit and doesn't have to get personal. It was actually fun. I did find his penchant for Mexican food as his favorite either brown-nosing or adorable. Can't tell which yet.

Ping. A text comes through on my phone.

Tomorrow night? ~ Mark

Sure ;-) ~ me

I answer immediately as I always do, but this time, a new feeling of worry washes over me. Knowing Garrett is causing these foreign feelings is irritating but not something I want to do anything about. Not yet...

I CAN'T BELIEVE how exhausted I am. The past few weeks of working, partying, and juggling these damn new emotions for Garrett have done me in. I'll just lie here for a minute while Mark showers, then I'll get dressed and head home.

"Toni, it's time to get up." I'm vaguely listening. "Come on, Toni, you know the deal."

His voice registers, and I think, *Fuck, I know better. I should never have gotten comfortable.* I quickly sit up to look for my clothes.

"Sorry about that. Late night at the club and early morning class must have done me in. I'm out of here in a sec," I lie while I'm quickly dressing to head home.

"No worries. Just making sure nothing has changed," he responds skeptically.

"Nothing has changed. I'm out of here," I answer while moving a little faster.

"Good." He comes up to me as I pick up my purse from his nightstand. "This is all I can do, but I like spending time with you." I tip-toe to reach his lips and give him a quick peck so I can scurry out. "Take a few bills from my wallet."

I walk to the door, turning around to give him a flirtatious wink to ease his mind about our non-existent relationship. I open his wallet to find several hundreds and twenties. I pull out four hundreds and place his wallet back down.

Driving home is sometimes the hardest. Knowing men just let you down, I don't want any more than this, but tonight, the cheapness I feel is irritating me. I've never apologized for anything I have done to survive my life, always doing what is needed. I've never felt guilty or bad about it. Until now.

LOLA HAS BEEN TEXTING non-stop the past couple of days, arranging a night of bowling. Never in a million years would I have thought so much work needed to go into a casual night out. When we get together in the hood, we just announce whose place, and everyone brings their own drinks and snacks if you're feeling generous.

Garrett has insisted on picking me up this time. I couldn't think of a reason for him not to, so he is heading here. My feelings of uneasiness are somewhat tempered due to Lola's insistence of making her way into my place already.

Just as I'm finishing up my mascara, a knock on the door announces his arrival. A deep breath. Here goes nothing.

I open the door. "Hey!" He makes casual look good.

"Hello, darlin'." He places his hand on my cheek and gives me the softest kiss on the corner of my mouth. "Almost ready to learn how to bowl?" His dimple gives away that he is trying to contain a full-blown smirk.

I move to the side, allowing him to come in. "I guess. Not much I can do about that now. Lola will have a fit if we change her plans." That is one thing I have quickly learned about her. She loves to do for others and is fiercely loyal.

"She may be little, but she's quite feisty." He goes to sit on my small second-hand couch. "I'm waiting on you to finish. Hurry on up. She said our reservations are at nine. I'd hate to see how mad she'll get if we're late."

I glance around my small studio, the one room with nowhere to go for privacy except the bathroom. He pulls his phone from a pocket and begins scrolling social media. I'm glued to this spot. How have Lola and Garrett pushed past my normal walls of extreme privacy?

He turns back and looks at me, confused. "Ready?"

"Almost." I scurry into the bathroom, closing the door behind me. I lean against the wall and take a few deep breaths. I take a quick look at my face and glide on some gloss. I walk out of the bathroom and slide on a pair of sandals. "Okay. Now, I'm ready."

Garrett stands up and takes me in from head to toe. There is a hunger in his eyes. It may not be helping that I'm standing in front of my bed.

"You will want to wear socks." His eyes come back to mine.

"Right. Socks." Not something I have done before, I forgot about the shoe rental. It kind of grosses me out, but if Lola—Miss Sorority—does it, how bad can it be? I slide off my sandals and take a pair out of a drawer. I sit on my bed to switch into a pair of Converse. He continues watching me as I make the change. "Okay. Now, for real, I'm done." I wink.

I walk beside him, not knowing what he drives. He clicks the button on his keys, and the lights of an oversized, older truck light up. Not surprising, but shocking at the same time. The truck fits his cowboy look. It does not, however, resemble the luxury cars parked at the frat house. He opens the door for me before walking to his side.

The drive to the bowling alley is filled with bowling jargon and tips. I can't believe he is suggesting I use bumper guards, as he calls them. He explains they are for children learning to bowl.

"I'm not a child. I can't use them," I protest, a little insulted.

"Of course you can. Anyone can. It's just a setting you add," he continues, teasing.

"I'm not using them." I stand my ground.

"If you insist. Just don't get mad when you gutter ball." I notice him giving me the side eye before adding, "Quite often." And with that last jab, his snickers turn into a full laugh.

Rolling my eyes dramatically at him, I inform him, "Just wait. I may surprise everyone with beginner's luck." I'm not too sure that will be the case, but I have to have some hope of surviving bowling. Bowling. How could anyone suck at this game? It's literally rolling a ball down a lane.

THE BOWLING ALLEY is filled with high school and college-aged people. Most of the lanes are filled with people already in the middle of games. The music is much louder than I expected, and the black lights make everyone look ridiculous. I can't help but smile at the good-natured fun everyone seems to be having. So completely different than the parties on the south side. The way everyone dresses, their mannerisms, the carefree laughter, is something I've only seen on TV. I grew up with "parties" in dark parks with alcohol purchased by someone's older relative. And that was in middle school. By high school, we had graduated to finding abandoned homes or whoever's place adults were gone or didn't care if we were there. And booze was no longer the central theme. Weed was easier to score and did the trick faster and cheaper.

Garrett leads me to the counter where Lola is already congregating with three others I remember from the party.

"Yeah! You're here. I feared you all would be late and we would lose our lane," she gushes while giving us each a friendly hug—another strange practice of hers. She turns back to the counter to speak with the attendant. "We are all here now."

We sit at the benches in our lane to swap our shoes. I hesitate, watching the others, before I make the switch. I don't want to wear these absurd shoes if no one else is. Surprisingly, they all begin changing, so I do also. Rene, one of the guys I met at the party, stands in front of a small screen.

"Okay, guys, real names, initials, or are we choosing characters?"

"Characters!" each person replies except for me.

Garrett turns to me, explaining quietly. "If we choose character names, the loser can hide their embarrassment behind a fake name. And any pics people choose to post won't give away who sucks." He winks at me teasingly.

"Ha....ha....ha." I say each like a slow clap.

He kisses my cheek and whispers, "You got this. You're probably a hustler." His description of me is too close to my truth.

Each person gives a character, so we have: Mickey, Superman, Flash, Daisy, Winnie, and I chose Eeyore.

Rene stays at the screen while everyone else goes to pick out their balls. Who could have known there were so many steps that needed to be done before a game could even begin? Garrett recommends I choose a six- or eight-pound ball, nothing heavier. Listening to his direction is becoming necessary. I place my fingers in the holes to make sure they are big enough. Getting your fingers stuck in a bowling ball is not my idea of fun. I'm hoping Rene places my name last. I wouldn't want to be the first one up without seeing someone do it first.

"Come on, Daisy. You're up first." Rene points at Lola.

I look up at the screen and see he placed the game girl/boy. I'm second to the last. It gives me a moment to watch before I make a fool of myself. Trying to decide whether or not I want to announce my bowling virginity, I choose to wait until after my turn. Maybe I can master this with no problem.

Lola's small frame picks up a ball and walks to the lane. She stands with her left leg in front of her right leg, pulls back her right arm, bending slightly, and lets the ball go. It travels down the center of the lane before angling to the left. She hits two of the corner pins.

Her body slouches as she turns around to face us. "I'm just warming up." She moves her head from side to side and stretches her arms. "That's better." Just then, her ball comes up through the machine.

Her next ball hits a few pins, staying more centered.

Rene, AKA Winnie, goes next. He takes a couple of steps before releasing the ball. His ball flies down the lane and crashes into the right side pins. The screen up top tells us six pins are down.

"Can I get y'all anything?" A waitress arrives to take our order.

"A couple of pitchers of Dos XX," Garrett tells her then turns to the group. "Snacks?"

"Yes, please. Get the appetizer sampler platter," Lola chimes in for the group.

"I need to see everyone's IDs," she responds.

Once our drinks and food order is settled, I watch each person who goes. With each of them having their own style, I'm left more confused.

My turn has come quickly. I slide my fingers into the holes, lift the ball, and test the weight out. I swing it back and forth a couple of times, making myself familiar with it. The decision is made to take the couple of steps then release the ball. My heart is beating fast and hard with nervous energy. I bring the ball up to clutch with my other hand the way I saw others do it, take a step, then bring the ball down and back. The next step, I bend and release the ball... It lands on the lane and quickly strays right into the gutter.

"Gutterball!" is yelled behind me from a couple of Lola's friends. I knew it would be coming as they had done this with a couple of others before me.

My head drops from embarrassment but more from frustration. How can this seemingly easy game be beyond me? I turn around slowly and catch Garrett's gaze. He's smiling, and he gives me a slight nod and mouths "Go again." A soft smile forms on my face at his encouragement.

I grab my ball again, testing the weight. I quickly ponder my game plan, unsure if I should take the steps again. Decision made—steps it is. The ball leaves my hand, lands on the lane, and rolls toward the pins. It's staying on the lane but slowly veering right again. It seems to be moving in slow motion, the anticipation of hitting at least one pin hanging in the air. Rolling...rolling...and crash...three pins on the right down.

The excitement of hitting just three pins hits me, and I jump up and down like I'm in elementary school, forgetting the people behind me. I turn around to walk back to the benches with high fives waiting. What is this alternate universe? I never thought throwing a ball down a lane would bring such happiness and excitement.

I sit down as Garrett stands for his turn. As he bends over to pick up his ball, he sneaks a glance at me and winks. His dimple is pronounced, making my stomach flip. These feelings are getting annoying, but at the same time, I don't want them to stop.

The waitress comes by and drops off the couple of pitchers of beer. One of the guys quickly gets to work, helping the waitress pour the beers. After everyone's are poured, there is only a bit left in one pitcher.

"Can you bring us a couple more when you see our glasses running low?" He waves the almost empty pitcher at her. "Thanks!"

My attention had been pulled from Garrett during the pouring. I missed his turn. I was only made aware of his accomplishment of knocking all the pins down by his loud declaration of "Ha" and his pointing at us on the benches.

"Don't get a hard-on for that, dude. It's only a spare, and it's only the first frame," the other guy pipes up at him, laughing.

Garrett plops down next to me after picking up the lone

beer sitting on the table. He drapes his arm on the back of the bench behind me. He seems so relaxed right now. Each time we have been together, a lingering tension seemed to fill the air around us.

"What do you think of bowling so far?" Garrett whispers in my ear, the intimacy of his breath so close, sending chills down my arm.

I turn to face him, our faces so close. "As long as I don't gutter them all, I think I'll be fine." I smirk at him.

The mischievous look in his eyes has my body begging to be touched. I'm not sure how long we sit watching each other until Lola snaps her fingers at us as she walks past us to sit down.

We both turn to look at her.

"Just checking to see if you were still with us." She smirks knowingly.

The game continues with laughs and teasing. I'm not too bad, hitting pins here and there with some gutter balls thrown in. It may seem like everyone is competitive, but it is all in good fun. This really is an All-American past time that is lost in translation to the poor.

Garrett emerges as the winner of the first game. His winning dance is silly, not what I would expect to see. But I guess this whole night is not what I had expected. I didn't know what to expect, but I was sure TV and movies exaggerated the "wholesome" fun they portrayed bowling to be. I guess not.

"Be ready to go down!" Rene points to Garrett. "I'm ready and warmed up." We watch him as he jumps around as a boxer would, spinning his arms, stretching his neck, and hopping.

Much more teasing and yelling continues through the second game, but this time, it's directed at Lola. She is looking like she may have hustled us, because she is knocking down pins like it's nobody's business.

After the fifth frame, she walks back to the benches, picks up her beer, and kisses the glass. "Thank you, friend, for my superpowers."

Appetizer trays and beer continue to flow throughout the second game. Garrett waves the waitress down for the check, ready to close out. She hands it to him, and he opens it, looking it over.

"Forty-five bucks each. It includes the tip," Garrett announces to the group as everyone is finishing their beer and changing their shoes.

Crap. No wonder I've never been here. I can't be spending that kind of money on a night out. I concentrate on tying my shoes as I watch a couple of them pull out bills from their wallets and the others get on their phones.

"Cash App or Venmo?" Lola's other female friend asks.

"Venmo," Garrett answers as he pulls his phone out. I watch her scan a barcode on his phone.

"Done," she lets him know.

I had a good time, but this won't be my regular. I grab my purse and stick my hand in to pull out my wallet.

"I got you." Garrett places his hand on my hand, stopping me from pulling out my wallet.

"Thank you, but I can't let you." I try and pull out my wallet with his hand still placed on mine.

"I insist. I'm not taking your money," he whispers to me.

"Okay. Thank you." I move my purse to the side, not wanting to draw attention from the others.

Garrett slides money he was handed into his wallet and takes out his card to place in the folder before handing it to the waitress as she walks by.

"I'll start closing out the lanes." Lola jumps up with her beer in hand and heads toward the shoe counter.

Closing out the lanes? I thought we just paid. I stay with Garrett while he waits for his card.

We meet her at the counter, placing our shoes on it.

"It's twenty-three each," Lola announces to us.

I watch as everyone is taking more money out. What did we just pay for? There would be no way I could afford this type of going out. What have I gotten myself into? I should never have let myself get befriended by them. Almost seventy bucks just for one night out? I'm truly sticker-shocked.

I'm grabbing for my wallet a second time tonight when Garrett comes in close to my ear. "How many times do I have to tell you I got this?" His cocky smirk stirs me but not enough to overcome the uneasy feeling of knowing I don't fit in.

I have no problem letting guys pay for me when we both know that's the deal. All my "dates" have been purchased. I provide company in whatever form they need, and they treat me well. This is new, and I am in uncharted waters. Garrett is not a customer, and I would never want to have that conversation with him. I don't want him as a customer. I want more... *What the fuck?!* That thought did not just happen.

My heart feels like it's about to thump out of my chest. This is not happening. I can't let this happen. NO. I'm not falling for some guy.

Garrett

"WE'RE TAKING OFF. LATER," I say to the group as I hand Lola a fifty. Toni's spooked and looks like she wants to make a mad-dash getaway, and I'm not about to let her.

I grab her hand, squeezing it, letting her know I have her without bringing attention to her. I doubt anyone else sees this. I've learned this look from the past couple of times she has tried to leave me. She closes her fingers. She's still with me.

Lola comes up to Toni, giving her a hug. "I'll call you tomorrow just in case you need to remember the bowling rockstar I am." She winks and turns back to the counter.

Everyone else says their byes quickly, and I lead her out. As we begin driving, I am wracking my brain for something to lighten the mood and bring her back to me. She is quiet and distant. There is so much more than what she lets on. She has a story behind those eyes, and I want to know what it is. I'm figuring money is an issue. She may not have looked like a deer in headlights when we were throwing money around paying for the night, but I sensed her unease.

"Salty or sweet?" I ask as she is looking out her side window.

"Huh?" She turns and looks at me.

"What do you prefer to snack on? Salty or sweet?" I repeat, pretending to be oblivious to her change in mood. I want her back with me.

"Hmm..." She pauses for a few seconds. "I'm not sure. I guess now it is salty, but it was sweet when I was little because my grandmother would sometimes have atole for me after school. I loved the days when I got home to the smell of cinnamon. It was my favorite."

A peace washes over her as I suspect she is picturing that time. I say nothing in return, not wanting to break the spell I just cast.

A few more seconds pass before she speaks again. "Atole is—"

"Rice pudding," I interject before she can finish, cocking an eyebrow at her with my knowledge.

"Yes, rice pudding. Not everyone knows. And you? Salty or sweet?"

"I've always been a sweets guy. My mom makes the best homemade cookies. I have to say, snacking on store-bought is just not the same." I decide to share a piece of me in return. "She makes all kinds: peanut butter, chocolate chip, oatmeal."

"I like cookies." I'm rewarded with her rare, real smile. The one that reaches her eyes. She's back with me.

Food seems to be a safe subject, keeping her out of her head, so I continue with the food conversation until we reach her place.

"THANK you for being such a good sport and bowling with me even though you had never bowled before." The unease in her surfaces again in an instant.

"You're welcome. But I do feel bad you paid for the entire night." Her gaze drops to the ground.

"Hey. It was my pleasure." I reach for her, placing one hand on her waist and the other on her shoulder. I gently pull her closer to me. "Call me old-fashioned; I feel better paying on a date."

She brings her gaze up to me, not pulling back but not saying anything. Seconds tick by. She slowly closes the few inches between us, leaning her body into mine as her arms snake around my waist. I wrap my arms around her shoulders, wanting to shield her from whatever ghosts seem to haunt her. I place a small kiss on the top of her head.

Our moment is broken when her next-door neighbor opens their door to walk out. She pulls back, looking up at me.

"Good night." Her lips come up to mine.

Don't get me wrong, it was a good kiss, but it was tempered.

CHAPTER NINE

HER SECRET LIFE...

Toni

LAST NIGHT WAS NOT what I had expected. I wanted to invite him in. I wanted to surround myself in all that was Garrett. I lay in my bed for what seemed like eternity, thinking of him. Wondering if he was seeing anyone else. Wondering if he wanted more. Wondering how I could keep my past a secret. Wondering if I wanted to. All this continued floating around until my mom called.

"MOM, seriously. When is enough going to be enough?" She just finished telling me about her newest boyfriend woes. Not wanting to be exclusive, blah, blah, blah.... I tune out quickly because this is a broken record.

"I don't understand your hostility. I'm going through something, and I don't even think you were listening." Ding, ding, ding...she's

right. I wasn't listening. My eyes roll at her dramatics yet again.
"What should I do? Should I let him take his break? Do you think
he'll come back?"

*"Why don't you take a break? If he comes back, fine, but if he
doesn't, then learn to be with yourself. Have you ever been alone?" I
know the answer to this. No, she has not, but she needs to see this for
herself.*

"By myself? Why would I want to do that? Men are supposed to
take care of their women. I don't understand why I can't find the one
to take care of me."

*Her pursuit of men has never stopped, but she is not concentrating
on the big bucks like she did before. If the bucks are there, she's ecstatic,
but now she really just wants someone to take care of her.*

"Maybe because they smell the desperation," I let slip, frustrated
with her once again.

*"Really! Well, thanks for the pep talk. I gotta go." She hangs up on
me before I can apologize.*

HER CALL THREW ice-cold water on the what-ifs I was just
imagining with Garrett. Perfect timing, waking me up to reality. Frustration with myself sets in because I can't want
anything with him. Eventually, they all leave. No matter how
nice he seems, he is still a male and so then untrustworthy.

I WAS GOING to pop into the club and pick up a shift until my
phone pinged with an incoming text.

Bitch, get your ass over here. No working

My best friend from the hood. Her way of telling me it
has been too long. Ditching the club may be what I need
tonight. I have ignored my real life, pretending to be the
perfect college student for too long.

. . .

"HEY, BITCH!" Amelia yells across the small apartment filled with bodies as I open the door.

"Hey, ho!" I respond.

We have been friends since elementary. Our shitty lives have been entwined with my grandmother and her mom taking turns watching us when we were little so they could work. Her mom is actually a pretty good mom, working several jobs just to make ends meet—but never enough to leave the hood. Her mom's concentration on Amelia, never leaving her in search of a Prince Charming that does not exist.

"What are you doing here, pendeja?" Alex's voice breaks through the music and chatter.

"What do you think, asshole?" I flip him off, walking into the kitchen to put my 12-pack in the fridge.

"Why do you keep coming back? Stay over there. Leave this fucking place." Alex follows me into the kitchen and begins his lecture.

"I told her to come. You can't take her away from me, fucker," Amelia responds angrily. While she is proud of me for attending a university, she is still trying to work and complete an associate's degree at the local community college. She would like to make it out, too, but won't drop the jackass boyfriend who mooches off her. If he would keep a fucking job for longer than a few months at a time, she wouldn't have to work so many hours.

"I know. But she needs to get used to those other people. The ones she will be working with and for. There is nothing for her here. She's going to leave the fuckin' ghetto." Alex holds his ground. "Maybe you need to learn and assimilate yourself over there with her. Instead of bringing her back here, you go to her."

"Fine. Next time," Amelia concedes to Alex, pacifying him.

He comes over and places a kiss on the top of my head. "Have fun tonight. But don't keep coming back." He places his hand under my chin and lifts my head to look at him. The firmness in his words is heard loud and clear.

As soon as he walks out of the tiny kitchen, Amelia starts in on him, "What the fuck, Toni? Why is he trying to keep you away?"

I shrug my shoulders, not wanting to answer. She knows the truth, but the truth is painful to bear. She may never leave this shithole life. She knows I have the ticket to leave, so she clutches me so hard sometimes, scared to face what happens next.

I see a bottle of tequila sitting on the counter. A cheap bottle that will certainly cause a horrendous hangover if we do too many shots, but one or two will kickstart the night.

"Shot time!" I point at the bottle.

"That's Eddie's. He'll blow a fucking gasket if we drink his bottle." Eddie is her loser boyfriend.

"Who paid rent this month?" I ask, knowing she did.

"I did. You know that."

"Then, he at least owes you a couple of shots." I raise an eyebrow, waiting for her to falter.

"Fine. We just won't admit it." She grabs two glasses and pours us a generous amount each.

"Pa vajo." We click our glasses together and shoot the awful-tasting alcohol.

"Where is he, anyway?" I ask, curious to his absence.

"He's filling in for a bartender at The Hole."

She's being generous, calling it bartending. Grabbing customers their beers and mixing cheap booze with sodas of their choice is not exactly bartending. But on this side of town, that's all we can afford, and it's always a treat to indulge at a bar.

Back in high school, Amelia and I did much of our drinking at The Hole. A few places on this side of town never checked IDs. They risked it for the business. Luckily, no one was ever shut down for serving minors. Bartenders knew who was who—one big, dysfunctional, poor family. They served who they knew, never chancing it when an unknown walked into the bar. You had to be introduced by family or a friend before they served you. Another one of Alex's gifts to me.

"Nice. At least he'll come home with cash in hand." No waiting on a paycheck when there are tips involved.

"Yup. And I'm taking those fucking tips from him, too."

She opens the fridge and grabs four beers. "Come on."

I take two of them from her and follow her out of the apartment. She walks to a couple of benches several yards from her door. She sits, folding her legs under.

"What happens when you graduate? Will you really stay away for good?" Her voice is low even though there is no one around to hear our conversation.

"Not for good. I have my grandmother. When I can finally afford a place for the two of us, I don't know. Maybe." I don't want to blow smoke up her ass.

"It's changing already. Alex doesn't want you here, and I'm losing my best friend."

She's not exaggerating about the best friend status. We have had each other's backs throughout the years.

"THE FUCKING COPS ARE COMING," a whisper yell breaks through the hissing of the spray-paint can. My middle school boyfriend is busy spray-painting his gang symbol on a slide at the neighborhood park.

Four middle school kids run. My boyfriend grabs my hand, pulling me. "You two head toward 11ᵗʰ street, and we will head toward the paseo. Meet at my place."

Amelia and her guy veer off as we continue on our path. Just when we think we are in the clear, a cop car pulls up beside us a block from his house.

The juvenile detention center was our next stop. I refused to name who was with us or give up any of my friends' tag names. I'm not a fucking rat. I got a month because it wasn't my first time breaking city curfew. That and because boys can't be trusted. The boyfriend admitted it was him and me tagging the bench.

Amelia stayed out of trouble that night. Her history is clean, no need to hide a juvenile record. At least mine "went away" as soon as I turned eighteen. I'm not naïve enough to think it's completely gone, but at least it's not there for easy viewing.

WE HAVE COVERED for each other our entire lives, it seems, never letting the other fall if we can avoid it. I don't know how this next phase will work. I want to leave and am ready to say good-bye to everything except her.

"I know. But we'll figure something out." I stay somewhat optimistic, not wanting to think about it yet.

"I'm still fucking sober. Shot gun." She pulls her keys out of her pocket, ready to poke the can, waiting for me to agree.

"Do it," I encourage her, wanting to be shit-faced and not think of what happens next.

She pokes the bottom of the first can and hands it to me, then does the same to the next.

"Go." We each pull the tabs back and finish a beer in seconds.

"Not enough." We click the ones we had already opened and chug them too. We head back into the apartment.

The night continues with more drinking, games, and conversation. I may not come around often anymore, but I'm known well enough for people to leave me the hell alone. My reputation and familial relations keeps girls and their cattiness quiet.

———

MY EYES open with the usual hangover that accompanies nights out with Amelia. When I'm with her, I've never been able to control the amount of drinking we do. It's like we want to forget the crap around us, so we send ourselves into oblivion. Temporarily, we can ignore the glaring sign of life on the southside.

I look around the small bedroom she shares with Eddie. I see his arm hanging off the side of the bed as I'm on the hard-ass floor. I have a pillow and blanket, so I'll be grateful for that. Memories of the night come back, and I really don't want to be around when Eddie wakes up. He blew up when he got back from The Hole. I don't remember why he was pissed, but the large amounts of liquid courage I drank had me intervening. At least he knows his place, and if he would have gone after me, he would have had Alex to deal with. Alex has made a name for himself, so no one messes with him or our family.

I get up, glancing at the bed with my best friend still passed out and the jerk she is hanging onto.

In my car, I send her a quick text, not wanting her to be worried about me. I open the texts waiting for me.

Lola: *Text or call me if you want to hang tonight*
Garrett: *Hello gorgeous! When can I see you again?*

IT TAKES a few moments to decide if I want to respond. The headache wins out, so I close out the texts and drive home.

Sleep and a greasy burger are the only things in my immediate future.

Garrett

A FEW OF the brothers decided on a hole-in-the-wall bar for cheap beer and liquor, but mainly to avoid all the usual girls wanting to hang all over us. They felt they needed some new meat.

While the guys are trying their best, trying to impress the ladies enough to take them home, I sit at the bar, only wanting to take one home. Unfortunately, she is nowhere to be found and hasn't responded to my text, either. The bartender is nice to look at and even pleasant to talk to, so I stick around.

"No game tonight?" Kevin sits on the stool next to me.

"Nah. Just not in the mood. This will be my friend tonight." I lift the beer bottle.

"Please don't tell me you're stuck on Toni?" He's trying to act casual, but I notice an edge to his question.

I pause a moment, deciding how I want to approach this.

"Why would I be?" I shrug, sounding as uninterested as possible. "Shots?"

He is not too far from drunk. Getting him loose-lipped about Toni may not be too hard.

"Hell yeah!" he responds.

I wave to get the bartender's attention. "Two jager shots, please."

Here goes nothing, hoping I don't get too drunk in the process so I can finagle more information about her.

A tequila shot and a couple fruity ones the brothers joined

in for later and Kevin was ready to begin talking. Luckily, I was able avoid a few by excusing myself to the bathroom.

"Who do you have your eye on now?" A casual question which is often asked of him. His reputation of going through women is well known in the house.

"I want to bang the shit out of Leslie in Kappa, but she's playing hard to get. I may drop her and watch her come crawling back. I know she wants it but thinks I'll respect her if she waits. Little does she know that as soon as I get her, I'm done. No need in pretending otherwise." He slurs through his jackass comment which was expected.

"Are you ever going to keep one around?" I tease him, knowing he won't settle down—at least, not in the near future.

"Nah, man. No need. Too much pussy around to play with." He laughs at the absurdity of monogamy.

"How do you keep them from clinging?" I know the answer to this, but I have to get him talking and pretend he's helping me solve a problem.

"Drop them. You're too fuckin' nice." And there it is. My unease of being a dick to women. This is what gets me in trouble, why they keep coming back thinking there is a chance.

"I feel guilty, dude. It's just not my style." I drop my head on my arms on the bar. If I play like I have no game, he may offer information without me having to ask.

"That's why you're stuck with Toni, dude. You need to let that one go. Don't get yourself saddled with that one." His laugh is grating on my nerves as he talks about the girl I'm falling hard for.

"I haven't thought about dropping her yet." My shoulders shrug.

"I'm telling you. That one is not one to take home to

Mama." He slaps my back firmly. This now has me wondering what he knows.

"Not the plan. But what's wrong with her?"

"Go by the gentleman's club off of Walters Road. You'll understand then."

"Huh?" The shock of his statement has me wanting to go now but also wanting to punch the shit out of him.

He slides off his stool, patting my shoulder. "Just believe me, drop her and drop her fast. I gotta take a piss." He walks off, leaving me in a stupor.

Not wanting to believe him, on one hand, but knowing she has been hiding something has me doubting my belief in her.

The room begins to feel too small for all the people traversing around. She has not responded to my text. She has mentioned a job. I wave at the bartender one last time as I drop money on the counter. There is only one place I need to go now.

I WALK into The Pass Gentleman's Club. I creep the side, not knowing what I will come face to face with. I scan the place, watching a few waitresses working tables full of men. I don't see Toni anywhere. I don't know if I should be relieved or worried she will be coming out onstage. I find an empty table in a dark corner and sit down. I probably look like the worst type of stalker here by myself.

An overly done waitress stops by the table. "What can I get you, handsome?"

"Bud Light, please," I say, not really wanting to drink any more but knowing I can't take one of her tables without buying something.

"That's all?" The perturbed feeling is showing.

"Yup," I answer. I'll leave her a good tip and make it up to her.

A tall blonde walks out to the stage with some high-energy music. She sways and shakes everything before she jumps on the pole.

"That'll be six." The waitress is back.

I hand her a twenty. "Keep it." She smirks before walking away.

I stay for three more performances before I decide Kevin must have been full of shit. Either that or she may have changed professions.

I WAKE FEELING WORSE than I did last night, confused with what she could be hiding and all the damn drinks.

A glutton for punishment, I send another text.

How about staying in? Dinner and a movie. I hit send.

I jump into the shower, hoping it will help me feel human again.

CHAPTER TEN

IT'S ONLY DINNER

Toni

MY PHONE HAS BUZZED CONSISTENTLY through the nap I needed after last night's escapade with Amelia. I haven't picked it up, not sure I want to face the day or who is on the other end of the texts.

While I enjoy spending time with Garrett, I know it can lead nowhere. I have nothing to offer him, and he has nothing to offer me. It would be different if there were an arrangement. Then, we would be on the same footing.

I'm not going back to sleep. No use in pretending. I might as well get up and get something productive done. I take the couple steps to the bathroom, letting the shower heat up, the steam and water washing away the stink of afterparty.

After the long, hot shower, I decide to check my messages. There are several from Lola, wanting to hit up a club tonight with friends. I text back, letting her know I am in no shape for another night out. She asks who I was out with. I leave it ambiguous and just respond "a couple of old friends." While I have begun to like her, there is still no way I will admit where I'm from.

Alex sent a couple, reminding me to stay away from the south side.

Amelia was worried where I had snuck off to this morning and apologized for Eddie's behavior—something she does often but doesn't realize or won't admit. The only reason I put up with him is because she "loves" him. As soon as that shit is over, I don't have to play nice anymore. I guess I wouldn't need to play nice if I stayed away like Alex wants.

And, of course, there are a couple from Garrett. He's asked me over for dinner and a movie. It actually sounds good if the meal is homemade. I've been eating too much crap lately. The last one is his attempt to sound casual and funny, asking if I am still alive and well.

This is the trouble with having him around. He is so damn cute, funny, and persistent. As soon as I make my mind up to stay away, here he comes again, breaking through my defenses. It's almost like he knows they are there and refuses to acknowledge them.

I should know better and should say no, but a night in with a fun person is better than the Ramen I would be eating alone here in this tiny apartment. Before I can respond, my phone pings again.

If you don't want to come here, I can come to you....maybe???

See, he doesn't give up.

Yes, dinner and a movie sounds like a good plan. I can go to you. If that's ok?

I hit send, knowing nothing good can come of it but doing it anyway.

That's a plan. Come over at 7. Tower apartments #1590 Know them?

I do know them, and they are very nice apartments. That's where Kevin lives. How can Garrett afford to live there, too?

I'll be there.

Kevin does not live in that building, so I don't think I need to worry about running into him. He is one person I don't want to run into. He knows enough of my secrets. I'm regretting going home with him that night last year. I only did it that once because I fell for his good looks, but I have stayed away since. It wasn't even an arrangement. I was just horny and wanted a good lay. I thought he would be one, and I was right. Now, he just shows up at the club sporadically. I thought he was older based on the men he is usually with.

I KNOCK on Garrett's door, looking around, wondering if he lives with anyone. A roommate would explain how he could afford living here. He opens the door in athletic shorts and a t-shirt. I'm glad I decided on leggings and a loose tee. I was unsure how casual I should dress.

"Hi!" The smile creeping on my face is impossible to stop. I really am happy to be near him.

"Hello to you." His dimple tempting me, I use all my strength not to touch it. "Come in." He moves to the side and lets me walk by.

Looking around his apartment, I'm amazed to see the simple décor. It is all really nice, the furniture matches, and it is clean.

"This is a nice place. Is your roommate here?" I ask, trying to learn more.

"Thank you. And no. I don't have a roommate. I'm all alone here." His smile turns into a sexy smirk.

"Oh." I'm confused. The living room and kitchen are so much bigger than my small efficiency. I haven't even seen the bedroom. No. No, I can't see the bedroom. He could definitely crash through the defenses if we went there.

"You sound surprised." He walks toward the kitchen. I follow.

"No. I just thought most people had roommates." I try and save myself.

"True. And I did, too, for the first couple of years. Last year, I decided I didn't want to put up with anyone else's crap, so I got my own place." He begins stirring what looks like spaghetti sauce in a pan. "But you live on your own, too."

"Yes, but my place is a dump compared to this." The statement flies out of my mouth before I can stop it. No reason to bring my crappy life to his attention.

"No it's not." A sweet smile that reaches his eyes fills his face. "It's yours and you don't have to put up with anyone else's crap, either. I think that's a win."

"Yes. I like having my own space. I sit at one of the stools overlooking his kitchen. "So, how many roommates did you have?"

"The first year, I was in the dorms with one roommate. I don't see him as often since he rushed a different frat. The next, I was in the frat house. That was madness. I couldn't do it anymore, so I talked my parents into this place. All for better grades." He winks at me.

I laugh. Even 'normal' kids tell white lies to get their way.

"And you?" He asks in return.

"I had one roommate my first year. It was horrible. She wanted to party all the time. People in and out of our room. I couldn't take it, either, so I found a scholarship that would cover living expenses." Again, word vomit. Why did I share this?

"Cool. I didn't even know there were those types of scholarships." He takes a pot off the stove and walks it to the sink.

"Not many. I really had to search," I added, no need to hide it now.

"In case you couldn't tell, spaghetti is for dinner." He pours the pasta into the strainer. "Hope that's okay."

"Perfect," I answer honestly. "I haven't had a good meal in too long."

"Well, I'm not sure how good it is, but remember, I tried." A short, nervous chuckle escapes his lips.

"It will be fine." I try and make him feel better for attempting.

"Do you want a drink?" He looks back from the stove as he is pouring the pasta in the sauce.

"I'll take a water, please." I'm not sure if he wants to drink, but I need to abstain after last night. Still hydrating.

"Sure. Help yourself. There are bottles in the fridge." He nods his head in the direction. "Can you pull one out for me, too?"

I pull two out and place one on the counter close to him. Bottled water is an extravagance I don't splurge on. I don't understand it. Water tastes like water to me.

I watch him. He looks a bit out of sorts in the kitchen, so it makes me even more appreciative of the effort.

"I need to be honest here." He looks my way and pauses. "I'm not the best cook. This is one of the only meals I feel comfortable making for another person." His eyebrows lift with his admission.

"Then I'm flattered you went through the trouble." Which is the truth. "Do you eat out all the time?" I'm curious. He does not seem like the type of guy who would eat sandwiches and Ramen on the daily.

"Thank you. No. I will eat my own cooking, because I'm only subjecting myself to the torture. I keep telling myself if I continue practicing, maybe it will get better."

I laugh at his honesty.

"Go on and sit at the table. It's all done." He is lifting a bowl and a basket.

He places the items on the table and walks back to pick up his water.

"Do we have everything?" he asks.

"I think so. Pasta and bread. What else do we need?"

"Cheese!" he exclaims before opening the fridge and pulling out a small plastic container.

That is not like pizza Parmesan cheese. He sets in down in front of me. It's shaved chunks of cheese. The real stuff. He's either really trying hard to impress or this is his life. I haven't figured out which.

"Help yourself, please," he prompts.

I pick up the serving spoon and help myself to a plate of his pasta and grab a piece of bread from the basket. It dawns on me—he has a basket...for bread. What kind of guy is this?

I watch him serve himself before I try my first bite. He takes his first bite, so I pick up a piece of the cheese from my bowl and place it in my mouth. It's good. This is the real stuff.

"I have wine and beer in the fridge if you'd rather. I'm still hydrating from last night," he begins the conversation.

"Me too," comes out quickly. Crap. Again, my words escape without thought. I may have to come up with something quick.

"Well, good. I am still feeling some of the effects from last night. I just didn't want to ruin it if you were in the mood to have a drink."

"I'll abstain tonight, too. What did you do?" My curiosity about whom he was with gets the best of me.

"My frat brothers and I went to a hole-in-the-wall bar for cheap booze. Too many shots later, and I'm feeling like this." His shoulders shrug as he takes another bite.

"This is really good. No need to be worried," I compliment him, hoping it changes the subject of last night.

"Thank you. Like I said, it's edible."

"It's more than edible. It's good. Thank you. Especially if you are hungover." I just brought up last night again. Ugh. "Why would you ask me over if you are hungover?" I'm wondering why he would want to torture himself.

"Because I wanted to see you. I was not going to jeopardize my chance of seeing you tonight."

This is what gets me. He is always so sweet, and my usual defenses are not accustomed to it. Guys are usually all in for themselves, so it's easy to keep them at arm's length. Garrett. Well, Garrett creeps under your skin with his grace and charm. He always seems to put me and my needs first.

"I think that is the sweetest thing someone has ever said or done," I answer honestly.

Garrett

"If you just give me a chance, darlin', I'll continue to show you sweet." She is more relaxed tonight than ever before. I don't know if it's her hangover, the casualness of the evening, my cooking for her, or maybe she's starting to trust me, but I'm going to milk this for all it's worth. Even after Kevin's crazy announcement last night, I still want to be with her. Her strength, beauty, and mystique are driving me crazy.

"Don't push your luck, mister." Her lips pull up, reaching her eyes as she twirls a large portion of noodles on her fork and shoves them in her mouth. She chews a bit then adds, "You don't know what you're getting into."

"I'll take my chances." I shove a large piece of bread in my mouth, mirroring her. And with my mouth full, I respond, "I'm a big boy."

She quickly covers her mouth before a laugh escapes. She picks up her napkin with her other hand and brings it up to her mouth.

"I was not expecting that. And the first mental picture that came to mind was your face on Baby Huey."

"Not who I wanted to remind you of." I need to redeem myself now.

"What movie are we going to watch?" she asks, sobering me from my embarrassment.

"Whatever. I haven't picked one out. Thought I would wait and see what you enjoyed."

"Cool. I haven't paid attention to what is at Redbox lately."

DINNER CONTINUES with more conversation about movies. She helps me clean up before sitting on the couch for an action movie—her choice, not mine. Most girls—when given the chance—will subject guys to rom-coms, hoping we'll act like the guys in the movie. She never responds the way I think she will.

We start innocently enough on the couch. Not wanting to push my luck, I stay on my side. But eventually, she moves closer, snuggling into me. I drape my arm around her shoulders, letting my fingers graze her shoulder. Her hand on my thigh is testing my willpower. She begins to lazily drag her hand up and down—nowhere near my boy, but just as enticing. Her clean, out-of-the-shower scent, her body molding into mine, and the heat building between our two bodies has me hoping my cock doesn't show through these loose shorts.

As the movie drags on, the caresses become a little more urgent. More pressure. Closer to places we are purposefully avoiding. I've looked down at her a couple of times. Her eyes are fixed on the TV. But this time…this time, she looks up at me, and her breath hitches, hunger in her eyes. I freeze, not wanting to break the spell. She brings her hand up, caressing my cheek before bringing her lips to mine in a hunger-filled kiss. It is the most passionate kiss I have ever experienced.

Breathing is not an option right now, as I have the one thing I have been waiting for. Getting lost in her is the only thought consuming me. Tasting her lips, our tongues are in a manic dance for more. Her arms creep around my neck, pulling me closer. Then, she pulls away, breathing shallow and fast. I watch as a storm passes through her eyes. She's deciding whether this will end or go on.

A few seconds pass in silence, just watching each other. As the thought of her getting up and leaving begins to pass through me, she rolls her body over, straddling my lap. I know she has to feel the hardness that has been building. She picks herself up slightly and comes down again, rubbing herself on me as a small moan escapes her lips. If she keeps this up, it will be my undoing.

"Do you want me?" Her voice is husky with need.

"Only if you want me to, darlin'." I place my hands on her firm ass, pulling her closer to me.

"Then what are you waiting for?" Her lips crash back into mine.

Hands are roaming and groping, lips are tasting, and bodies are pressing so tightly I need to take a step back or I'm going to unload before the actual party.

I place my hands on her shoulders slightly, pushing her back.

"What's wrong?" Confusion mars her face.

"Absolutely nothing. I just need to get a handle, or you're going to make me come before I'm ready."

The sexiest smirk known to man crosses her face before she puts her hand between us and cups my dick.

"Okay, that's it." I push forward, standing up, holding her by her ass, and her legs wrap around me instinctually. Her arms come up as she licks and suckles my neck.

I walk us to the bedroom and place her down, standing in front of me.

"Pick up your arms." I watch as she slowly complies. I grab the hem of her shirt, pulling it up over her head. A lace, see-through bra greets me. I come down, taking one breast in my mouth as I slide her pants down her legs. A small little triangle thong is exposed.

Here she is, in all her beautiful perfection, in front of me for the taking. I guide her back until her legs hit the side of the bed. She sits down and pushes herself back.

"I'm going to kiss every last inch of you before we even get started." And I mean it. Her flawless, tan skin is begging for attention. I crawl on the bed until I reach her mouth.

CHAPTER ELEVEN

TRUST

Toni

AS MY EYES open to a new day, memories of last night flood my memory. I stay perfectly still, not wanting to wake Garrett yet. My need to process everything first is crucial. So much of last night was out of character for me. When have I "hung out" with any guy? Sleep over? That's just asking for trouble. Sex. Sex complicates things.

But as these thoughts pass, I can't help but be content. Can I even say happy? His demands, firm but gentle. His attention to my needs rather than his own. His insistence on keeping me close. His ability to please. All of these things are not something that I have experienced. Or maybe I just haven't let myself experience it? Is this a usual relationship beginning? If you have never experienced a beginning, how's one to tell?

My mind is made up. I need to stop this now. This is all a

mirage, and the only thing that happens now is getting burned. Better to be the burner than the burnee.

I sit up quickly, keeping the sheet high, covering my breasts to search for my clothes.

"Morning, darlin'," a voice, thick with sleep, greets me.

"Good morning." I move to stand, but his arm comes around my waist, quickly pulling me back down.

"Are you trying to leave me already?" He looks directly into my eyes, searching for an answer.

"Uh..." I say, not expecting him to ask directly. I'm not sure what I expected, but not that. "Uh...I just have to get home." I stumble over an explanation on the urgency of my departure.

"To do?" His gaze does not leave mine.

"Homework," flies from my lips.

He brings his hand up and rests it on my cheek. "Don't leave because that's what you think I want." He brushes his thumb across my lips. "I want you to stay. We don't have to do anything but spend the day together." He brings his lips gently to mine and pulls away. "No more games. I want you in my life."

I'm surprised by his admission. I just don't know if I can do this. Everything from my past is telling me this is a bad idea. But every time I've been with him, he has broken a little piece of my wall. And last night, it felt as if he demolished it.

I want him so damn much, but I am terrified. All relationships end badly. And how can I even be honest about my past? My life is not worth sharing.

"I'm not sure why this seems so hard for you, but give me a chance." His plea has my heart thumping loudly.

I can't think clearly anymore.

"What do you want from me?" It's a question I have wondered.

"All I want right now is your time"—he props himself on

one arm, releasing the one from my waist—"and attention. I want to know about the storm behind your eyes. The hesitation to trust. What drives your determination and willpower. I want to know about it, and I want to walk through it with you. Be your shoulder if you need. Be a listening ear." He stops abruptly, taking a deep breath, holding it as he lets himself fall back onto the pillow, his gaze on the ceiling.

I stay silent, not knowing what to say, as he lets out his breath in a long sigh. This is movie kind of talk, so I know it isn't real. This is not what happens in real life. This is all a set-up for the ultimate demise with broken promises and hearts. Something I don't do.

"And what if I said I can't?" I challenge him, knowing all males walk away when the going gets hard.

"How can you say you can't if you haven't even tried?" he counters.

"I know I can't." My resolve is building.

"And how do you know that?" He finally turns over toward me again, his eyes burning for an explanation.

"Because relationships are for suckers. And I...AM... NOT...A...SUCKER!" I emphasize each word to drive my point home.

"And why, pray tell, are relationships for suckers?" His eyebrows raise in question.

"Okay, but first, tell me of a healthy relationship that has lasted."

"My—"

I interrupt to clarify. "But not only lasted, but they like each other too. Not some 'we are staying together for the kids but secretly hate each other,' or 'we are together but haven't had sex in a billion years,' or 'we are too fuckin' broke to divorce, so we are still together making each other miserable' type of relationship."

"Like I was saying, my parents. They are still together,

twenty-seven years later. Still working together, sleeping in the same bed, and if I'm honest, grossing me out a bit with their PDA."

Not wanting to diss his parents, I have no comeback. After a few moments of silence, he continues, "So are you now going to share your 'relationships are for suckers' theory?"

The word *theory* raises my hackles. And all I have been trying to keep in explodes out.

"It is not a theory; it is a fact. At least, it's a fact in my life. My mother has gone from guy to guy with them promising the world only to go back to their wives or girlfriends or lives. Or better yet, they keep her like a dirty little secret, never exposing her to their friends or family. My best friend's boyfriend is a loser that sticks with her so that he can mooch off of her. Fucker does nothing but lie around the damn apartment all day, drinking or hanging with his buds while Amelia is trying to work and just get a fuckin' Associate's degree. How about all my friends whose dads split because raising a kid was too hard or not fun? How about all the guys who hit it and quit it?" All the emotions about men that I have bottled up my whole life come tumbling out in one hot breath. All I can see is red, and I need to bolt.

I quickly move to get out of the bed and stand, looking for my clothes. Garrett does the same, quickly pulling on boxers before I can get anything other than my shirt on.

He grabs my shoulders, holding me still. My gaze drops to the floor. My heart is pounding, ready to escape my chest, the anger lingering but not having anyone to direct it toward.

"I'm sorry," he whispers out. "But please don't judge me by some assholes who have no respect."

"I can't." I want to, but I can't. I need to leave, but I can't.

He lets go of my shoulders, bending down and picking up my thong. He holds it out so I can step into it. He slides it gently up my legs. He then guides me back to sit on the bed. He drops to his knees in front of me, peering up.

"Look, I'll be patient and show you not all males are assholes. Over time, I'll prove to you I'm worth the hassle." His words are soft and slow.

"I can't," I repeat.

"You can."

I've never placed myself into a situation where I could feel vulnerable. How could I do it now? I want to. There's something about him that draws me in.

"Okay…" slips past my lips. This has to be my heart speaking, not my head.

"Okay?" His hesitation if my answer is true is glaring.

I nod slowly. He comes up a bit, wrapping his arms around my waist, pulling me toward him as a long breath leaves his body. My breath is still stuck, unsure if I'm making the right decision. He's holding me like his life depends on it. My head falls on his shoulder.

After a few short minutes, his arms leave my body, leaving me wishing I could read the future. He stands, extending his hand to me. Not knowing what he has in mind, I place mine in his.

"Let me, at least, make you breakfast." I'm not sure if his unsure smile is trying to calm me or him. "Grab one of my shirts in that drawer. It will cover more." He winks as he scans my body. I'm standing, braless, in my short tee with a thong that really covers nothing.

He walks out of his room, leaving me to my thoughts and his personal items. He even trusts me to go through his drawer to pick out a shirt.

I walk to the kitchen barefoot to see him pulling eggs and bacon out of the fridge. It didn't dawn on me last night that he had a fridge filled to the brim with food. And he lives alone.

. . .

Garrett

"HERE, LET ME." She nudges me away from the counter and directs me to sit down. "You made dinner last night; I'll make you breakfast."

"Deal." I take my seat on a barstool and watch her look through cabinets and drawers to find what she needs.

Watching her in the kitchen, moving gracefully, prompts me to ask, "Who taught you to cook? You make it look so easy."

She takes a moment before answering. "When I was little, it was a necessity, because my mom was more worried about her life than mine. Then, when I moved in with my grandmother, she taught me. She was always in the kitchen if she wasn't working." Another pause before she continues. "My grandmother saved me. I don't know where I would be if she hadn't agreed to take me in... well, not only me but my two cousins, as well."

She's opening up a bit to me, and I don't want to ask anything that will shut her down. I decide on a safe route.

"Older or younger?"

"Huh?" She raises her gaze from the food to look at me.

"Your cousins, older or younger?"

She smiles. "They're older. Alex is four years older, and Javie is two. I guess I have to give Alex some credit, too. He is the one who has continued to encourage me to stay in school."

"You were going to drop out?" flies out before I have time to think.

"Sort of. No need to go into that now since I'm still here, less than a year away."

She's pulling back. On to safer subjects.

THE REST of the day passes quickly. She goes to her place to pick up her books, and we meet to study at the library before a long dinner at a hole-in-the-wall burger joint she suggests. My attention is always on her, reassuring her I'm not in this for a game. The touches and kisses we share throughout are never forced but genuine. A natural rhythm begins to form.

IT'S my afternoon on study duty with the pledges. Instead of reading to set an example, I'm busy texting Toni funny memes. That has quickly become our mode of conversation. Say it through meme. I guess for her it feels safe—not sharing too much. I'll take it if it keeps her responding and answering my texts. Plus, it's hilarious.

"I don't think that's considered reading." David sits across from me at the table, pointing at the phone and giving me a shit-eating grin.

"At least I'm reading something, not watching," I jab back, knowing he's just giving me crap.

"How much longer?" He nods his head to the recruits.

I look at the time and realize our two hours are five minutes away. "Five."

"They can handle the last five. Come on." He stands back up and begins walking out.

I follow him into the back den and shut the door behind me.

He sits on one of the sofas, and I take a chair.

"What's up?" I ask, wondering why he needs the secrecy back here.

He looks down at his hands clasped together. "Need a

drink?" He makes his way to the bar and pours himself a whiskey clean.

Must be something heavy, so I agree to one too. He hands me a glass and proceeds to sit again.

"Are you going to spit it out or not?" His cryptic attitude is starting to grate.

"Are you seeing anyone?" He looks up at me quizzically.

"Yes." I take a sip, focusing on the burn.

"Who?" he continues.

"I don't know if you know her. Toni. I met her at one of our parties." I don't want to share too much. He takes another drink, and I can tell he's pondering his next statement.

"For fuck's sake, just spit it out." My anger is beginning to show. Who the fuck cares who I'm seeing?

"It seems Kevin also knows Toni." Another sip.

"I know. I got her number from him." I calm myself at Kevin's name, wanting to know what the big secret is between the two of them.

"You did?" He seems surprised.

"Yes. I saw them talking at one of the parties. I talked to her that night, too, but didn't get the digits. Since I saw them talking, I decided to ask. He gave them to me." I make it all sound as casual as possible so he will spill whatever he knows.

"Oh..." He seems surprised. "I guess never mind." He begins to backtrack.

No he doesn't. I want to know where this was going.

"Never mind what?" I push.

He takes the last in his glass in one large gulp. He looks nervous, which is putting me on edge, so I follow his lead and gulp the last of mine also.

After a few breaths, he begins. "Remember the night we were at that hole-in-the-wall?"

"Yeah."

"That night, after you left, Kevin began talking about her. Toni..." He pauses again, his unease with recounting the story evident.

"And what did he say?"

"First, he asked if you had left. When someone confirmed, he began talking about her sexual prowess." His gaze drops to the floor, not wanting to meet my gaze.

"Is that it?" Smoke is beginning to escape from my ears.

"Just about. He was just calling her some pretty nasty names."

I'm stunned. No wonder Toni feels as she does. "Any more?" I ask, wanting to ensure I have the full story.

"No."

"And these names?" I want clarification.

Again, he pauses in discomfort. "Look, I just didn't want you to be blindsided if someone brought it up."

"Thank you. And the names he called her?" I stand my ground.

"Whore, easy, money-hungry, stripper. You know, all the names he likes to degrade women with. It's not like she's the first he has tried to degrade."

He has a point, but that he was doing it to someone I love is intolerable. Love. I love her?

"Look, thanks for the heads up, and don't mention you told me. No need to start shit here." I appreciate his friendship and don't want the house in on this crap. No need for Kevin to dig in his heels and start a rumor about her and the club on Walters he tried to make me believe.

He looks up, relieved, as I make my way out of the house.

CHAPTER TWELVE

DATING

Toni

ANOTHER FUN meme makes its way to my message inbox. My hesitation about a relationship with Garrett is still a constant thought, but he is holding up his end of the bargain and letting me set the pace. Well, the sharing-of-my-life pace, because well, I can't seem to keep my hands off of him. I have even agreed to more sleepovers. His apartment, with every modern convenience known to man, is hard to resist.

As soon as he places his strong hands on me, I melt. That is what I now trust whole-heartedly. I trust him to take care of my body and needs. He never rushes to get me off for his own release. He takes control. And I listen. He takes his time, almost worshipping me, his soft kisses and caresses foreplay to what I can expect later.

I'm on campus, having lunch with Lola. She is trying to

convince me into another group night out bowling. While it was fun, I can't spend that much if I'm giving up the club. I have enough tucked away for the year if I'm careful. I can't work there while "dating" Garrett. I refuse to lie about something current. My past is only an omission, not a lie. And I won't let Garrett spend that kind of money, either. While I assume he's comfortable, I won't let him support me, either.

"We have to go bowling. It was so much fun!" Lola is pleading with me again after I have told her no twice already.

"Why bowling?" My mind is scrambling on finding something else for her to grasp.

"Because we aren't just drinking. We're interacting. It's not some party where we are just getting shit-faced. Or a club where we can't even talk." I'm beginning to understand her why. She likes being with people and not just the "party" aspect of it.

"Got it." I put my hand up to stop her from interrupting me. "How about a game night at your place? Like Pictionary or something cheesy like that?" I don't really know many "family games" since it wasn't part of my childhood, but I have seen enough TV to imagine.

"Game night!" Her eyes light up. I can tell I'm onto something.

"Yes. And we can each bring snacks to share and whatever we're drinking." This will also help my budget.

"O.M.G." She shakes her head back and forth. "I can't believe I hadn't thought of that. You're a genius. It's set. Saturday night, game night at my place." She quickly takes out her phone and is typing at a furious pace.

My phone pings an incoming text a few seconds later with the group text. She has already begun inviting everyone over and coordinating the evening.

"Now, are you going to tell me about Garrett or not?" She places her phone on the table and stares at me.

"Tell you what?" I feign ignorance.

"Pah-lease. You all have been together for the past couple of weeks, and you have not said anything."

"What do you want me to say?" I ask.

"Well, I don't know. How much you like him. Usual girl banter about boys. Come on. Let me live vicariously through you, because I'm still looking for someone worthwhile." Her smile is genuine.

"He's sweet."

"Argh...I know he's sweet. That's not what I'm talking about. Are you all exclusive, still dating others, has he told you how he feels..." Her eyes are bright with wonder.

"I don't know. We haven't really talked about that yet. It's only been a couple of weeks."

"You are so avoiding this, aren't you? I can tell. That boy is head over heels, and you have him guessing, don't you?"

A laugh escapes my lips with her dramatic, spot-on analysis. Well, I'm not sure he is head over heels, but I am the one keeping things as light as I can—for now.

"Stop pressuring me," I tell her once I get my breathing under control from the laughter. "I'll tell you when I have something to tell." I roll my eyes in a dramatic fashion, which has her now cackling at me.

I think I will tell her. She has pushed her way into my life like Garrett. She insists on getting together, never taking no for an answer unless we make alternate plans. She is supportive. It amazes me how these two people came into my life at the same time.

I PICK UP THREE CHEAP, large pizzas and a bottle of vodka with mixer. All this for under forty dollars. Garrett is not pleased I am buying the things to take to Lola's, but I insisted since he paid at the bowling alley and continues to pick up small tabs here and there. It is nowhere near equal, but at least I'm contributing.

"Why wouldn't you let me get the stuff?" Garrett begins again as I get in his truck from the liquor store.

"I told you already." I climb across the console and kiss his lips.

I sit back down in my seat, buckling up as he begins reversing. "You thought that shut me up." He looks over at me, smirking.

"Didn't it?" I glare at him teasingly.

"Nope. It's not happening next time. I'm paying or buying next time." I roll my eyes at him. We'll fight about that when the time comes. I'm not using him for his money. He's not a client or customer, so I can't let him pay.

WE GET to Lola's before everyone else as I promised her I would help set up. She has purchased a dry-erase board for the evening, and Garrett has brought some card game they all seemed excited to play based on the text reactions.

"I don't have enough seating, but pillows on the floor are okay, right?" She has a sofa and a chair for four, and there will be six or seven of us.

"Lola, stop stressing. We are all here to have fun. And if it makes you feel better, Garrett and I will sit on the floor pillows."

"Speak for yourself, woman. I'm taking the chair." Garrett throws himself into the chair dramatically.

"Stop teasing her. Look at the girl." I point at Lola placing bowls of chips and dips on her table.

"Lola. Really. It's fine," Garrett chimes in to try and help. "Why are you so worked up anyway? It's a casual night out."

He seems as curious as I am about why she's acting like she is expecting the queen.

She sits at one of the kitchen chairs she has pulled into a corner and sighs deeply. We wait as she gains the strength to let us in on why she is obsessing over the little things.

"The last time I had people over was before I took my year off. And it was horrible. My 'sisters'"—she air quotes with her fingers—"bashed the dinner I had at my apartment. They criticized the food, the games I brought out, what I wore...just everything. I never had anyone over after that. It's one of the reasons I took a year off. I just didn't want to be around them anymore." Her shoulders slump.

I drag a chair closer to her and sit. "You have to remember, we are not them. You have chosen who you let into your life now. We aren't judging. We are here for food and laughs. That's it."

She looks up at me and smiles. "Thanks. I just let the memory drive me crazy today. When you mentioned it, I was all in. Then today, the nerves of being criticized hit."

This is another reason why she has become a person to trust. She has been hurt and judged. She won't do the same maliciously.

"No worries," is the only thing that comes to mind as I'm not the sentimental type. "Now, chill out. Everything is good."

And just as she is getting up, someone knocks on the front door.

It is the same group we bowled with. Everyone is casually dressed for a night in, carrying in more food, from wings to mini burgers to taquitos. They all settle in with food and drinks, ready for an evening of laughs.

Garrett

135

. . .

As the night progresses, I watch as Toni grows more relaxed and comfortable with the people around her. It is amazing what a few weeks can do. I know there is still so much to learn about her, but there's no going back now.

"Time to head out, darlin'," I inform Toni, knowing it's time we leave. Maybe if we leave, the others will too. Give Lola some quiet.

"Okay." She gets up from the floor.

At the door, I kiss Lola's cheek. "Thank you for the evening."

She gives me a hug and turns to Toni and hugs her tight. She whispers something in Toni's ear I can't hear. Toni giggles and tells her, "Stop it." The devilish, matching grins they wear is enough to make me curious.

I head out of the complex toward Toni's place.

"Where are you going?" she asks.

"Your place. It's closer."

"Are you dropping me off?" she asks, her tone changing.

"Nope. We are sleeping at your place," I inform her.

"You want to spend the night at my place?" We have not spent any time at her place. I've been there but only to pick her up, but we always end up sleeping or hanging at my place.

"Sure."

"Why?"

"Like I said, it's closer. No need to drive too far." I can tell she's unsure about this.

"Okay." She sits back in her seat.

Why is she nervous about going to her place? All of the worst scenarios run through my head on the short drive there.

We walk into her place, and everything is just like the last time I was here.

136

"Here we are." She sounds really nervous, which makes my stomach turn.

I can't take it anymore. "Do you not want me here? Should I leave?" I'm beginning to get angry, but I can't explain why.

"No. I want you. But here?" She looks at me and waves her hand sadly.

"Yes, here. Why not here?" I come closer to her, placing my hands on her cheeks, pulling her gaze up to me. I want to see her eyes as she explains.

"Because your place is so much nicer. Your bed is bigger. This is it. This is my place. No other room to go to unless you count the bathroom." She comes forward, hiding her face by placing her forehead on my chest.

"Nuh uh. Look at me." I wait until her eyes are on me again. "This is your place. No roommate to worry about intruding on us. A fridge with food. A TV to watch. So what if it is small? It has everything we need." I place my lips on hers greedily, the kiss heating up quickly. "Undress for me."

She takes a hesitant step back, pulling her shirt over her head. She kills me with her bras. This one is mesh, and I can see her perky nipples harden as she works off her jeans. This is one thing I admire about her. She is confident in her skin. She can parade around me in the barest of clothing or completely naked with no qualms.

I place my hand in between her legs to feel her wetness, and she widens her stance.

"Lie down." I watch as she lies on her back in the middle of the bed.

I strip down to my boxer briefs before joining her.

THE MORNING SUN is coming through her blinds as I hear her phone ping a message. *Lola, it is too early,* is the first thought that comes to mind. Toni is tucked in my side, naked. I don't think we have ever made it to bed clothed. She is still blissfully sleeping, so I quietly get up to silence her phone. I pull it out from under the clothes we have discarded on the floor when it pings again.

Call me asap

It's from Alex. Guessing it may be important, I decide to wake her.

"Darlin'." I shake her shoulder a bit then kiss it. "Wake up."

"Hmm..." She turns her face toward me and peeks one eye open. "Go back to sleep. It's too early." She turns her face away from me.

I kiss her shoulder again then state, "Your phone has been going off. Alex said to call him ASAP."

"What?" She sits up quickly. "You read my messages?" Her tone is accusatory.

"No. I was going to silence it because it went off a few times. When I picked it up, it went off, and that is what the text said on the screen. Besides, I don't know your password." And with that, I drop her phone next to her and get out of bed for the second time this morning to slip my clothes on and leave.

She quickly follows me out of bed, leaving her phone. "I'm sorry. I don't know what else to say. I was wrong."

I stop, keeping my back to her. The accusing tone stung. But more than that, what is she still hiding?

"I'm sorry," she says again, pressing herself into my back. My resolve is fading.

"So can I ask who Alex is?" I slowly turn around to see her face as she answers. She stays mum, so I press. "Well?"

"It's my cousin." She pulls back, crossing her arms to hide her breasts.

"And your cousin is needing your attention this early in the morning because..."

"I don't know yet. I haven't looked at my phone." Her tone is hard, but there is fear in her eyes. Fear of what?

"Be my guest." I wave my hand over to the bed where I left her phone.

As she makes her way back in bed to check her phone, it pings again. I begin dressing to make my exit. My instincts are telling me to leave, but my heart is willing me to stay and find out what is going on. I know very little about her family. Each time they come up, she vaguely answers and changes the subject. I haven't pressed, giving her the time to share. I know she does not come from much. Scholarships and her apartment tell me at least that much.

As I slide on my clothes, I watch as she is furiously typing out messages.

"Is everything okay?" I ask, not knowing if she will answer or even give me any information.

"No, it's not." As she looks up, her eyes are watery as if she wants to cry. "I'm not sure what is up, but if I had to guess, it's either my asshole uncle or bitch of a mom that has screwed something up again."

"What can I do?" I ask, hating to see the pain in her eyes.

"Nothing." She shakes her head. Her gaze drops to her lap, and the faintest whisper I barely hear says, "Absolutely nothing." It's as if all the spunk and fight I have come to love about her has been let out.

"Please...let me help," I plead. The direction this is going feels over.

"I need to go to my grandmother's house. They are expecting me." She is from town. I had assumed by a couple of things she has said but didn't know for sure.

"Okay, call me later?" The statement comes out more as a question.

She only nods before getting out of bed and pulling a shirt on. She walks over to me, hands on my shoulders, and pulls me down for a long kiss. There is a sadness in this kiss. If I didn't know any better, she is telling me goodbye.

CHAPTER THIRTEEN

REALITY BITES

Toni

I WALK into Guela's house to find her with Alex and Javie at the kitchen table, drinking coffee. Not ready to face whatever damage is going to be revealed, I pour myself a cup and have a seat. I sip slowly, looking around at the solemn faces. The only sounds are of us taking sips of our coffee and placing them back down on the table.

The quiet and suspense of what has happened becoming too much, I say, "Spill it."

Alex and Javie look at each other. The seconds it takes for one of them to begin is agonizing.

"Guela needs money," Alex begins.

A slight sense of relief hits. She always needs a bit more money. She makes squat cleaning houses.

"That's fine. We always help her out. How much and why the big meeting?" The dread slowly begins to melt away.

"No, Toni. She needs money," he states again.

"*Va estar bien, mija. Tengo suficiente dinero hasta la próximo cheque.*" (It's fine. I have enough until the next check) Guela chimes in.

"No, Guela, you don't," Alex cuts her off, surprising me with his anger. "How are you going to pay for your medications and bills?"

"*No los nesesito horita.*" (I don't need them right now) She states.

"Wait!" I cut in, still confused with what is going on. "Tell me the whole story."

"She lent money to your mom, Toni," Alex informs me.

"What?" I look directly at Guela, confused why she would sacrifice herself again for a conniving, self-centered bitch.

"*Va esta bien.*" (It will be okay) She states again.

"*Y tu medicina?*" (And your medicine?) Javie decides to jump in.

"*Ya te dije, no la necesito. Me siento bien.*" (I already told you, I don't need it. I feel fine) Guela defends herself.

"*Cuánto le prestaste a Mamá?*" (How much did you lend Mom?) I ask her.

Guela looks down at her coffee, not answering. I give her a couple of moments, and when she still doesn't answer, I ask again. "*Cuánto prestastes?*" (How much?)

Alex and Javie stay silent, staring at the table in this one-way exchange. Their silence around the table exasperates me further. I finally lose it and yell in Alex and Javie's direction. "HOW MUCH?"

Alex finally looks up and answers, "A couple grand."

"A couple grand? Are you fucking kidding me?"

"*No hables asi, Antonia!*" (Don't talk like that.) Guela admonishes me.

"Guela, how could you?"

"*Es mi hija.*" (She's my daughter.) Her go-to explanation.

How many times have I heard this before? Every time Mom or Uncle Alex runs into trouble, she jumps in to save them, and her explanation is always "they are her kids." It's a good thing she only had two, because those two are bleeding her dry.

We all look toward the front door as someone has opened it. I watch as my mother strolls in without a care in the world. Her hair and makeup are immaculate as always with what looks like a new outfit.

I charge at her immediately. "What the fuck, Mom?! How can you take money from Guela?"

"I needed it, Toni. You don't understand," she defends herself.

"What the fuck don't I understand, Mom? Guela cleans houses. She shouldn't be doing that at her age," I yell at her.

"Well, I needed the money, Toni," she tries to answer superiorly, but I know she is as fake as they come.

"Get a second job then." I give her practical advice.

"I can't get a second job. That's absurd," she continues in her "I'm better than you" airs.

"Yah. Yah." I hear Guela yell at us from behind.

I step back and throw myself on the couch.

Javie decides to come in next. "So, are you here to pay Guela back the money?" he cautiously asks.

"I don't have the money yet," Mom answers automatically.

"Then, what are you here for?" he continues.

"I can't just come and see my mom?" She is getting annoyed now.

"NO. No, you can't." I shoot straight up again. "You never come to see Guela unless you need something. If you are here, you are ready to put your hand out again, I'm sure."

"What the fuck is the ruckus about?" my uncle asks from the hallway. He is only wearing a pair of jeans, his beer gut on display, completely disheveled, probably still hungover from the night before. "I was trying to sleep."

"Not now, why don't you go back to sleep," Javie tells his dad.

Ignoring my uncle's presence, I turn back to my mom and inform her, "We need to figure out how to get Guela all she needs this month and ensure her bills are paid. So, if you are here to help, then great, have a seat. If not, then turn your ass around and leave."

"That is no way to speak to your mother." Her frustration is clearly showing now.

"My mom? Really? You want to pull the mom card now? The only mom I know is Guela."

"You disrespectful bitch!"

"It is this bitch that is going to solve Guela's problems. So have a seat or leave."

"What problems could she possibly have?" My mother is as haughty as ever.

"How to pay her bills if you aren't here to pay her back the money."

She rolls her eyes. "What bills? The house is paid off." This is how little my mom knows. She doesn't know anything about her own mother except what she can do for her.

"Well," Javie begins behind me. "You borrowed everything she had. All her bills need to be paid."

I'm still blocking Mom's way into the house.

"Look, Jacob left me with nothing, just a bunch of mess," Mom tries to defend her actions and deflect.

"You're an adult, Mom. Handle your own shit," I answer.

"That's what moms do, take care of their daughters," flies out of her mouth before she has time to think who she is speaking to, her narcissism clearly showing.

"Really, MOM?" I respond as sarcastically as ever. "That's what moms want to do? Take care of their daughters?" I drive the knife of her selfishness in as deep as possible. I want to try and hurt her as much as she has hurt me throughout the years. She was never there for me. Never gave a damn. Never invested any time or attention my way. All she does is leech on and drain you dry.

The sting of a slap bites on my cheek. Never taking a couple of steps into the house, she spins on her heel and walks out the door.

"That was entertaining," my uncle laughs, still leaning on the hallway wall. "What's going on?"

"Nothing to concern yourself with, Dad," Javie answers him. "Just go back to bed."

He pushes himself off the wall, and I watch him retreat to his (my old) room.

As soon as we hear the click of his door, we all sink into the couch and chairs in the living room. I'm already exhausted, and we have not figured anything out yet.

"Alex, you are freaking me out. You haven't said anything," I begin, dropping my head on the back of the couch to stare at the ceiling.

Many silent moments pass, and still, Alex does not say anything.

I pick my head up off the back of the couch. "WHAT? Tell me WHAT?" I practically yell in Alex's direction for information.

"I'm sorry, Toni," he begins, speaking almost in a whisper. "Sorry."

"Sorry for what?" I'm beginning to feel sick.

He leans forward in the chair and places his elbows on his knees. His head drops into his hands. "I can't cover Guela this time. I need you to do it." He continues to stare at the floor.

"Why are you sorry?" I'm confused by his apology. We —

Javie, Alex, and I — have always taken care of Guela. It's been our unspoken rule to ensure she has what she needs.

"Because..." I watch as his jaw clenches as he sits up again, running his hands through his hair roughly. "I am trying to keep you away from this place. You mentioned last time you could stay away from the club because you had enough stashed. I figured if you ran low at the end of the year, I could cover you." He takes a deep breath and blows it out in a huff.

"You don't—" I begin.

"Don't what?" he interrupts. "Need to take care of you? I know I don't. But I want to. If you make it out of this place, if you find something steady, I won't worry about you and Guela anymore. I know you will take her wherever you go. Away from the fuckin' leeches. But now you need to go back to work and not mingle with the people who you should be spending your time with."

My stomach drops at the reminder of *the others*. This is why I've always kept superficial friends who have come and gone. I never wanted them knowing what I did for money. It's none of their business. I need no one's pity or judgment. But now I've made friends. People who know more about me than any others—but not what is truly behind the curtain.

"Oh." My head drops back onto the couch once more, and I close my eyes. I can feel tears starting to form. Tears are a rarity. I cried enough as a child for a mother who didn't care. I learned there is no use in tears.

"Javie and I are still playing it safe with my dumbass dad living here. Not to mention supporting his lousy ass since he can't keep a job. Better we do it than he start asking from Guela. Lucky for us, if we keep enough beer in the fridge and enough for him to hit up The Hole, he's good."

I have never needed anyone other than these three people in the room. I should have never allowed myself to build friendships. Maybe when I've graduated and started working.

Guela has stayed quiet in our discussion. She has always been there for us but has that soft spot for her own children.

"*Mañana pago todos las cuentas*." (Tomorrow I'll pay all the bills). I look toward my grandmother. The pain on her face is evident.

"*Está bien, mija. Puedo limpiar más casas este mes*. (It's fine, sweetie. I can clean more houses this month) She informs me.

"*No. No vas a limpiar más casas. Yo tengo dinero*." (No. You will not clean more houses. I have money) I rebute her firmly.

"I'm going to pick up her meds from the store." I stand to leave, not trusting my tears to stay at bay.

She stays silent as I rise and walk to the door.

"Toni," Alex calls.

I turn around to look at him.

"I'll try to figure something out," he adds.

I shake my head at him. "No, you won't. We have always been in this together. I'm doing my part."

With that, I exit the door, knowing tears of sorrow are coming fast. In the safety of my car, I drive to a dead-end road used only for illegal dumping or horny teens at night. It is here where I can finally allow myself to feel the pain of leaving behind this newfound life. I can't date Garrett and work at the club. I can't date Garrett and be with Mark. I wouldn't want Lola to know about this side of my life.

While I've assimilated and learned the ways, I won't have people judge me for what I need to do. And that's what I'm sure will happen. I was born into this shit life, and I have been desperately trying to claw my way out of it. Sins of my mother have haunted me my whole life. All I want is to wake up one day without a past that disturbs me.

I allow myself a couple of minutes of self-pity before I turn up the radio, blaring angry music. Because that's what I feel now. Anger.

. . .

Garrett

THE DAY HAS PASSED and I never heard back from her. Texting her once this evening, I leave it at that, not wanting to press, especially since she looked crushed this morning. My bed feels empty without her in it. It's only been a few weeks since she began spending many nights over here, but I've quickly begun to crave them. The absence on her side has never felt as ominous as it does now. Before, it was giving her space and taking the time to let her adjust and consider *us*.

Tossing and turning throughout the night, I wake to Monday classes. I look at my phone. Still no text or message from her. I'll catch her at the coffee shop, knowing she will probably need caffeine today.

I LEFT class a couple of minutes early so I could make it to the shop before she arrived. I didn't want to miss her if she decided to take it to go. And knowing her, she may to avoid a discussion about yesterday's events. My mood is quickly matching that of the hot, bitter coffee. Over an hour passes, and Toni has yet to come in. She wouldn't have any more time to make it in before her next class, so I decide to leave.

Aimlessly walking around campus before my next class, I search for her. I'm left worrying what could have happened to have her ignore me completely.

"Hey, stranger!" Lola's voice comes at me from behind.

I stop, letting her catch up to me, debating on asking if she has heard from Toni.

"Not wanting to help clean? Is that why I didn't hear from y'all yesterday?" she continues teasing.

Her question prompts me to ask, "You haven't heard from Toni, either?"

"No. Why?" The quizzical look she gives puts me on edge.

"She left yesterday, and I haven't heard from her since," I admit, defeated.

"Have you called her?"

"No..."

"Then what are you fretting about? Call her," she interrupts me.

"I've texted her, and she still hasn't responded," I add in my defense. I don't want to share why I won't call her. Everything I do with Toni is opposite what I would have done for any other girl. Any other girl would have wanted me to save them. But not Toni. Toni can take care of herself, and I give her that control. I'm just along for the ride.

"Then call her." Her eyes roll with annoyance.

"I can't," I simply state.

"Why not?" she pushes.

"I don't want to scare her away."

"Aaahhh." The lightbulb of comprehension goes off. "Closed off with you, too, I see."

"Yes."

She takes her phone out of her back pocket. I watch her as she messes with her screen and places the phone to her ear. She is looking around, avoiding eye contact.

"She didn't answer," Lola states as she is messing with her screen again. "Sent her a text for dinner tonight. I know that girl likes to eat, so I'll get a text soon."

Should I ask her to share with me if Toni texts or calls back? As I'm pondering this, she adds, "I'll let you know if I hear from her. Okay?"

I nod.

"I have to get to class now. I'm going to be late if I don't jet." She rushes off toward the closet building.

Realizing the time, I start to run to my class also.

NOT HEARING from Toni or Lola all day, I decide to text Toni again.

Why the silent treatment?

Then, I text Lola. *Any word?*

As I am making myself a bowl of cereal, my phone pings a text. My heart pounds in anticipation of finally hearing from Toni.

She hasn't texted or called me back either

CHAPTER FOURTEEN

AVOIDANCE

Toni

I SILENCE MY PHONE, not wanting to hear any more texts come through. I spent the afternoon at my grandmother's again. I went to the bank and placed money in the escrow account for her taxes. I spent the rest of my time at her house, on my laptop, paying the rest of her bills. I had set her up with online accounts, but she still kicked it old school and went in to pay for her things. I wasn't in the mood to deal with people, so I hid behind my screen, getting things done.

The only thing I can be grateful for today is a home-cooked dinner. She is going all out, cooking arroz con pollo with homemade tortillas to us. To keep the peace all evening, I never mention my mother's name. What is done is done. My mother is never going to pay Guela back, so I might as well drop it.

Seeing Garrett's text makes my heart drop into my stomach

again. I need to break it off. What am I saying? We weren't together, so there is nothing to break off. I just can't talk to him anymore. The suckiest part of everything is I miss him. How can I miss him if I was just with him yesterday morning? Knowing I can't see or be with him again is messing with my head.

I grab my phone to text Sasha. I need to keep my head in the game.

I need to pick up shifts again. Can I come in on Thursday?

Not wanting to head to my apartment, I pull up homework due later this week. If I'm going to ignore everyone successfully, I will need to stay busy. There's no going back now. Garrett and Lola know where I live. They can easily 'drop by' if they choose to. I can't see him yet.

"What are you still doing here?" Alex asks, coming into the kitchen.

"Homework," I state bluntly, never looking up from my screen.

"No you're not. Might as well tell me," he pushes.

"What does it look like I'm doing?" I refuse to be baited.

"It looks like you're avoiding." He sits across from me, twisting off a beer cap.

"I'm doing homework. I don't want to start again if I'm on a roll." I try and get him off my back.

"And that's all?" I can feel his stare. "It has nothing to do with the guy whose texts you have been ignoring? What is his name? Garrett, right?" He's playing dumb on purpose.

I push my laptop back and let my head fall to the table on my crossed arms. I can't do this now. I don't want to do this.

"Just talk to me, Toni."

Trying to hide the frustration of the situation I'm in is no longer an option. "What do you want to hear?" The tears I have kept locked up since letting go yesterday come back. I look up at Alex. "I let Garrett in. He knows where I live. I actually started to like him. He's not like other guys. He's different. Always letting me lead. Never pushing too hard. Never boasting about himself.

"Those texts will keep coming. And what do I tell him? Oh, by the way, I have to go to work tonight—at a strip club —where I openly flirt with every single guy there so I can make good tips. And sometimes they get handsy, but don't worry, because I don't like it." I pause and the anger continues to build. "Now, if a guy named Mark calls, don't worry. I just shag him for money. But it means nothing. There are no feelings involved. It's just the cash I need.

"HOW THE FUCK DOES THAT SOUND?" I yell. The house is too small. I need to leave. I stand quickly, knowing I can't go home but not able to stay here.

Alex stands with me. His large stature is scary to most but has always been my safety. He walks past me to the cabinets. He opens a bottom one and pulls out a bottle of tequila. He pulls out two small glasses and pours. He hands me one and takes one for himself.

Without saying anything, he clinks his glass on mine and swallows the contents in one shot. He places the glass back on the counter and raises a brow at me. I follow his lead and take the drink. He pours his glass and holds the bottle out to me. I hold out my glass for him to fill up.

He walks his glass and the bottle back to the table and sits in front of his beer. I grab a beer from the fridge and take my seat again. He holds his glass to me again. I clink his this round, and together, we throw our heads back, letting the sting of the alcohol slide down. Ready to feel numb, I twist the cap off and chase it down with beer.

· · ·

153

AFTER CLASS, I head back to my apartment, knowing I won't be able to hide from them forever. I walk in to find Alex on my couch, watching TV.

"What are you doing here?" I ask, confused. He hasn't hung at my place since last year when he began pushing me to stay away from the hood.

"I thought about what you said last night. If you don't want to explain why you are staying away from him, use me. He doesn't know me, does he?" He says this as if it explains everything.

"What?" I'm still lost.

"You said it yourself. You were falling for him but never talked about being exclusive. Maybe you are seeing someone else. If he sees me here, he can assume whatever when you tell him you can't see him anymore. This is really the way to ensure he doesn't come back." He shrugs his shoulders. "That is...if you are sure you can't see him anymore," he adds.

"I can't see him." Can I really do that to him? He has been nothing but a gentleman, and this is super effing shady.

"Your call. Just thought I'd offer." He is scrolling through shows on Netflix.

"I don't know..." I leave the statement hanging because I really don't know what I want to do. I walk into the bathroom—the only other room in my apartment—to breathe in private.

Alex is a really good-looking guy. He's not as tall as Garrett but has more muscle bulk. His dark hair and eyes complement his tanned skin. His chiseled facial features must have been inherited from his mom's side. His full-sleeve tattoo, brooding mannerism, and constant five o'clock shadow makes him every girl's bad-boy wet dream. Many in the hood have tried to tame him, but he just goes through them. When I asked why he uses them, his response was, "If they think spreading their legs will get them a relationship, they need to learn a little more about self-respect."

I'm not sure what he's looking for in a girl, but I do know he doesn't want her to throw herself at him.

What do I want to do? Can I really hurt Garrett like that? Will he even be hurt? Of course he will. Why would he have been so patient with me if he didn't care? Why did I put myself in this position? A person like me can't have normal. It's just not in the cards. At least, not while I'm still tethered to the south side. But it is exactly what I want now. I was able to taste normal. Normal may be vanilla, but it's steady. It's long-lasting. It mixes with everything. It is a flavor everyone likes. It's normal.

Wanting so desperately for a transformation, I wish I were a butterfly. Needing a transformation. Wanting so much to be from somewhere else. To be the person who doesn't need to hide who she is.

A shower is the only thing I can think of to do. I don't want to make a decision—at least, not yet.

Garrett

MONDAY CAME AND WENT. No texts. No calls. Not even a response to Lola. Now I'm getting worried. Why would she just drop off the face of the Earth like that? I decide to swing by her place this afternoon, because I wasn't able to run into her on campus or the coffee shop either. It really is like she disappeared.

On the drive over, my mind keeps bringing me to a dark vision of her dead. She doesn't live in the safest complex. It is not one I would have chosen for a single girl, but it's not my place to dictate where she lives. If this is what she can afford to live on her own, then this is what it has to be—even if I don't like it. Why else would she stay silent? As I drive into her parking lot, I see her car parked next to her building. At least it looks like she is home.

I park and make my way to her door, nervous about what I will find. I knock and wait.

"There's someone at your door." I hear a male voice yell on the other side. My heart drops. Who the fuck is that?

There is discussion, but nothing I can make out. I can't even tell if it's Toni's voice. I wait, not knowing what I'm about to see.

A few moments pass before I hear the sound of the dead-bolt turning, and the door opens. Toni is in a towel, fresh-faced with her hair wet.

Stunned at seeing her, words do not leave my mouth. Standing there, speechless, relief she is okay is in battle with the curiosity of the male voice I heard.

"You are alive?" I begin, trying to tone down the anger I was beginning to feel.

"Why wouldn't I be?" she counters. The coldness in her voice is not to be missed.

Weighing my options on whether to go all in or play it safe quickly run through my mind. "A text or call the past two days would have been nice. No need to ghost me." The anger is beginning to take over.

"We weren't exclusive." Her stance is firm. Her eyebrow cocks, challenging me.

"Who's at the door?" I hear the male voice again from inside.

"Don't worry about it. It's nothing." She answers the voice without breaking eye contact with me.

"We were NOTHING?" I ask for clarification. If what we had begun to build didn't really mean anything, I want to hear it from her.

"Get ready, I'm starving." The male voice sounds closer

this time as he appears behind her at the door. He's a tatted up, rough-looking guy. "Are y'all done?" He looks to me, asking.

"Sure does look like it," I answer him, turning around and walking away.

I won't look back. I want to know if this bothers her, but I can't look back. I don't want to give that fucker the satisfaction of glancing back at her. If she doesn't care, then neither do I.

THE BOTTOM of a bottle seems to be the best place to be right now. I left Toni's, not wanting to go home, or face the guys at the house, or even face people in general. The best place I knew was a hole-in-the-wall on the outskirts of town. A place where no one knows crap about my life other than being a rancher. I slapped down a hundred dollar bill and told the bartender to leave the bottle. It seemed appropriate at the time.

"Hey, guero. *Por que estas aqui?*" (Why are you here?) I hear Juan's voice behind me.

I don't answer, staying hunched over the bar and my drink.

He takes a seat on the stool next to me and lets out a low whistle, shaking his head.

"Who pissed in your cereal?" Juan asks.

"Why did someone need to piss in my cereal? I'm just enjoying my fucking drink, man," I retort, frustrated, not wanting to tell anyone what happened but wanting to yell about it at the same time.

"Well, fuck, enjoy the drink."

I watch him out of the corner of my eye wave at the bartender. Without any words, she knows to bring him a bottle of beer. Before taking his first drink, he clinks his bottle to my glass.

"To no one pissing in cereal." He takes a long pull before placing the bottle back down on the bar.

Several quiet minutes pass before he utters another word.

"Why are you drinking so far from home?"

"No reason," I lie. There is no reason to announce what a loser I am right now.

"Hmmmm." He mumbles something under his breath quickly in Spanish that I don't catch. The last thing I need is everyone's judgment. Maybe Kevin is right. How could I have been so fucking stupid?

We sit in silence for my next two pours. He finally gets up and walks away, probably because I am still ignoring his presence. I look around the small dive, and a few more people have come in. Most I do not know, but a few of the ranch hands have congregated at a table in the corner. Their laughs carry all the way to the bar. Their laughter and ease is what I'm missing right now. I slide off my stool on unsteady feet. I look at the bottle in front of me and am surprised to see almost half the bottle is missing.

I have to concentrate on putting one foot in front of the other, making my way across the room to leave. Juan gets up and meets me at the door.

"*No vas a la casa de tu mamá así.*" (You are not going to go to your mom's house like that.) Juan begins.

"*No, pendejo. Voy a el apartamento.*" (No, stupid. I'm going to the apartment.) I answer angrily. What the hell is he doing in my business?

"*No vas a manejar.*" (You are not going to drive.) He tells me, holding out his hand in front of me. I place my keys in his hand. I watch him as he gets the attention of one of the guys at the table. He tosses his keys to him. "*Lleva mi troca al rancho.*" (Take my truck to the ranch.)

. . .

I'm awoken by a car door slamming. I look around and realize I'm at the workers' house on the property. I watch as Juan walks into the house, leaving me outside. As stubborn as I want to be, I really don't want to sleep in the truck.

I make my way into the house, and the smell of coffee hits me. Juan is in the large kitchen, pouring a cup. The house is set up dormitory style, many rooms with double beds. When there are late nights and early mornings, it's easier for the workers to stay on property. The house is always ready for them, stocked with all the essentials.

I take a seat at the banquet-style table. He places the cup in front of me with the creamer and sugar. He pours a cup for himself then sits across from me.

"She's dating someone else." Refusing to look up, I fix my coffee instead. My head is already beginning to pound.

"Who?"

It was still so new; no one knew about her. How did I fall as quickly as I did?

"The girl I thought I was dating. But she was dating someone else. I was the fucking pendejo."

"Nah. You probably let the little head do the thinking for you." He lets out a small laugh before continuing. "It happens to the best of us."

"I thought she was different. She wasn't like all the other money-hungry ones I keep meeting. All of them just stand around with their hands out. She didn't. She wasn't after me for what I could give her."

This elicits a booming laugh. "Of course she didn't have her hand out, because she had another one."

With this realization, my head drops to the table. I was flying blind on this one.

"Take the back room and sleep it off," he says, getting up and heading outside.

Not wanting the coffee, I get up, looking around the cabinets for some pain reliever and a Gatorade. I hope my dad doesn't come back to this house tomorrow morning and see my truck here. He won't be thrilled I'm back.

The room spins as I shut my eyes, begging sleep to take me.

CHAPTER FIFTEEN

MISSING YOU

Toni

I MAKE my way through the next few days on autopilot. Not wanting to spend my days on campus and not wanting to go to an apartment that is closing in on me, I struggle with where to go. Who knew actual physical pain accompanied heartbreak? Always thinking my mom was being a drama queen, I didn't think it was possible. Now, I can't deny the pain in my chest. The tightness will not let up, but I refuse to cry. I made my decision and I will stick to it. Mingling with people from campus is not an option anymore. My life is too complicated, and not wanting to share makes this my only option. All I need is time to readjust to how my life was before.

Checking my phone for texts from Garrett has become second nature, but there have been none since before he came over that day. As much as it is a relief, I wish my phone to ping with his name. Lola is the one I cannot shake. She has texted daily. I haven't answered them, so being the persistent one, she found me on campus. I made an excuse to hurry off, but I had a feeling she was not giving up that easy.

SASHA CALLED to let me know she has too many waitresses at the club tonight, so she got me in at El Mundo instead. The money will be good, because it is an upscale club that caters to rich, Mexican internationals. While I will make a decent amount, the gentleman's club has always brought in the most. I change quickly, knowing I need to dress for the women as well as the men.

As I am getting my things to walk out, a knock stops me in my tracks. Panic on who could be on the other side of the door grips me. I freeze, not wanting them to hear me inside. Another knock. A few moments pass. I hear movement. Have they left? I quietly walk to the door and look through the peephole to find no one. I unlock the door, and when I open it, Lola falls back into my apartment. She is sitting on the floor, book in hand.

"So you are here and avoiding me?" Lola questions as she stands up.

"Not avoiding you. Just in a rush to meet friends," I say quickly, trying to explain my club attire.

"Cool. Where are you headed? I'll go home and change then meet you all. I haven't been dancing in forever." I know there are no ill intentions with her genuine smile and excitement. How in the hell do I explain this now?

"Well..." I'm stumbling for words, not knowing how to lose her.

"Well, what?" she asks, confused by my hesitation.

"I'm not really going for fun." I decide to let her know I

work. At least it's at a club today. She didn't catch me on the way to the strip club. "I'm actually going in to work."

"Really? Why didn't you just say that?" Her brows pull together in question.

I shrug, not knowing how to explain.

"For reals, Toni. Next time, just let me know. Where are you working?"

"El Mundo, downtown." This time, I can answer honestly.

"Cool. I heard that people throw money around like it's nothing there. Is it true?" As well off as she is, this is what amuses her.

"I guess so. Most of the people that come in are internationals. They are on vacation, so having fun is usually on the agenda." I smile at her and the fascination she is exhibiting.

"Is it true the line is outrageous?" She is full of questions.

"Yes. Unless you are on the list."

"To be on the list must be cool." She shimmies her shoulders. "Line. I don't do lines, darlin'. I'm on the list." She takes a couple of steps, trying to impersonate a wealthy snob. I can't help but laugh.

"Yes, being on the list must be cool, but the drink prices are not cool." I bring her back down to my reality. "But I do have to go. Work is calling."

She comes in for a hug. "Call me tomorrow. Since I haven't seen you all week, I'll take you to brunch. I miss you."

And just like that, she turns and walks away, waving. It's so hard to ignore her. She doesn't give up, and she makes everything in life seem normal. But I do have a sneaking suspicion she could go to that club and be VIP if she truly wanted.

AFTER A REALLY LONG NIGHT, I open my eyes, trying to find my phone to check the time. I remember the other reason the strip club is a better place to work: hours on the job. The strip club closes right after last call. No hanging out for coffee. El Mundo caters to the Mexican clientele who are used to being able to party into the wee hours of the morning. The booze may have stopped, but coffee, agua frescas, and munchies flow. I didn't walk into my apartment until after six a.m.—about the same amount of money, but way more hours.

It's almost one in the afternoon. I guess I should get up and get my day started. Should I text Lola like she asked? I take a few minutes, playing out every scenario I can think of, and I come back to the same conclusion each time. She won't let me just disappear. She is persistent, and there is no way to scare her off the way I was able to scare off Garrett. Funny thing is, I don't want to. I didn't want to scare him away either, but it was necessary.

Just woke up hungry. I hit send.

Perfect. Heading your way in a few. She responds right away.

WE WALK INTO THE CANDLELIGHT, which is a coffee and wine bar in the evenings but hosts brunch on the weekends. Lola has brought me here a couple of times already. The first time, I was nervous with the swanky décor and upscale atmosphere—a hipster haven. We sat down, and I was surprised with the not-so-exorbitant prices. It's not an everyday hangout, but I can swing it every now and then. This is a great place, letting all feel the swanky lifestyle for a normal price.

Walking in this morning, I feel like I am coming home. This is the type of place I hope to be able to walk into, never worrying if I belong or if I can afford the bill. We place our order at the bar, take our pager and lattes, and find a small table in the corner.

"I always hate to mess up the pretty designs they make on the coffee," I begin. I always hesitate pouring sugar in my lattes when the baristas take the time to place designs on the top.

Lola takes her phone out of her pocket and snaps a pic of hers. "You know the drill. Take a pic and post." Her smile is infectious. I follow her lead and take the pic to post. Her openness and likability is hard to ignore.

"How is it you are always in a good mood?" I ask, curious. We have been friends now for a couple of months, but I have avoided asking her meaningful questions for fear she would turn them around to me.

"Am I?" she asks before taking a sip of her latte.

I nod.

"I don't know. I guess I don't think about it anymore." She pauses and looks pensive before beginning again. "I wasn't always so cheery. After my mom died, I was a mess. Then, my first year in college, I was in a deeper hole of misery. I hate to put it like that because there could be so many more reasons for life to suck than 'I don't like my shallow friends,' but that was me then. My dad saw it. He was worried. I mentioned before that I took the year off and traveled. That year helped me refocus on what was important and helped my mindset."

"How so?" I am really invested in her transformation now.

"I was grateful for what I had, but I don't think I truly understood gratitude. All the material possessions are nice, and money does make life easier, but my friendships were lacking. I always hung out with people like me—materially speaking. But sometimes, when you have so much, it's taken for granted. I was there. I was taking things for granted. All the money couldn't bring my mom back. I wanted to express my sadness to my friends, sorority sisters, and all they wanted to do was party and shop. I wasn't where they were anymore."

"I will admit I don't have many friends, but I keep it that

way. I have chosen to isolate myself because I don't trust others."

"Why?" she asks. I figured my statement could cause questions and I would have to open up. For some reason, at this moment, I'm not uncomfortable with it.

"Before I answer, how did the traveling help your mindset?"

Just then, the pager starts vibrating at the table. I jump up. "I'll get it."

I walk back to the table with our food to proceed with the conversation.

We fix our plates and get comfortable again before she begins again. "Traveling."

She lets this word hang for a moment. "I was alone in my travels. I was forced to either build new friendships or stay alone in my thoughts. I was aching for real connections. The European culture was so open to speaking truths—or at least the people I met and began forging friendships with. In meeting them and opening up honestly, I found myself. The original intention was for me to do one semester abroad, but I didn't want to come back after a semester. One turned into two. And to be honest, two was almost three. But my dad pleaded with me to come home. I couldn't see him as often as he would like, so I packed up and came home."

"You found yourself? Explain." I want more.

"I realized, while I love the material things money can get me, those things weren't as important as the friendships I made. Our circle was diverse in every way imaginable. I wasn't surrounded by cliquish, cookie-cutter friends. These people all had their own styles and thoughts. They weren't scared to share them for fear of being on the 'outs.'" She air quotes with her fingers.

I am stunned silent with her admission. Could I be just as honest?

"Why have you isolated yourself?" she asks after a few quiet moments.

I take a deep breath in and exhale slowly, buying myself a little more time. I have never considered sharing my truth to anyone. At least, not while I am still in college. There are very few people who can handle this type of truth. I hope Lola is one, or I am alone again. The realization of not wanting to be alone again is not where I want to be anymore.

"I was raised on the south side." I decide to start with my easiest truth.

"Okay," she responds when I don't elaborate past this. "And this means?"

"I'm poor," I add for clarification.

"Why do you feel you need to isolate yourself because of that?" Confusion mars her face. She really doesn't care how much money I have.

My life is about to be on display, exposing all my vulnerabilities. "That part of town is like quicksand. Once you are in, there is very little chance of escape. The stereotypical vicious cycle of poverty. I have a chance of escaping, and I don't want anything to mess up my chances. Which means I do what I need in order to survive."

I pause, collecting my thoughts on how to proceed. Now that I'm talking, I want to continue, but there is so much.

"My grandmother raised me. My mom is a leech who is always looking for her next white knight who is going to support her and sweep her away from her life. But all she ever finds is losers who use her and dump her. She gets a few bills here and there, but they go back to their respectable wives or girlfriends and leave her back on her hands and knees, begging for another chance. She blamed me when I was little. That was why no man wanted her—because she was strapped with a kid. So she up and dumped me on my grandmother.

"My grandmother did the best she could. And I'm grateful

to her. She didn't have to keep us, but she was our stability. I guess you can say I'm smart. That's how I got into college, because my grades weren't the best. I was a National Merit Scholar, so the university offered me a free ride. If I hadn't gotten that scholarship, I wouldn't be here. I would be working some dead-end job and living at home until I died."

A single tear escapes. My admission is stirring emotions I didn't realize I had suppressed. Lola places her hand on mine and squeezes.

"I don't know what to say other than...thank you. I knew you had a story. I was just waiting until you were ready and trusted me enough to share with me."

She doesn't realize there's more.

"I'm not done. Are you sure you want to know the rest?" For the first time in my life, I'm not afraid of who I am or where I'm from.

"Absolutely. If you want to share."

"I work at a strip club." I drop what I think is a bomb.

"But I thought you said you worked at El Mundo?"

"I did last night, but I don't usually. My manager at the strip club got me in because she had too many waitresses and I needed to work. I'm a cocktail waitress, not a stripper." A hint of a smile appears on her face. "I work there because it's easy money, and I make enough to where I don't have to work all semester as long as I stay on budget. I thought I was not going to have to work at all for the rest of the year. I had squirreled away a good amount. But then my mom messed it all up again." My anger is rising, thinking of what she did to my grandmother.

"How did she mess it up?"

"She borrowed money from my grandmother. My grandmother doesn't have money to be lending. She barely makes it. My cousins and I help her out. When my mother borrowed money and didn't repay, I had to cover. That took a large chunk out of my savings. Now, I'm back at the club, working."

"Oh... That's really crappy. I'm sorry."

"It is what it is." I shrug.

"So how many nights will you be back at the club?"

The normality of her question stuns me.

"Uh... If I'm only working once maybe twice a week, maybe four to six weeks. Now that the semester is on the way, I hate to work more than that. I need to stay on top of my work to graduate on time. If I have to, I will pull several shifts during winter break to cover the spring semester."

She finishes chewing and swallows before adding, "I can understand why you wouldn't want to share where you work. There are so many judgmental assholes." She takes a sip of her coffee.

I can see a question beginning to form on her face.

"You can ask," I prompt her to end the suspense.

"I'm happy you told me, but what does this mean now? You have to admit, you were avoiding me. Will you continue avoiding me again, or will you hang the way we did before? If you have to work, just tell me. No one but me needs to know what your plans are."

I've opened up enough for today. There is still so much more, but maybe it will just go to the grave with me.

"I was avoiding you. I can't stand the judgmental assholes, like you said, or the looks of pity. I do what I do, and I don't need anyone's damn pity. And because you are taking this so well and aren't showing either, we can go back to before," I answer, feeling a small weight lift.

"Good. As you know, I have no problems with stalking you." She winks at me before shoving a large forkful in her mouth, smiling.

. . .

Garrett

I NEED to get my head back into the game. I can't continue pining away for some chick who had no respect for me. She is a complete bitch. Who knows how long she had been with that dick? Every time I think about that day, I want to go back and wipe that fucking superior smirk off his face. Who the fuck do I think I'm kidding? I'm pissed because I still want her.

I knew she had an edge to her. There was more to her. She kept everything close to the vest, but for her to be dating me and another ass was not a thought that had crossed my mind. That guy looked rough. One of those guys who you don't want to get caught with in a dark alley cause shit may get real.

Crossing campus to my next class, I catch a glimpse of her walking with Lola. I stop in my tracks even though I want to start running to intercept their path. She is smiling and seems relaxed. As angry and hurt as I am, I'm also happy to see her smiling. That true smile. Not the one she wears to hide herself. I stand in place, letting them pass, not wanting to interrupt the lightness she very rarely shows.

I just have to face the facts that I'm just not what she needs. Class is the last place I want to be right now, but I force myself there.

THE SUN IS JUST BEGINNING to peek over the horizon as I finish saddling my horse. I grabbed a couple of waters and snacks to ride the property. The city and the frat house were not the safest places for me at the moment. If I had seen Kevin and he had told me one more time she was bad news, I was going to lose it on him.

I lift myself up into the saddle, ready to spend the day in peaceful solitude—my horse and me with the beauty of the land. That's all I need right now. I head to the west side of the property, ready to ride the perimeter of the land and check all the fencing myself. As the sun continues to rise, the pastel shades of the sky remind me of her. Even with the tough exterior Toni likes to project, there is a fragile center she hides. Even with her insistence of masking it, I saw it. I just wanted her to let me in.

I still can't figure out how I could have been so wrong. How did I not see her dating someone else? When and how was she seeing him? Was she sleeping with both of us? As these questions continue to swirl, the anger continues to build. The peace I was hoping for on the quiet ride soon changes to a race. The faster I go, the quieter my mind seems to be. I don't realize how long we have been charging until my horse begins to slow on his own. He gallops toward a small pond. I know I have worn him out and need to give him a break. I leave him next to the water as I make my way to the shade of a nearby tree.

I sit with the snacks and water I had packed, not really wanting either. When he is done drinking, I walk to him and guide him back to the shade of the tree and tie his reins to a branch. I lie down, watching the leaves dance in the breeze.

The sound of a truck wakes me from an unexpected nap. Juan is opening the door to the ranch truck.

"Your parents are looking for you, guero," Juan yells as he walks in my direction.

"Not surprising. I left before anyone was up. I needed to get away," I inform him. "I thought I was going to check the perimeter for myself, but I decided to ride in chingas instead." I shrug as I sit up.

"Still bothered by the girl?" His question is simple but loaded.

171

"You can say that." It is the best answer without boring him with it again.

"Perimeter check then?" He points to the back end of the property.

"Yeah. I'm going." I stand, getting the horse ready to go out again.

"*Vamos tomar hora?*" (We drinking tonight?) He asks as he's walking back toward the truck.

"I'll be there," I yell as he's lifting himself up into the truck.

THE SCENT of a mom-made dinner is wafting upstairs as I exit my room. Surprising my parents with my unannounced visit last night was not the best idea. My dad was upset, wanting me to 'focus' on my studies. He doesn't believe I need to be driving back and forth or worrying about what is happening here. Dinner will either be the normal affair it usually is or I'm in for a lecture. Since I've been out all day, they haven't been able to corner me for an explanation.

"Smells good." I butter my mom up with the truth. She can be the greatest referee known to man if I can keep her happy.

"Thank you, honey. It's all ready. Come serve yourself." She motions toward the stove and counter where she has laid everything out.

"Didn't know we would be seeing you this weekend," my dad says as he walks toward me.

"It wasn't planned. Not much going on at school, so I thought I could use a quiet weekend." I tell a partial truth.

"Not much going on means good study time," he continues. It's not looking to be the best dinner after all.

I take my plate and sit down at the kitchen table, staying quiet. I know no response will be the best one. I watch as my

172

dad finishes serving himself and as my mom dotes on him. She then begins serving herself. She brings her plate to the table, and before she sits, she asks, "Anything else?"

"Sit down, Mom. Everything looks delicious." Which is the truth. This is the part I miss most about living on my own.

Her smile brightens as she takes her seat.

"Stop giving him such a hard time. He does not come home that often, and I miss my baby," she directs at my dad, her mad skills bringing my father's temper down in full gear.

Wanting to please my dad and show him I can handle the ranch, eventually, I begin to tell him about my ride—the one after I tried to race away from her memory. "I rode the perimeter of the line. The work we did before covered the most critical areas. There are a couple at the far north end we should look at. I could get those done during winter break. The herd very rarely heads in that direction, so it could wait."

"You rode the property?" my dad questions.

"Sure did. It's been too long since I've done that. I want to make sure I know everything about the land. You told me that." I use my dad's words to soften the conversation.

"Enough about that," Mom sidelines ranch talk. "Tell us how school is going. You haven't been calling as often. Someone taking up your time?" A light teasing can be heard.

She is right. Those weeks spent with Toni, I didn't place the usual good-morning calls. I drop my gaze to my plate, not knowing how to and not wanting to answer.

"There is someone!" she exclaims.

"What? No." I quickly try to shut the conversation down. "I also had to lead number 137 back to the herd. She had wandered off." The ranch talk is much safer now.

"Don't you go changing the subject on me. Spill." She sees right through me. My father's brows pull in, wondering if my mom is right.

I shove food in my mouth, buying a little more time to figure out what I'm going to say. I chew as slowly as I can before both my dad and mom have stopped eating and are staring at me for more information.

"Fine. Yes, there was someone, but now there's not." I shove more food in my mouth, hoping the explanation is enough.

"Okay. Thank you for that. But I'm going to need a little more," Mom continues.

"Her name was Toni. She wasn't one of those annoying girls who want me for my name. I don't even think she knew who I was. But now she's gone. End of story."

"And why is she gone?" She continues to probe.

"I don't know. Maybe it's because she chose someone else." I lay it all out. Why hide it now?

"Oh, honey. I'm sorry. I don't know who she would have chosen over you." A mom's biased statement for sure.

"Yeah, well, she chose some rough-looking dude. I guess the stereotype of girls choosing the bad boy is true."

"Maybe. But I know for a fact, you, my son, will come out on top." She winks and places a bite in her mouth.

HOLE-IN-THE-WALL BARS ARE the only place I need to be. There is no need for 'airs' or good impressions. Alcohol and more alcohol is the only thing I'm concerned with. Juan drove us, but I'm figuring someone else may be driving us back, because he's going one for one with me tonight.

"Mind if we have next game?" a pretty blonde asks.

"How about teams, sweetheart?" Juan answers before I can. "You with my friend, Garrett, and your friend with me."

"Sure." Her smile widens. "I'm Carrie, and this is Sara."

Juan motions the waitress over. "Two more for us, and

ladies..." He gestures for them to give their order. I collect the balls to re-rack the table.

Blondie is hot, and I could really use the distraction.

I break to start the game. As the girls each take their turn, the flirtation is on full blast, their asses swaying as they bend to take their shots, and their tits showing through low-cut shirts as they lean over the table. Blondie has made it a point to brush past me, grazing her hand by my length each time she's passed me.

I'm not big on one-night stands, but tonight is looking good.

"I gotta take a leak." I excuse myself.

As I walk out of the bathroom, blondie is standing against the wall, biting her lip with hunger in her eyes. I take a step to her and pin her against the wall.

"Tell me what you want."

She grabs my face, bringing it down to hers forcefully. A first kiss it is not. She opens instantly, greedily shoving her tongue in my mouth. Her hands come around and cup my ass as she pulls me against her. I grind into her as she moans loudly. My hand comes up to rub her breast as I begin kissing down her neck, her nipple hard underneath my palm.

"My place, Garrett Anders?"

That one statement is like a bucket of ice-cold water. She knows who I am and probably only wants two things—my name and my money. I pull away quickly.

"Sorry. We gotta go." I turn to walk back to the table.

"What?"

I get to the table with her hot on my heels.

"Let's go, Juan." I motion for the door. He nods at me, walking to a table of ranch hands. One follows us out to drive us home.

. . .

Sitting in bed, willing the room to stop spinning, I scroll through my old texts with Toni. We had just turned a page, and the formal planning texts had become fun with a teasing quality. Why would she have made this change if she was just going to date someone else? I type out a message.

I miss you

I never meant to send it, but the knock on my bedroom door startled me and I hit the send button. Shit.

"Are you home yet?" My dad's voice comes from the other side of the door.

"Yes, sir."

"Good." I hear his footsteps going down the hall.

CHAPTER SIXTEEN

HURTING

Toni

I miss you

Three words. Just three words that can gut you to the core. He sent it after midnight. Drunk text? What's the saying...children and drunks are the only honest people. I miss him too. But I can't explain my life to him. He's good. Too good for me. At least, right now he is. Asking him to wait around on the weekends as I flirt at the club to make money is a gigantic no-no.

Those three words have me spiraling through the few weeks of memories I had with him. He's so unlike anyone I've spent time with. He's generous, kind, patient, and he never expected anything.

Even that description does not do him justice. People can be generous and kind. But he was different. He was generous without being flashy. All I know is he was comfortable enough to be able to do things without worry, and if he did worry, he did not show it. His only concern was making sure I knew he had me. And his kindness was pure. Many people are kind for what it will get them in return, but he never expected anything. He was—or is—an anomaly.

I want so badly to text him to come over. The feeling of nothing being able to touch while I'm wrapped in his arms is what I want again. His gentleness. His calmness. His humor. His smile. That dimple. That damn dimple that pulls me into him.

I miss you too...come over?

I type out the words, wanting so much to be able to send them.

Garrett

THE CRUSHING pressure in my head I knew was coming wakes me. As much as I dislike hangovers, I hate the feeling of missing her even more. The alcohol numbs it—at least for now. I roll over on my back and feel my phone at my shoulder. I swipe the screen, and the text I sent her is staring right at me.

Why did I even type out those words? I can't erase or delete that damn message. My only hope is that she deletes it before reading it. Just as I am about to close and delete the whole damn thread, the typing bubble comes up. She's responding?

I wait, staring at that bubble like my life depends on it. It is there for what seems like several minutes, then disappears and no text. She saw it. She wants to respond, but decided against it.

Fuck. I drop my phone back on the bed and decide breakfast and driving back to the city is what needs to be done.

Toni

I HIT backspace until all those words are erased. It may be how I feel, but I should not be feeling this way. What has my mother taught me? Why am I letting some guy turn me into a weak bitch? No, that life is not for me. No man will have me begging, saying I miss him. I've seen the life where that road leads, and I have no desire to pine for someone only to be left at the end.

He may be a unicorn, but he still has the ability to hurt me. They all do. I have to stay in control.

Even as I say these words, I don't believe them. I want him. But my life is too jaded and screwed up for his white picket fence. My only consolation is he misses me, too.

It is useless trying to study today. I can't focus. Looks like today is turning into a laundry day. I roll out of bed to begin collecting my laundry, which is strewn all over, and head to Guela's house. It may take me all day, but at least I can treat her to lunch.

I have not bothered picking up my things since the day Garrett came to my door. This is not my normal. Today, I get myself back together. I will not turn into my mom. I grab all the clothes from the bathroom and toss them into a heap on the floor by my bed. I walk around, continuing to grab and toss. I'm going to be there all day by the looks of the pile. I shove clothes into a large laundry sack. I grab the last item that is peeking out from under the bed.

One of his shirts. I have had one of his shirts this whole

time, and I didn't know. I bring it up to my nose and inhale. His scent is barely noticeable anymore. At least I have this.

"HEY, GUELA!" I exclaim as I walk into the house, laundry in tow.

"She's not here," Javie informs me from the couch, remote in hand.

"Where is she?" I drag the bag through the living room.

"She got an extra house to clean. She left early this morning. She should be back soon."

"She shouldn't be cleaning more houses." I turn back, hearing this.

"I know. But with the mess with your mom, she didn't want you to have to cover it all. She worked last Sunday, too."

"What the fuck? Why didn't you or Alex stop her?" My anger is building.

He lets out a huff before responding. "Yeah. You try stopping Guela from doing what she insists on doing."

I shake my head, defeated, knowing their interference would have done no good. My grandmother is headstrong.

"Sorry. I know," I apologize. "I'm just pissed at my mom for putting us in this situation."

"No biggie." He turns back to whatever he was watching.

I place the first load in and sit at the kitchen table, phone in hand, waiting for her to get home. I scroll social media, stalking him. He hasn't posted anything for a couple of weeks, since we went out the last time. If he doesn't post, there's nothing to stalk.

With nothing to do but wait, I make my way to the couch and lie down and place my head on a pillow on Javie's lap.

"Miss him, don't you?" Javie's question surprises me.

"Uh...how?" I respond.

"Alex told me."

I turn around to look at him. His eyes are sad. I nod in the affirmative.

"I'm sorry it couldn't work out." He looks up to the screen again. I turn around and close my eyes, wanting to sleep away the emptiness he left.

BACK AT THE APARTMENT, I pull Garrett's shirt out of my laundry basket. I take off my clothes and pull it over my head and hug it to my body. This is all I have left. It's possible to have normal. Just not yet.

CHAPTER SEVENTEEN

NOT ANYMORE

Garrett

I WAS SO curious what she had typed out but never sent. The whole week was consumed with thoughts of the text bubble and all responses it could have been. My mind has given me everything from *"Fuck off"* to *"I miss you too"* and everything in between.

Waiting on an Uber was not in my plans tonight, but avoiding the frat brothers the last two weeks has not gone over too well. David talked me into meeting them. He said it will be a tame evening, the guys bringing their girlfriends and some of their friends.

I walk into a bar we rarely frequent due to its location, but I figure it is the safest option. I don't want to run into Toni by accident—at least, not yet. It's still too fresh. I don't know if I could hold a drunken tongue.

Walking in, I see the guys already have a table with

pitchers of beer in the center. Knowing a beer isn't going to do the trick, I stop at the bar and order a tequila shot. I tip my head back, enjoying the liquid heat. Moving my way to the table, I greet everyone as a beer is handed to me. I tip it back, taking long gulps until half is gone.

"It's going to be one of those nights?" David asks.

"Nah. It was a long one last weekend at the ranch. All work no play," I fib about the time away.

The beer, conversation, and laughs continue to flow easily. I sit next to a friend of David's girl, Amy. She is easy on the eyes, funny, intelligent, and doesn't throw herself at me. Not that I want anything from her, but at least I'm not having to turn her down in front of the guys and having to explain why. Harmless, friendly flirting feels good.

"I'll be back," I excuse myself to the bathroom.

Standing up, I meet her eyes. Am I seeing sadness? We stand like this for several moments until Amy notices I haven't left and pats my ass.

"I thought you were going to the bathroom." I break eye contact with Toni to look down at her.

"I am." I look back to where Toni was standing, and she is gone. I scan the bar with no sight of her.

I move quickly, wanting to find her. I cannot find her anywhere around the bar. I walk outside and see her driving away in Lola's truck. She drove away. Was she hurt? Why would she be hurt?

TONI

"NOT TONIGHT. I can't right now," I tell Lola as she drops me off in front of my building. I don't want to talk about him. Not now. Not ever.

How could I let Lola talk me into going out tonight? I knew it was a bad idea. I told her so, but she's so persistent. As soon as we walked in the bar, I heard his booming laugh. His uninhibited one. The one that told me he was comfortable and really enjoying himself. That laugh. That laugh was being shared with another girl. Some perfect little sorority girl, no doubt.

A wreck I couldn't pry my eyes away from. His arm draped over the back of her chair. That small protective gesture. The one I came to crave. His leaning into what she was saying and his dimple on display with a mischievous smirk.

I was glued to the floor when he stood up and saw me. I couldn't move. I wished for him to walk to me, but he didn't. He was shocked I saw him. Caught him. But I didn't catch him. He was free to do whatever his heart desired. And then she patted his ass. My heart dropped into my stomach, and I knew I couldn't handle any more. I wanted to go southside on her, yet I had no right to.

All that could have been mine. But it wasn't, isn't, and never will be.

Garrett

I EXIT the men's room and walk straight to the bar. Tequila is a necessity right now. After ordering, I take out my phone to text her. I stare at the last text sent, my fingers hovering over the keys.

"Don't do it, man. It's not worth it. Told you before, tell you again, she ain't worth the trouble." Kevin is by my side. He grabs the tequila the bartender left in front of me and shoots it back. He nods in her direction, lifting the glass and putting two fingers up.

I place my phone back in my pocket, knowing Kevin will not let this one go. She places two more glasses in front of us. He grabs his, clinks it against mine, and shoots it back like the first.

"She's a wild one. There is no taming a girl like that," he continues. A couple of whiskeys are placed in front of us.

"How do you know?" I challenge, the couple shots and plenty of beer I've had this evening boosting my bravado.

"I just know. No need going into specifics now." He shakes his head. "Just thank me and move along."

"Fuck that, man. You can't give me cryptic crap and expect me to buy it. Fuck you!" My anger is rising at his description of her. I can't tell if I'm mad because she fooled me or because I want to protect her. I just want to hit something, and punching the hell out of Kevin is sounding more and more like a good idea.

"Look." He places his hands in front of him in surrender. "I'll tell you tomorrow. I'll pick you up tomorrow and show you. Deal?"

I've never been the one to start shit. I keep to myself, not getting involved in the politics of the house or other people's shit, so Kevin adding his two cents in my life is not going over well.

What choice do I have? "Fine," I concede before downing the rest of the drink in one gulp. "I gotta go."

"I'll take you," he offers.

"Nah." I shake my head at him, pulling my phone out to schedule an Uber.

Toni

. . .

185

I GET IN MY CAR, needing to get away, and the only safe place to head is back to the south side. This is the only place I don't need to hide who I am. My past is in this place. Here, I can do whatever I need to survive and no one blinks an eye.

Where's the party? I text Amelia, my south side savior.

I'm at Leo's. But Alex is here. She responds right away.

Heading your way

Alex may be pissed I'm back, but he does not have a leg to stand on now. I'm back because I have to be. I can't pretend to fit in when I'm still too busy hiding who I am. He can't expect that of me now.

Tears that used to be so foreign to me but lately have been making an appearance more often begin to escape. I have no claim to him, yet I want it. I let him think I am dating someone. How hypocritical of me to expect him to stay home, pining away. I thought I hurt him, but maybe it was what I wanted to see. Not what was really there. I park and turn on the interior lights to check my makeup. No one will see me break.

As I walk up the sidewalk to the small, rundown home, Amelia is sitting on the front steps, a beer in one hand and a lit cigarette in the other. She motions for me to sit next to her and hands me the beer.

"What happened?" she begins. "And no shitting me anymore," she adds before I have a chance to open my mouth.

I take a long pull of her beer, finishing it. "I let a guy get to me."

Her eyes widen at my confession. She stares at me in disbelief. "The unattainable Toni got caught?" She sounds skeptical.

"He didn't know he caught me." I grab the cigarette from her hand. "Where's Alex?"

"Inside. I sat out here, waiting for you, in case you didn't want to run into him. We can get out of here if you want."

"Nah." I stand to find Alex. "I need to find him. Meet me in the back."

"Are you sure?" She knows what I'm going to get from Alex.

"Yes." I scan the crowd as I walk through.

All the usuals are standing around, drinks in hand. A few different couples, but the faces still the same. No one new. No one leaves. As much as you try to push yourself away, this place has a way of pulling you right back. It never lets you forget just who you are and where you came from.

"I need one." I put my arm through Alex's, placing my head on his shoulder.

"Nuh-uh. Not going to happen, Toni." He looks down at me as I look up at him. He knows. He can tell. I may be able to mask everything from everyone else, but he can see right through it. He places his hand in his pocket and pulls out an Altoids box. He opens it and grabs a single joint out. He holds it up to me. "Hand me your car keys."

I roll my eyes at him. "This isn't my first rodeo."

"It may not be, but you are almost out. I'll be damned if a stupid driving under the influence ticket brings you back." He holds firm.

"Fine." I slap my keys in his hand before he offers me my relief.

"And I'm driving you home. You are staying at Guela's. None of this shit staying at Amelia's," he adds before I can walk away.

I look back at him, shaking my head. He nods and walks away. He knows I'll listen and come to him when I'm ready to leave. I've never crossed him. I can't. He'd give up an organ for me.

I meet Amelia in the back, grabbing the lighter out of her hand.

"That bad, huh?" she asks as I take my first drag in years.

"Um-uh," I mumble out, holding the smoke, nodding my head. She watches me because I still haven't passed it along. Her curiosity is evident, but she's waiting for me. I exhale everything I was holding. "I don't even know how it happened."

She raises a brow. "No, I'm serious. It was just fun at first, being chased. He wouldn't give up. And somewhere in there I fell. I didn't even realize how far until I had to cut him loose."

I take another drag before I pass it off to her. I let the calm of the drug flow through me. My brain is the first to relax, and soon, everything else will too. I exhale slowly, watching the smoke I promised Alex I would stay away from.

"Did you cut him loose because you fell, or did something else happen?" she asks as the smoke leaves her mouth.

"Something else." I don't elaborate. She knows my mom is a loser, so there is no reason to go announcing our family dysfunction, especially since everyone around here has their own family secrets.

"So why mope around? Go back to him," she says, passing the joint back to me.

"Not in the cards." I inhale again.

Not wanting to explain or reveal things I don't even understand myself, the urge to find another quick relief comes quickly. I scan the small backyard, zeroing in on Jay. The southside hot guy I never gave the time of day to due to his reputation. But needing something to help erase memories of Garrett, I decide to give in.

"Think I'll hit that one up tonight," I tell Amelia as I nod in Jay's direction. I take another hit before handing her the last of the joint.

"Okay," she responds, sounding skeptical.

Jay spots me walking to him instantly. He smiles knowingly before taking the last steps to meet me.

"What are you doing back here?" Jay inquires.

"Letting off some steam. Wanna help?" No reason to beat around the bush.

"What do you think?" The smirk which used to aggravate me is welcome right now.

I grab his hand and walk him around to the quiet side of the house. Leaning against the building, I wait for him to make his move. He comes in hard and fast, his tongue invading my mouth while pressing up against me. I fall into him for a few seconds, my mind quiet, until my thoughts catch up, realizing the kiss is not right. His roaming hands have no rhyme or reason. It's sloppy and gross. I push him back, regretting my decision instantly.

"I gotta go." I walk away to find Alex.

This has always been my safe place. I belonged here. I knew how to survive here. But looking at myself now, I have changed. As much as I wanted to get out before, I always came crawling back to the safety I knew existed. Somewhere in the middle of all of this, things changed, and the safety my neighborhood had provided is now suffocating. A lightbulb comes on. This isn't my life anymore.

"Alex!" I yell across the room to get his attention.

As soon as he sees me, he knows. I see him wave someone over to him. Javie's heading in my direction with my keys in hand.

"Ready?"

I nod, walking to the front door.

CHAPTER EIGHTEEN

EXPOSED

Garrett

I'M LOOKING for a reason to cancel on Kevin. I don't know what he has planned, but I know whatever it is won't be good for me. He is insistent I need to know the 'real' Toni, but I think I may know her better than he does. She doesn't let people in, giving them only the mask she wears. There were very brief moments where it slid off and I was able to see the real her before she realized and placed it back on.

If he knows something about her, it's not the important part. It's superficial and is a waste of my time. But even so, I am curious what he thinks will change my mind.

My phone vibrates on the table.

On my way

No backing out now. Since he lives a couple of buildings away, the Uber has already been ordered. I do find it strange it is only the two of us going. When he goes out, he's infamous for inviting everyone, ensuring he has a posse surrounding him. He basks in his position, unlike me. We are polar opposites in the attention department. He enjoys girls throwing themselves at him. He doesn't mind tossing them when he's done. He will probably end up marrying the next 'Real Housewife' while I want to repel them all.

The knock on my door cues the beginning of what I fear will be a very long evening.

"Hey," I announce as I open the door.

"Uber is here. Ready?"

It's already awkward. It is at this moment I realize I have never been anywhere with Kevin on our own. He is a frat brother, but not my favorite person, so I have never had the inclination to hang alone with him. I should have taken a couple of shots.

"Yeah." I grab my keys from the counter to lock up.

Since he ordered the car, I don't know where we are headed. Small talk about upcoming mixers and duties are the only things we have in common to discuss. The driver parks at a bar we frequent.

"I thought you had things you had to show me?" I ask, confused why we are here.

"I do and I will, but it's still too early. Drinks first," he answers, exiting the car.

I follow, still not understanding where the night is going to take me.

"If any of the other guys are here, do not invite them with us when we leave to our next location."

"Okay." This is sounding more cryptic and has me wondering what we will be doing. "Where are we going?"

"I'll tell you later."

We take two seats at the bar and wave the bartender over.

"A couple of Shiners and Patrons." He is quick to order.

I take my card out to hand her for the tab. He pushes my hand with the card back.

"Let me. I'm not sure you are going to be happy with me after tonight." He slides his card to her.

"If I'm not going to be happy, why take me or show me? Leave well enough alone." My frustration is at an all-time high.

"I'm doing this because if it were me, I would want to know. That's it." The bartender places our drinks on the bar in front of us. He grabs his shot glass and holds it up, waiting for me. I grab mine, tapping the bar before tossing it back quickly. I need something to calm the edge.

"What can you tell me?" I ask before bringing the beer bottle to my mouth. As it flows down my throat, I can't seem to want to stop. Half the beer is gone before I place the bottle back down. I wave her down to bring another. No reason to sit with an empty in front of me.

"I can tell you what you won't do after." The seriousness in his voice cannot be ignored. He lets the statement hang before continuing. "You won't be chasing her or missing her anymore. You will realize you dodged a bullet."

"Then just tell me and forget about this cloak-and-dagger routine you have going. Enough with the fuckin' dramatics. Man up and just say it." I wish he would spit whatever it is out.

"I can't. You need to see to believe. If you don't, then there will always be a what-if."

I can't decide if he is doing this for himself or to 'save' me. I know he has a history with her—one that they do not speak about. He has never been this invested in any girl I've dated. Although, no girl has brought me to my knees before.

"Then tell me your history with her," I push back.

"I can't. Not yet. But it will come." His calmness is irritating.

Not comfortable with where the night is going, I move to something stronger to numb whatever may come my way.

MANY DRINKS LATER, we are back in an Uber. I am, again, ignorant to the next location. The ride is completely silent until I recognize what part of town we are on. We are heading back to the strip club he mentioned before.

"Why are we heading to the club?" I ask in irritation. "I came already. You threw out the bait, and I took it that night. Nothing came of it, so why are we here?"

"I figured you did. But I did my homework." His ambiguous answer increases the annoyance.

I drop my head back on the headrest, not ready for what I may see.

KEVIN PASSES the bouncer at the door and nods at him in recognition. He waves at the woman collecting the cover without giving her any money. He knows this place and knows it well. I follow him along the wall to a table in the back, close to the one I sat in the last time. He takes a seat, so I follow suit.

I scan the area. There is a woman onstage, performing to an upbeat older song. She oozes sexuality as she discards each piece of clothing she removes. It's not Toni. The suspense of waiting for the other shoe to drop is nerve-wracking.

I watch as women are walking the floor, hoping for private dances. The cocktail waitresses flirt while keeping everyone filled and happy. I watch as a waitress seductively walks around the table, taking orders, passing each man, slightly rubbing herself on them. A hand dragging across a back, her side up against one, and another, she is leaning her breasts on his upper arm. I stare in agony of what may be in my very near future.

The wait has come to an end. It's Toni. She walks out from behind the bar and stops at a table. She is wearing very short black shorts with a top exposing her midriff and cleavage. Her flirtatious mannerisms can clearly be seen. Jealousy comes hard and fast.

"Don't." Kevin places his hand on my arm. "If you don't want to be kicked out in the next thirty seconds, you will keep that in check," he warns.

My body is tense, watching the men at the table much too friendly with her. I hold myself steady to watch her. I can tell she's flirting, but her smile is too big, and her body stiffens as one tries to touch her. She moves swiftly out of his reach. I watch the other waitress again and clearly see the difference between the two. Unless you are studying them, you wouldn't see the difference. All men notice is a beautiful woman who is paying attention to them.

The tension, while still there, begins to slowly dissolve. I don't want her here, and I still don't understand what is going on, but I can see through the part she is playing. I watch her as she turns in my direction. Her eyes meet mine, and time stops. I want nothing more than to go to her. Kiss her. Claim her. But there is still so much that hasn't been said.

TONI

WHAT. The. Fuck. How is he here? I can't move. Everything I have tried to hide for so long is coming undone. Kevin is sitting right next to him. His smirk is in complete opposition to the pain marring Garrett's face. This is not the first time I have been hurt, and it won't be the last. This seems to be the story of my life. The cards I was dealt. There is no other choice than to go over there and get this night over with. I can't see them staying long.

"Funny running into you here." I try and make light of the agonizing situation we are in.

"I would say so," Kevin pipes in, even though my comment was directed to Garrett.

"Usual?" I look directly at Kevin this time. He has never been in here without a large party of older men. I figured they were all his daddy's partners, clients, or something of the sort. Kevin has always been the youngest in the group. The usual for them is bottle service. If Kevin wants to out my secret, I won't bother keeping his.

"Nah. It's just the two of us tonight."

"Then what will it be?" I place my hand on my waist and cock a hip, impatient with the shenanigans already.

"Just bring a pitcher of Dos XX."

"Fine." I turn to face Garrett head on. He has been watching our exchange. "Want anything?" My bravado is slipping.

He shakes his head slowly, no sound leaving his mouth.

I turn quickly, needing to find a place where I can breathe again. I walk to the back and enter the dressing room, because those damn tears want to escape again. No. This will not happen. I gain my composure back. I find the closest machine to place in all my orders. Tonight will be like any other. He is like any other.

At the bar, I yell over the music to get Sasha's attention. She may manage, but she spends the majority of her time at the main bar.

"What's up?"

"Two shots. I didn't ring them up," I ask for a favor. I never do this, so she quickly obliges.

She hands me two Jager shots with my order. I make my way to drop off drinks at another table, saving Garrett and Kevin's table for last.

I place the pitcher with two glasses on the table first. I then place one shot in front of each of them.

"These are on me. Cheers! Have a good evening." And with this declaration, I quickly glance at Garrett and walk away. He still has not said a word to me. He's probably sorry he spent so much time chasing.

Garrett

WORDS DON'T SEEM to want to leave my mouth. Everything I think I would want to say is either stupid or too personal I won't want to say it in front of Kevin. I don't want to give him the satisfaction of knowing how hurt I feel right now. I don't want him to know that this doesn't change much for me. I don't want to have the conversation with her out in the open.

I lift the shot she placed in front of me and down it. I pour a glass from the pitcher and finish it in a couple of swallows.

"Ready to go." I place a few twenties on the table for her. I know this should cover everything and leave her a good tip.

"What are you doing, man? I got this." He picks up the money, handing it back to me.

"Like I said, ready to go. Leave the money there and let's go." I stand, waiting for him to follow me.

"We still have more beer." He's having too much fun at my

expense. I grab the money from his hand and walk to the bar. I get the attention of a cute blonde.

"Can you have our waitress close us out?" I point to our table. I'm not sure if waitresses go by their names or use 'stage' names like the dancers. "This should cover it." I hand her the money.

"Sure thing, sweetie."

CHAPTER NINETEEN

NOW WHAT?

Toni

HE LEFT without a single word said to me. I placed myself behind the bar, hidden by a tower of bottles, to watch them. There was nothing to watch. He left. The hole I felt before widened a bit more. A couple of minutes after Garrett walked out, Kevin followed. I wanted to ask him why he would do this but decided it wouldn't be worth it. He did it because he thinks he's better than me. End of story. No reason to get into a no-win argument.

The rest of the night was a blur of delivering drinks and keeping the fakest smile I could muster plastered on. I doubted my tips were going to be anywhere what I was used to, because I had put no effort into the tables except to take orders and deliver. I didn't chat, flirt, or tease. The energy it would have taken seemed so out of reach.

. . .

FALLING into my bed after tonight is needed. Now, if I could find a way not to leave. The possibility of running into Garrett somewhere on campus is too much. Now, my reason for not running into him is so much more dire. Before, it was for my heart's safety, but now it is me needing to save face. The lonely college student persona I've had in place for the past three years has come undone. One look at me and where I work can have him assuming correctly about my past. Past? It's my present. I haven't left. I've been playing pretend. I never really belonged here. It was me hoping to take enough steps forward. Enough steps away to break the bands that tether me to the south side.

I drift, drowning in dread and despair.

As soon as I open my eyes with the sun shining a new day, the hurt and anger I felt last night comes roaring back. There is only one thing left to do.

MY PLACE. Both of you

I hit send. I'm sinking in quicksand, and the more I fight it, the faster I sink. A list of things I have to do is forming in my head, so I begin typing them out in the notes app on my phone.

What happened?

Now! I respond angrily.

Fine

I THROW on some leggings and an oversized hoodie over Garrett's shirt—the only thing I will be taking home from my time away.

A knock on my door announces their arrival as they walk in.

"We're here. What happened?" Alex walks in first with Javie close behind.

"We need to move me out. I don't know where your dad is going to stay, maybe the couch like he did when we were little, but I need my room back." I sit up, crossing my legs underneath me. I take out my phone, opening the notes app to check my list.

Alex drags a chair close to me, and Javie sits at the foot of the bed. They are both just watching me, not sure what to say.

"Why are we moving you out?" Javie breaks the silence that has loomed for the past several seconds.

"Because I'm dropping out." This all needs to be done expeditiously. "I believe if I'm out before the end of the month, I won't have to pay anything. This place always has a waitlist for apartments since they are so cheap and close to campus. I'm sure they can fill it quickly with no penalty." I glance up from my phone. "We need to collect boxes from the grocery and liquor store today so I can start packing up."

"And don't forget to borrow a truck. We have a week. I need to start looking for work too. Figure out what I'm going to do. I can't wait tables at a strip club my whole life. Long-term plans. That's what I need."

"STOP!" Alex raises his voice to break through my ramble. He takes a moment before he continues. "Before we do all that, you have to let us know why."

The walls I had constructed so carefully to protect myself crumbled last night. If I explain, they will see just how broken I've become. I stare at Alex, hoping I win the war of wills. Javie crawls up the bed to sit next to me and envelopes me in his arms. My head drops into his chest, and all the feelings I was trying to ignore flood out of my eyes. Hot tears stream down steadily.

After several moments, I turn my face to look at Alex. "He found out."

"How?"

I sit up so I can face both Alex and Javie. "At the frat party where I met Garrett, I also ran into a guy who frequents the club. Kevin comes in quite a bit with older gentlemen. He wanted me to leave the party, but my stubbornness won. I stayed and met Garrett. They are frat brothers. I didn't know Kevin attended here. I never share my life, so I don't ask about anyone's either."

I pause, everything a jumble of memories and no real good explanation now that I have to say it out loud.

"I was worried about Kevin at first, but when it seemed he kept my secret, I let my guard down. Now Garrett also knows where I work."

"How?" Javie's brows pull in question.

"He and Kevin came to the club last night."

"Did he make a scene?"

"No."

"Then it's no big deal," Alex chimes in.

"You all know I hadn't made friends with anyone here. I came to classes and stayed true to my southside roots for friends—until this year, when Alex made me venture out, not come home. I started making friends here, but now that people know what I do, I know they will either judge me or pity me. And I don't need either of those things in my life."

"Two guys know what you do to support yourself through college. You wait tables. Lots of people do. Who gives a flying fuck, Toni?" Alex spits out angrily. "You are not dropping out, and you are not coming back. End of story." He stands, arms crossed in front of him with a scowl, daring me to challenge him.

"I am and I will." Alex may scare half of the neighborhood, but he doesn't scare me.

"Guys. Just pause." Javie is the mediator, knowing how stubborn both of us can be. "Toni..." He pauses until he knows he has my attention. "Explain to me, please."

"I al—" I begin, but Javie places his hand in front of me to stop and interrupts.

"No, you didn't. All you have said is you are dropping out because two pricks know. Tell me more. Tell me why them knowing has you throwing everything you have worked for these past three years away."

"I don't want people's pity or judgment. Yes, I wait tables —but at a strip club. Girls would love to start shit with that piece of juicy gossip."

"Yes, you work at a strip club, but who cares? When have you ever cared what another girl thinks of you? And guys? They go to the strip club."

"But there is still a double standard. Guys are fine frequenting them, but girls can't work there or they are sluts. Even you and Alex do it—call girls 'hos' all the time."

"Don't place us in that asshole category. We don't call anyone a 'ho' who doesn't deserve it," Alex informs me with a smile, taking a seat at the edge of the bed, then adds, "Are you a 'ho'? Because if you are, then maybe you need to re-evaluate, and if you aren't, then don't worry about it."

I swipe his arm playfully, knowing he is right.

"You fell." Alex looks at me directly. "And you never wanted to fall."

I nod my head, looking down at my hands clasped in my lap.

"I thought he was different. He wasn't the typical asshole guy, talking about himself or boosting himself up to be better than he was. And every time I thought I was brushing him off nicely, he kept trying harder. He never pushed. He let me set the pace."

They stay quiet, knowing if they say anything, I may close

up again.

"He is in that frat, so I'm guessing he is, at least, comfortable, but he doesn't show it. Not like some of the other guys who try to be flashy with cars or...I don't know. There is just something about the rest of them that grates me. Like they are trying too hard to be cool. Garrett wasn't that. He was protective."

A peaceful silence lingers before Javie asks, "If he is that guy—the one that's different—then why are you worried about him saying anything to anyone?"

This thought has never occurred to me. I automatically think the worst of situations and people. He didn't cause a scene. He looked hurt, but walked away. It's almost like he knows I do not want attention brought to me, and he has sheltered me from it the whole time. Quietly paying even if I don't want him to, making sure I'm comfortable every place we go, following my lead are all things I hadn't thought about.

Garrett

MY MIND always wanders back to her. I wonder how long she has been working there. Her confidence and secretive nature makes perfect sense now. A woman has to have confidence to work there and survive the guys who make life difficult. Handling yourself while being put on display is a necessary trait to survive working under those conditions. She kept all this hidden away, too scared to share.

This explains so much—except the guy in her apartment. Is she really dating someone else? A knock on my door pulls my attention away from the invading thoughts.

Opening the door, I find Kevin on the other side, two coffees in hand.

"What do you want?" Anger greets him.

"Look, I'm sorry, but you didn't believe me the first time I told you." He steps into the apartment and sits on the couch. I take the chair, astonished he has the nerve to be here. But since he does, I'm asking questions.

I take the coffee he offers me with the small bag he's clutching with creams and sugar. I settle in, organizing the questions in my head I want answered.

"So why tell me at all?" I ask a simple question to start him talking. He hasn't been too forthcoming in the past.

"I didn't think that was the type of girl you would want to take home to Mama." His brows pull in as if confused.

"Maybe not," I agree to keep him talking, "but she was fun."

"Oh, I bet she was." His booming laugh fills the apartment, and it takes everything in me to stay calm.

"How long have you known her?"

"Probably over a year. I had no idea she was a college student. I only ever saw her at the club until the party at the beginning of the year."

"Really?" I ask surprised. "You didn't know she came to school here?"

"Nah, man. I just thought she was a working girl."

My jaw clenches tight at his description of her. I drop my head and rub my neck out. I can't let him know he's getting to me.

"Working girl? She's a..." I can't bring myself to say the word.

"I'm not sure. I took her home the first night we met, and I gave her something for her time. But it was a one-and-done for me."

That does not sound like Kevin. He is no one-and-done man. He strings them along for his pleasure. He showers them with money so they worship his feet until they bore him. And when they do, he cuts them off, and he's not so nice about it. The heated talk I saw them in that first night, he was trying to get rid of her, not the other way around. He's not giving me the whole story.

"Who were you at the club with?" Are all the brothers hanging there and know?

"My dad and his clients when he's entertaining them."

This makes sense now. No one else knows what he is doing. Trying to process the limited information he has given me, I take sips of my coffee, letting the silence drag.

"Look man, I just didn't want you hung up on a piece of ass that wasn't worth it. So many better options out there."

She is worth it. I just need to know more. "All those other options are only out for one thing: my future money. Fuck that."

Again, his laugh is annoying every fiber in my being, "It's the money that will get you what you want. You can be choosy when you have money. Get the one that is exactly how you want her to look, and you can control her. You have the money. If she wants it, she will behave exactly the way you want her to."

What a fucked up way to think about women. His poor mother. I wonder if she's just hanging on to be able to shop at her leisure. What an incredibly depressing way to live. Not having an equal partner but a servant who fills in as arm candy.

With not much more he can offer me by way of explanation, I tell him, "I have to get going. Thanks for the coffee."

"Sure, man. I just didn't want to see you drowning your sorrows for a cheap piece of ass."

I show him out the door, walk into my room, and punch the wall, leaving a hole in the sheetrock. I know better than to show him my true feelings. I just wish the wall was his face.

205

CHAPTER TWENTY

THE BOTTOM DROPS

Toni

ALEX AND JAVIE have convinced me to stay. I have done too
much these past three years to be run off. I'm better than
that, and I just needed someone to remind me. A week has
passed, and there are no rumblings of rumors about me that I
know of. Lola is on her way over with some dinner. I decided
to ask her if she has heard anything to make sure people
weren't just hiding shit from me. She knows the whole story
anyway.

She walks right in, without knocking, with bags from her
favorite taqueria.

"I'm starving, so my eyes are probably bigger than both
our stomachs combined." She laughs, placing everything on
the coffee table. "Did you decide if you are finally going to
venture out into the world of college parties again tonight?"

She sits on the floor, taking things out of the bags and

spreading them out. I sit next to her, placing drinks, napkins, and forks on the table.

"Not yet," I answer honestly. I won't know until I'm honest with her about what happened and if there is talk going on.

"Why not?" she whines as she stuffs a nacho in her mouth.

"I have to tell you something, and you have to be honest with me." I start by raising her curiosity. I grab a quesadilla and take a bite. This restaurant is really good.

"Shoot." She's piling avocado and sour cream onto another nacho.

"Something happened last weekend… Kevin and Garrett came to the club. They know where I work."

Her quick intake of breath causes her to choke on the food she was chewing, and she begins coughing. She spits her food into a napkin and takes a drink. "What?" Her eyes are wide.

"Let me start at the beginning." I tell her the whole story, beginning to end, leaving nothing out while we continue eating. At the end, I ask, "So please tell me the truth. Are there any rumors or talk about where I work?"

She shakes head her. "No. Not that I've been told."

"I don't want to go out if people are talking. I would rather just avoid it."

"I understand, but I swear, I haven't heard anything."

"You don't think Garrett has said anything?" I ask nervously, my feelings for him still raw.

"No. He wouldn't. He really cared," Lola tries to convince me.

"You have been saying that. How do you know?" I ask her, still doubtful.

"He chased you. Even when you made it hard, he was still coming around. Guys don't do that unless they care."

"I didn't make things hard," I deny.

She puffs out a sarcastic laugh. "Sure. You made it so easy for him." She rolls her eyes. "So, tonight? A yes?" She pushes a little harder. "I want my bestie with me." She knows I hate that term and uses it to annoy me because she trusts in our friendship.

"Fine." I give in to her as I have since we met.

Now that the hard topic is over, we can scroll through Netflix, finding a mindless show to kill the afternoon.

My phone rings on the counter. I ignore it, not wanting to get up. It silences then begins ringing again. Odd, since no one ever calls.

"Want something while I'm up?" I ask Lola who's still on the floor, leaning back on my small couch.

"I'm good."

I pick up my phone to see Alex calling me.

"What's up?" I ask, wondering why he's calling me.

"It's Guela. Meet us at Sacred Angels Hospital," he clips out.

"What's wrong with Guela?" I ask, my legs feeling weak.

"I don't know. She didn't wake up this morning, so I went to check on her, and she was not making sense. The ambulance took her, and Javie went with her. I'm following."

"I'm on my way." I hang up, frazzled, not knowing what to do. I look at Lola. "I've got to go."

"What happened?" she asks, worried.

"They don't know. The ambulance took my grandmother. I have to go." I grab my purse and shoes, walking out of my apartment.

Lola follows me out. "I will clean up and lock up behind me. What hospital?"

"Sacred Angels," I yell as I make it to my car.

Driving to the hospital, my mind races with what could have happened. Something happening to my grandmother has never been something I've ever considered. To me, she is invincible. Deep down, I know she is getting older, and that's why we take care of her—to lessen her burden. She has always been there for us; the least we can do is be there for her in return.

I didn't think my heart could hurt any more than it did when I walked away from Garrett, but it can and it is worse. My breaths are coming shallow and fast. A parking lot is just up on the right, so I pull in. I stop the car and place it in park. I open my mouth, and the loudest guttural scream comes out as I bang my hands on the steering wheel. Every fear I have is released in that moment. I check my surroundings, ensuring I haven't raised unnecessary attention. The partly empty lot is a relief.

With my foot on the brake, I place the car in drive. I need to have a clear head to get answers from the hospital staff. They may not take Javie—or especially Alex —seriously.

I'm here. Where r u?

I get out, walking to the entrance.

Still in ER

I speed up my pace, wanting answers. Hospitals are like mazes—hallways that twist and turn that all look the same. I think it's deliberate so that you walk off some of the anxiety before you reach the intended person.

"Where is she?" I ask them, walking into the waiting room.

"No one has told us anything yet. We were waiting for you," Alex informs me as Javie sits quietly, his head in his hands, refusing to look up.

My cousins are the epitome of what bad boys look like. It's not only their unshaven, scruffy faces, tattoo sleeves, or harsh looks; it's the way they hold themselves. They somehow project danger just by their presence.

"Hello," I greet the man behind the desk. "My grandmother was brought in a while ago. Can you get some information to share, or have someone come talk to us, please?"

His face has a scowl, probably from the long shift he's had, but a small smile forms when he sees me.

"Uh. Okay. What's her name? And relation?" he asks.

"Juanita Martinez. I'm her granddaughter. Thank you so much." I lay it on thick, trying to ensure some news quickly.

He picks up a phone. "We have the granddaughter of Juanita Martinez here. Is there any news to share?" I watch him as he listens to the person on the other end, wishing it were louder so I could eavesdrop. "Okay. Thanks."

"Someone will be down here in a moment."

"Thank you." I wish he could tell me something, but I know he can't.

I pace back and forth in front of the guys, having too much anxious energy to sit. Several minutes pass, no words spoken, the white noise of the busy ER waiting room our only distraction.

"Family of Juanita Martinez," an older woman calls from one of the doors.

The boys stand, and we walk together to meet her.

"Are you all family?" she asks.

"Yes. We are her grandchildren," I answer for us.

"Does she have a husband or any children here?" she inquires.

I shake my head. "She isn't married, and to be honest, our parents aren't really worth much. We are the ones who take care of her," I answer honestly. I don't want them to withhold information, waiting on our deadbeat parents. The guys nod their heads on either side of me.

"Okay. Please come with me." She begins walking to the door she came through. We follow eagerly, wanting any information she can give us.

We are taken to another waiting area on a different floor,

and a woman is standing in the middle.

"Family of Juanita Martinez?" the new woman asks.

"Yes, ma'am. We are her grandchildren. How is she? What happened?" Questions tumble out of my mouth.

"I'm Doctor Green. I evaluated your grandmother when she came in. She is still undergoing some tests and has not woken up, but our preliminary diagnosis is a stroke."

"What does that mean?" Javie asks, eyes filled with fear.

"It's too early to say. Right now, we are focusing on her waking up. When the test results come back, we will be able to give you more information."

"So that's it for now?" My hands are shaking.

"Unfortunately, yes. Give us a couple of hours to get the tests completed, and someone will be back to speak with you. You can stay in this waiting room."

The two women walk out quickly, leaving us to our fear and grief. At least the room is empty. I find a small bench and sit, the adrenaline quickly fading.

Garrett

MY PHONE HAS NOT STOPPED CHIMING incoming texts with plans for tonight. I'm not in the mood to do anything. Not wanting to run into Kevin has kept me away from the frat house all week except for my mandatory study session. An evening home alone is the only thing I want in my future. With this decision made, I place an order for pizza delivery.

I GRAB my wallet when I hear a knock on my door. Instead of my pizza delivery, I find Lola on the other side.

"Hi," I say, unsure why she is here. She has avoided me

since the split with Toni.

"One question. That's all I have," she states. I've never seen her so solemn.

"Okay..." I drag the word out slowly, not sure what she could ask.

"Did you care for her?" The way she watches me is unnerving.

Stunned by her question, I stay silent. Why would she be asking this now?

"Why?"

"Answer first," she says forcefully.

I pause before answering honestly. "Yes, I cared for her." I use past tense, hesitant of her intentions.

"Cared past tense or care?" she pushes.

"You said one question. Answer mine first."

She stares at me, unmoving. This is one stare off I don't think I'll be winning.

"Care. Okay. I care for her. Happy?" I exclaim, frustrated.

"Yes. Now, come on. I'll explain in the car." She turns around quickly, bumping into the delivery guy with my pizza. "Sorry," she tells the guy and continues walking.

I'm still trying to catch up with what she has said. I take money out of my wallet to hand the delivery guy. She stops midway down the stairs and turns around when she realizes I have yet to follow her. She looks up at me, waiting.

"I'm coming." I take the pizza inside.

"Are you going to tell me what's going on?" I ask as she's driving.

"Crap! I didn't think this out all the way." She looks in the rearview mirror and takes a hard right onto a small side street.

"What didn't you think through? What the hell is going

on?" I'm beyond confused and irritated with no explanation. How can this be happening again to me? Another strange adventure where I'm in the dark. I don't want to be blind-sided again.

"Sorry." She parks the car on the side of the road. "Look. I shouldn't have just asked if you cared for her. I should have also asked about last weekend."

The shock of her statement has probably drained the color from my face. Kevin is fucking spreading rumors about her. "What did that motherfucker tell you?" The confusion and anger is fueling my yelling at her.

"What motherfucker are you speaking of?" she asks calmly.

"Kevin."

"He didn't tell me anything. Toni did." she informs me.

"What did she tell you?" The surprise of this revelation catches me off guard.

"Everything that happened. You at the club with Kevin. Finding out where she worked. Walking away without saying anything to her." She pauses, watching me. "Why didn't you say anything to her? Or does that change things for you?"

She is throwing so much at me, and my mind is moving too slowly, trying to process. I take a few seconds before I open my mouth to explain.

"I couldn't talk to her there. First, I was with Kevin. He wanted me to know where she worked. He took me there, not telling me why. I didn't want him to hear anything I wanted to say. Second, she was working. I didn't think it was the best place, trying to yell our private details above the music." I stop. I don't want to say the third reason I walked away. The biggest reason I have to stay away.

Like she knows I'm not being fully truthful, she inquires, "That's it?" She cocks an eyebrow in question.

"No. The real reason I have to stay away. She is with

someone else." My head falls back, hitting the headrest. I hit it a couple of times for being the idiot.

I turn to her as I hear a small laugh. "What's so funny?"

"She isn't with anyone else." She seems so sure.

"What?" I'm still not following.

"She isn't dating anyone. Why would you think so?" she pushes.

"I saw her with a guy at her apartment when she said we were over," I answer honestly.

"Well, I don't know who was with her, but she isn't dating him. She hasn't dated anyone since you. That I do know." The confidence in her statement has me wanting to believe.

"So what's going on?" I ask, still unclear with where we are going.

"I figure she needs friends right now. I was with her earlier, and she got a call about her grandmother being taken to the hospital. She looked so scared." Her lips pull down.

"Oh."

"Will you go? I'm figuring she needs people she can trust."

"She trusts you?" A twinge of jealousy sparks.

"I think so. I forced her to." She winks at me. Lola is a force, and I could see her pushing her way into Toni's life.

"But she doesn't trust me."

"Not yet. But she will." She places her truck in drive.

WALKING THROUGH THE HALLS, my stomach is in knots, not knowing how I will be received. But that is an asshole thought. Worrying about myself when she is going through hell is selfish. I watch Lola reading and typing on her phone as we walk the corridors. I am following her, not knowing when I am going to come face to face with the girl who stole my heart.

We turn to the left into a waiting room, and there she is—

214

in his arms. I stop, the hole she left bursting wide open. They are sitting on a small couch, and he has his arm wrapped around her back, her head tucked on his shoulder with her eyes closed.

"How is she?" Lola asks, walking straight to her.

She looks up at Lola's voice, and her eyes immediately find mine. I'm frozen to the spot, unsure what comes next. The guy and another one sitting on her other side look up at Lola and see me watching. They stay seated as Toni stands, eyes still on me. Lola grabs her hand, squeezing it.

"We still don't know much." Her voice is filled with fear.

She heads in my direction. If I'm being helpful or not will soon be answered. She walks right into my chest, laying her head against me. My arms quickly come around her as I place a small kiss on the top of her head. Her soft sobs can barely be heard as she is clutching me around the waist. I look up at the guy she was sitting next to, and he is watching us with a small smile, which is not expected.

Lola watches us for a few moments before she sits next to him, extending her hand.

"I'm Lola. And which cousin are you?" I overhear her ask him. And a few things start to fall into place.

"Alex, and that is my brother, Javie, over there." He points at the second guy in the room who has moved to the corner.

Lola turns around and gives Javie a small wave.

"Have you all heard anything?" she asks Alex.

At this question, Toni pulls away and turns around but leans her back into my chest. "They are running tests, but they think it was a stroke. She still hasn't woken up," she answers Lola.

"Can we get you all anything?"

"I'm good," Toni answers, "but I need a few minutes."

Both Alex and Lola nod their heads at her as she turns around again, this time grabbing my hand and pulling me behind her. We walk down several halls. I'm letting her lead, not knowing where she wants to go. Once we are in the cafeteria, she sits at a table, and I mirror her.

I can hear her breathing as she stares at the table. I have all the patience now that I know she has missed me, too. I could finally breathe again once I had her in my arms. I was too stupid to know I was drowning, not understanding the reason she left.

"I'm sure you have questions," she begins, not looking at me.

I need her to look at me. I need to know what she wants and understand what I want. My fingers come under her chin as I gently push her head up.

Once her eyes meet mine, I begin. "I do. And before, I would have treaded lightly, scared you would have jetted so fast if I came too close to things you weren't ready to share. But now...now I think I need all the truth." A single tear falls, running down her cheek.

"I know we may not have time for it all right now, but soon," I continue. "The two most important things I need answered right now are..." I pause, giving myself a moment before I put myself out there again with her.

"What are they?" she asks.

I brush the tear away. "Are you dating anyone?"

Another tear falls from the brim of her eye. She shakes her head. "No. I haven't dated anyone but you in a very long time." A couple more tears follow as she blinks her eyes.

I can't hide the relief I feel when she tells me this. "Do you want me here? I don't want to intrude during such a personal time."

She nods at me. "Please stay."

The vulnerability she is showing at this moment is something I have never seen from her before. She always hid behind tall walls; emotions were rarely shown.

"Okay." I turn my chair to the side and open my arms toward her. She comes right into me again, sitting on my lap, her arms wrapping around my neck, clutching tightly. I give her a moment. "Don't you want to get back in case the doctor comes with any news?"

"Yes." She grabs a napkin from the table, wiping her eyes.

Before she stands, I grab her chin, bringing her gaze to me. "I'm here for the long haul if you let me."

Her lips pull down as she bites the corner of her bottom lip. "I can't believe it yet. Not until you know everything. I don't live in fairy tales, never have. My life doesn't even look normal. It's a train wreck. No one would voluntarily want to jump into the crazy which is our lives." She stands suddenly.

I quickly follow her, holding her by her shoulders before she can run away again. "Stop. Breathe for me. And don't tell me what I will or won't do." She's right, I don't know everything, but I do know I was a mess without her. "I'm here now. Let's get through today, and then we'll talk."

Grabbing her hand, I walk into the food area.

"What are you doing?" she asks.

"Grabbing some drinks and snacks for everyone. What do your cousins like?"

"You don't have to. It's fine. Everything is expensive in here," she whispers to me.

"It's good. I've got it. Grab some things. You don't know how long everyone is going to be sitting there."

We each load up our arms and hands with drinks and packaged snacks and place them at the cashier's stand. Her eyes widen when the cashier informs us of the total. I hand her my card and ask for everything to be bagged.

"Thank you," she tells me as we walk back to the waiting room.

"You're welcome." Little does she know I have a story of my own to tell.

CHAPTER TWENTY-ONE

TOO MUCH

Toni

LOLA IS LYING down on the small couch, her legs over the armrest with her feet on the next chair, Javie hasn't moved from the corner he was at earlier, and Alex is pacing. We place the bags on the small table by Lola's head.

"Alex, Javie," I call them over. "Garrett, these are my cousins, Alex and Javie." I point them each out.

Garrett extends his hand, shaking with both of them.

"*Estás seguro quieres el guero aquí?*" (Are you sure you want the white boy here?) Alex asks me. He's not really worried about etiquette, talking in Spanish in front of someone who doesn't and them knowing that's the reason he's doing it.

"*Claro que sí.*" (Of course.) I answer, knowing it's the truth. I do want him here. I just don't know if he'll want to stay when he hears the crazy that is my family.

"I'm relieved to know you want me here," Garrett chimes in.

"*Hablas Español?*" (You speak Spanish?) Alex asks him.

"*Si. Aprendí hace muchos años.*" (Yes. I learned many years ago) Garrett comes back with a decent accent.

"Wow. I didn't know," Lola chimes in.

"I guess speaking about the white boy in Spanish won't do us any good." Alex smirks at me.

"How did you learn Spanish?" I ask just as the door opens. I turn around, and the doctor from earlier comes through.

"How is she?" Javie is the first one to speak.

"Still the same. She has not woken up. But we did confirm that it was a stroke," she answers Javie then continues. "We have her in the ICU for constant monitoring. Right now, it's just waiting. We won't know the extent of it until she wakes."

"What now?" I ask, confused.

"We are still trying to wake her. Right now, that is all I have," she answers quickly.

I know it's serious by the clipped answer.

"A nurse will be out in a moment to give you her room number. Only two in the room at a time."

"Yes, ma'am," Alex answers.

The weight of knowing how serious the situation is feels daunting. I sit down, unsure my legs will hold me up. Garrett comes quickly to my side, holding me. I am numb with fear. What will happen to us? Who will care for her if she is able to come home? What if she doesn't make it? Will our asshole parents get the house? Where will Alex and Javie live? That house is our center. It's not much, but it has kept us together.

THE NURSE CAME and went with information on her room number. Javie is the first one to go in, and he insists he needs time alone with her. He is the sensitive one of the brothers. I don't think Alex feels he can be vulnerable with the responsibility of caring for me and Javie.

When Javie comes out, Alex and I go in. She is pale with so many machines beeping and running around her. The room is tiny with just one chair. I sit, holding her cold hand, praying silently. Alex is on her other side, standing and watching us, his cool exterior never broken. He has helped Guela carry the world on her shoulders, never asking for anything in return.

"I'M HUNGRY," I whine while looking through the pantry. There is nothing for me to eat because I'm not allowed to use the stove yet.

Javie is setting his things at the table to start his homework. This is the usual afterschool activity. The three of us home alone until Guela gets home from work. Alex in charge.

"Grilled cheese?" he asks me.

"Please," I answer, grateful for a snack. Our fridge was not always stocked with the usual packaged snacks, but Alex would always figure out something for us to eat. I watch him take out the bread, butter and cheese to begin.

I sit at the table, coloring and waiting for my sandwich to be done.

"Extra cheesy just for you." Alex places a plate in front of me.

THOSE ARE the things I remember fondly—my life at Guela's with my cousins who are more like my brothers. The four of us are a family. Somehow, our parents learned nothing from the wonderful mom they had. They took her for granted, and now the only mother figure we know is lying here helpless. I'm terrified of what comes next. My mind can't even fathom...

"What are you thinking?" Alex's voice breaks through my silent pleas to God.

"I...I don't know. My mind is everywhere and nowhere at the same time."

"And Garrett?" he continues.

"What about him?"

"You going to let him in? Honestly and all?" he pushes me.

"I want to." I squeeze Guela's hand, hoping she feels me here. "He knows more than I ever considered telling him, and he's still here. The most I can say is I'm going to try."

"And you never mentioned that spunky friend of yours." His smirk is contagious, and a small smile emerges through my pain.

"Yes, that she is. I became friends with her because she refused to be ignored. She knows pretty much everything, and she keeps insisting we are the best of friends. Since she won't let me go my own way, I'll keep her friendship."

"Come on. We can't do anything for her right now. Let's get some food and sleep and be back in the morning."

I drop my forehead to the bed, close to her hand that I'm still clutching. I can't think of leaving her here by herself. What if she wakes up confused and needs us?

"I'll stay here with her. Go on. I'll be fine."

"No you won't. I'm going to feed you, and you are going to get some sleep. We can get back as early as you want. You are not staying here in that measly little chair."

"What if she needs me?" I plead with him to leave me here.

The door opens, and a nurse walks in.

"Good evening. I'm here to remind you that visiting hours are over." She smiles apologetically.

"Thank you. We were just getting ready to leave," Alex answers for us. He looks to me.

I kiss her hand.

"I love you. I'll see you in the morning," I whisper in her ear.

Garrett

"I'M STARVING. Let's get something to eat," Alex declares to the room as he and Toni walk back in.

"I do need food," his brother exclaims behind me.

"Are you all hungry too?" Toni looks to Lola and me.

"Yes," Lola answers her.

"Let's head to my place. I'll place an order for some pizzas, and we can pick them up on the way there," I offer, not wanting them to worry about anything.

"No need, man. We can pick up our own food," Alex informs me.

Not wanting to insult anyone's pride, I nod.

"Darlin', did you drive?" I ask, not knowing any logistics.

"Yes."

"Can Lola go with you so I can take her truck to pick up some food? You go ahead to my place and relax." I don't want her driving alone, exhausted and emotional, even though I know she will insist she is fine. I look toward Alex. "I don't live far. Toni can send you my address if you want to head on over to be with her."

He looks over to her then back at me. "Nah. Javie and I are going to head home." Then he faces Toni. "Call us in the morning when you are ready to get back. We will meet you here."

She looks up at him and nods. I know she is doing everything she can to hold herself together. He knows this, too, because he takes a step to her, taking her into his strong arms, holding her. I want to be that for her. To be able to protect her from anything that could hurt her.

TONI AND LOLA are sprawled out on my couch. The TV is on, but the sound is so quiet I know they are seeing the screen but not truly watching anything. I have the second pizza that has entered my apartment today in my hand. I didn't want to offer them the cold one I left on the counter when Lola picked me up earlier. So much has changed in the last few hours.

I place a slice on a paper plate for each of them, grab two bottled waters, and take it to them. They thank me in unison but do not get up. I stand at the counter, taking bites, tired of sitting. As much as I want to talk to Toni, I know tonight is not the right time. After a slice, I head to my room to grab a couple of blankets for them to use.

"Here are a couple of blankets if you don't feel like moving. You are more than welcome to stay here," I extend the offer. I make it easy for her to stay so I know she is taken care of. I want to be the shoulder she leans on.

"As much as I love you, Toni, we both don't fit on this couch." Lola begins to get up.

"Y'all can take my bed, and I'll take the couch," I offer quickly so she does not leave.

"We can't kick you out of your bed," Toni quickly shoots my plan down. She sits up, looking at me. "Can I stay in there with you?"

"If you want, of course," I answer honestly.

"Go on then. Move out so I can rest." Lola pushes her teasingly with her feet.

She stands up and walks into my bedroom. I follow behind her.

"Do you need a t-shirt?" I offer, unsure if she'll go into my drawer on her own to get one like she did before.

"Please," she answers then begins taking off her jeans and shirt. I can't help but admire her body as she stands in her bra and panties in front of me. I quickly hand her the shirt, because the thoughts that fly through my mind aren't appropriate at this time.

She pulls the shirt over her head and crawls into bed, pulling the blankets up to her chin. Not wanting her to feel uncomfortable, I get into bed on top of the covers with my clothes on.

"What are you doing?" she asks.

"What do you mean?" I ask, not sure if she is upset I got in bed with her.

"Why did you get into bed with your clothes on, and why aren't you under the covers?"

"Darlin', I'm not expecting anything. I just want to know you are taken care of. If you are in my bed, I know you are as alright as can be expected."

"Then, get into bed like you would normally. I can't deal with us being weird, too."

"Are you sure?" I'm hesitant to say or do the wrong thing and have her flee again before we can work anything out.

"Yes."

I quickly strip down to my boxers and slide under the covers, making sure I give her space. As soon as I get comfortable and stop moving, I feel the mattress move as she curls herself into my side. I move my arm out, and she lays her head on my shoulder, draping her arm on my stomach. Her nearness is exciting the little man, but now is not the time for him to be awake. Her long, slow breaths let me know she is relaxed. Her long lashes brushing against my chest as she blinks lets me know she is wide awake. As tired as I am, I do not want to close my eyes. I'm savoring this for as long as I can, because I don't know how long it can or will last.

TONI

LIFE CAN CHANGE SO QUICKLY. I never in a million years thought I would be back in this bed again. He shouldn't want me here. He doesn't know who I am, what I've done. But even with all I'm keeping, he's here. He wants me in his bed. He was there to let me cry. To be scared. No questions. No inquisition. Just his protective presence.

I can't let myself get caught up in a fairy tale. I'm well aware of men's want to protect and control. That's all this is. It's in his kind nature, but he could never see me the same again. He will want out. It was so hard the first time to cut him out and avoid him. I don't want to start all over again.

"I'm sorry, I have to go," I inform him as I sit up.

"Woah." He wraps an arm around my stomach. "If you are going to bolt, I'm going to need to know the reason."

"No reason. We aren't together. Actually, we never were. I can't expect you to be there. It's okay. I was scared earlier, and I wasn't thinking." I'm rambling and trying to move out of his embrace.

"Stop!" He keeps his arm holding me while sitting up. "If you are leaving this time, I deserve a reason. Not that bullshit you just tried to give me."

"It's...it's not bullshit. It's the truth. We were never together."

"You're right. We weren't officially together, but not because I didn't want it." He lets me go as he reaches the bedside lamp.

The pain in his eyes is unmistakable.

"You know what? I can't. I can't go through that again."
He pushes himself up the bed and leans against the wall. His
gaze drops to the bed. "If you are going to go, pues vete (*just
go*). I can't stop you. You do whatever the hell you please,
anyway. I was just the pendejo (*idiot*) who was just along for
your quick ride."

*What the fuck? He's going to blame this shit on me. He's the
fucking guy. Guys are the ones who need a fucking wake-up call.*

"Fine. I'm out!" I yell at him, angry he thinks he can turn
this around on me. I stand, picking up my things. I open his
bedroom door to find Lola blocking my way.

"We're out." I motion for Lola to move.

"No, you're not." She doesn't budge, her arms crossed in
front of her with the most serious face I have ever seen
on her.

"Yes, I am," I insist.

She just shakes her head at me, cocking an eyebrow to
challenge her.

"How shitty did you feel without him?" she asks me.
When I refuse to answer, she continues, "Have you even
admitted you lied about dating someone else?"

"I didn't lie! He just assumed because he saw Alex." I try
and defend my actions even though I KNOW I'm in the
wrong.

"But you could have corrected him." She is like stone
except for her mouth moving. "Now, I am going to leave. And
I'm taking your keys too. Call me when I need to bring them
back to you. You are staying here and hashing things out."
She hugs me, pushes me back a couple of steps, and grabs the
door handle, closing it behind her.

I stand with my back to the bed, staring at the closed
door. He has heard the beginning, but there is so much.

"Why did you let me believe you were dating your
cousin?" his voice breaks the silence.

When he says it like that, it sounds absurd. I can't stop a small laugh that escapes. I turn around, leaning against the door. The space between us is necessary to keep me thinking straight. It is too easy to get lost in the feel of his arms.

"That wasn't my plan, really. It just happened that way. But if I'm being honest, Alex had thought of it."

"Why?" he asks, his eyes penetrating me, wanting answers.

I take a deep breath, building the courage to have a conversation I never expected to have. "I'm not the typical college girl. I don't hang at frats, and clubs, and bars, making friends. Well, that was until this year because Alex made me."

"I'm still not following." There's a slight annoyance in his voice.

"I'm poor. No one leaves the hood. They try and try, but it always pulls you back. I got a full ride, so Alex insists it's my way to escape. But I need money to live on, and that's where the waitressing comes in. It's easy money, and I don't have to work all year long. If I budget, I can take a couple months a semester off so that I can concentrate on school."

"Okay...."

"I don't want people knowing what I do. I don't want judgment or pity. I'm doing what I need to get by. Girls are catty bitches. I don't want fuckin' rumors to start because of where I work. I can hear it already—from waitress to stripper. Not that there's anything wrong with it, but I just don't need that shit in my life."

"I can get that. But we were together, whether you want to admit it or not. We weren't seeing anyone else. True or false?"

"True."

"Then why break it?"

"Because my mom is a worthless human. I was done working for the year. I was able to save for the entire year. I didn't think I was going to have to work again. But then my mom came around and ruined everything. She borrowed money from my grandmother. I needed to cover for her. Alex and Javie are strapped right now. They couldn't cover. They just covered for their worthless dad over the summer. So I had to go back to work. I couldn't date you and work at the club. I didn't want to tell you where I worked. I couldn't lie. That wouldn't have been fair to you."

"No, what's not fair is not giving me the choice."

"But that's not it. I've done other things. Things you don't want to be a part of. I can't stand judgment. And I especially don't want it from you."

"Tell me."

"No!"

"Yes."

He stares at me, waiting for me to blurt all my truths out. This is what it's going to take for him to let me walk away.

"I slept with men for money!" I yell out, hoping he kicks me out and I can go back to my life before him—the life I knew how to handle. I stare at him defiantly.

He's quiet for several long seconds before he informs me, "I assumed that already. And I'm still here."

His assuming lights a fire of anger in me. "What do you mean you assumed?" He thinks I'm a whore? I don't wait for an answer. I turn around, ready to walk home.

I hear him behind me, and as I am about to open the door, he is shutting it on me. I turn around to face him. He places his hands on the door on either side of my head, caging me in.

"I assumed because of what Kevin told me...or didn't tell me. He was insistent I should dump you, but I couldn't. You intrigue me. You don't fall over yourself for me. You call me on my bullshit. You are real." He places a small kiss on my nose. "Now, don't get me wrong and think it didn't bother me.

It did. It took me some time to think about it and come to terms with it."

He places a gentle kiss on my right cheek. "We all have pasts. I can't judge yours and think mine is squeaky clean. Our pasts are just that: pasts." He comes in close, our noses brushing against each other. "We haven't done the same things, but I can't claim I'm a wholesome virgin. And neither can you." He brushes his lips past mine quickly. "I just need to know if that part is over."

With his last statement, he pulls back to look me in the eyes.

How is it he can make me lose all the smarts I thought I had built with guys? No one has ever been able to make me feel weak, and that is exactly what he does. He makes me want him around.

"That part is over. I haven't since…never mind. Just know I haven't since we have been together," I admit to him.

As soon as the words are out, his lips are on mine, desperate. I welcome the feeling, wanting to get lost in him, but I'm terrified at the same time. As his arms encircle my body, bringing me closer, all I can think of is him. He pulls back, placing his forehead on mine as he takes a deep breath, slowing us down.

Wanting to feel every part of him, I bring my hands up to his bare stomach and let them softly and slowly slide up his abs and chest, savoring the ridges of his muscular, lean build. My hands come to rest on his shoulders, not knowing where to go from here. My big secrets are out, but there is still so much more. I still fear trusting him because he is a male. Rather than get lost in my thoughts, I pull him into me again, wanting to feel him instead.

His hands cup my ass as he lifts me to him. My legs wrap around his waist, and my lips find his. A desperate need fills every part of me. He gently places me down on the bed and crawls on top of me, his weight on his forearms.

"Are you sure?"

My hands are tracing the muscles on his shoulders. "Yes."

His lips meet my neck as his hand slides up my waist to my breast, squeezing softly then tracing my nipple with his fingers. His kisses are soft and slow as he makes his way from my neck to my lips. His hand slips down my stomach to my upper thigh, dancing close to my center but not giving me satisfaction. I can feel him harden, his wanting as desperate as mine.

I place my hands on his cheeks to bring his mouth to mine in a fevered kiss. He follows my lead, but his caresses stay slow and controlled.

"I need you. Now." I'm panting, feeling out of control.

"I've got you, darlin'." His hand comes to my center over my panties as he cups with pressure.

"Now," I persist.

He hooks his finger in the side of my panties and begins to slide them down. I reach down, pushing down his boxers, needing to feel him inside me. He gets up, pulling mine all the way off and finishes undressing himself before pulling a condom out of his nightstand.

I sit up, grabbing it from his hands, opening it and sliding it on for him. I lie back down, legs open, unashamed of my desperation, waiting for him.

He bends over and begins a trail of kisses beginning at my knee, up my thigh. He teases so closely with his breath then continues up my stomach, stopping at my right breast. He kisses and teases it as I'm writhing under him, lifting my pelvis, trying to feel any part of him. He presses himself in my center, my body grinding to his, wanting a release. He pushes himself in slow and controlled until he is in fully. He holds himself there, kissing my neck and bringing his lips to mine.

Staring at the ceiling as my breath is returning to normal after the best orgasm I've had, I begin to wonder again if this is something that can happen. Can I trust a relationship?

"Tell me what you're thinking," he asks as if he knows thoughts are swirling.

I consider how to answer. "My life has been fucked up. I'm telling you, we are a hot mess struggling to survive. And I don't know how to trust you. Not because of anything you have done, but watching relationships around me, I know they all fall apart, and the only person you can trust is yourself. I don't want to be the helpless girl who crumbles when a man leaves her." I close my eyes, unable to look at him with this admission.

"Darlin', my intention will never be to hurt you or leave you. You crushed me when you walked away. But that won't stop me from trying with you again." His hand cups my cheek, bringing my gaze to his. "Why do you not know how to trust me?"

I take a deep breath. If I want him, I have to lay it all on the table. He has to know and make the choice, like he said before.

"My grandmother raised me. My mom dropped me on her doorstep when she felt I was the reason men didn't stick around. She's a money-grubbing loser, but I saw her believe all the men she dated. She would lose herself in them, believing whatever lies they told her to get into her pants, have fun, then dump her. She was crushed every time. And it's not only her. Every single girl I know has had some guy jerk her around all while looking for his next. I won't be them. I will take care of me. I don't want to be let down. Not when I know better."

"I can't tell you any of that is wrong. You lived it. But it doesn't always have to be that. My parents are still married after 27 years. I'm sure it wasn't always easy, but they committed to each other and take turns carrying each other." He places a kiss on my forehead. "I want you. Even after all you've told me. I don't know if you are telling me in the hopes that I will walk away, test me, or are really just being honest, but you are not scaring me off that easy."

"Are you sure?" I ask, nervous about going forward.

"Yes." He brushes stray hairs from my face behind me ear. "And I guess since you have been honest, I should be too."

Here it comes. A lie to ruin everything.

"I'm not just some other guy. Like I said before, I'm relieved you are making me work for your affection and trust. You don't fall over yourself to be with me. You aren't chasing and making it easy, hoping to bag me."

I can't help the giggle that escapes. "You are a good-looking dude, but there are others too. Why would girls fall over themselves for you?" I inform him, trying to keep it real. No need for him to get too full of himself.

"Because they want my last name," he states matter of factly.

"They want to marry you?" I ask, still confused what the big deal is.

"Yes. Because of who I am."

He's still being cryptic, and I'm not following. "You are going to have to give me more, because I'm just not following you."

"I'm Garrett Anders." He pauses, watching me. "Anders Beef. My family owns the largest beef cattle distributor in Texas."

"Huh?" I say, confused with his statement. "You mean..." I don't know how to ask or say he's rich without sounding like an idiot.

"Yes. My family is wealthy. Most girls want me because they hope to be the next housewife. I want a partner, not some leech."

"Oh..." Now I'm nervous because I just admitted I have nothing. Less than nothing. He should be with someone worthy of all he has. The haze that has crept into my brain with his admission has me moving slowly. I sit up, needing to gather my things and leave him to his...

"What are you doing?" He pulls me back down and places his body on mine.

"I was gonna leave. I'm sure there is someone way more suitable for you than me. I just admitted to you I'm a peasant. I don't fit in your world."

"You, my dear, fit perfectly." He pauses, taking a deep breath. "Do you like me?" His voice is unsteady.

"Yes, I like you," I answer quickly.

"Do you care for me?" he continues.

"Of course."

"Then, you aren't leaving my life. Even the royals get to choose who they marry now." He winks before bringing his lips to mine again.

"We should get some sleep. You will want to head to the hospital early." He rolls away from me but extends his arm, letting me snuggle into his side.

Can this really be it?

CHAPTER TWENTY-TWO

PART OF CRAZY

Garrett

WAKING up with her snuggled into me is a glorious feeling. We are both holding back so much. Since she mentioned her mom and uncle briefly last night, I've been wondering where they have been. Neither of them were at the hospital yesterday.

It's seven a.m., and I know she will want to get to the hospital soon.

"It's seven, darlin'." I kiss the top of her head.

She stirs a moment before panicking.

"I've got to get to the hospital." She sits up quickly.

"Take a shower, and I will text Lola for your keys."

She jumps out of bed and heads into my bathroom.

. . .

BACK AT THE HOSPITAL, her grandmother's condition has not changed. She has not woken up, and they are fearing she may not. Her oxygen levels were too low, not breathing normally, so she was placed on a ventilator.

"You aren't going to mess with Toni's head, are you?" Alex questions me while we are in the waiting room while Javie and Toni are in the room with her.

"That wasn't my plan." Annoyance quickly rises since it was his idea to let me believe the lie. I don't want to offer any more information than needed.

"Are you sure you want to be a part of this shit? Because if you're not sure, you may need to step," he continues.

"Look, I don't know if this is big-brother talk or what, but when we figure out exactly what we are, she can let you know." I don't want to get on his bad side, but I'm still figuring out exactly where I stand.

"Look...it's not only that. She has been handed a shit hand. We all have. But she has the ability to leave it behind. I don't want some guy crashing everything she has worked so hard for. I haven't been pushing her to a better life for her to come back to the hood broken."

He's looking out for her and cares about what happens to her. "Yes. I care. Much more than I care to admit...especially since I still feel like I'm standing on shaky ground."

"Fair enough." He nods, satisfied.

The waiting room door opens, and an older woman with a face full of makeup, jeans, a low-cut shirt, and heels walks in. "What the hell, Alex? Why didn't anyone tell me what happened?"

"What would you have done, Maria? Called 911? Ride in the ambulance? Oh yes, that's what you would have done if there was a cute EMT." He stands from his chair defiantly.

"You're an asshole."

"How did you even know where we were?" His body tenses.

"I went by and no one was home, so I texted Javie. I figured neither you nor Toni would answer me. At least your brother has manners." She takes a dig at Alex.

By this exchange, I'm guessing this is Toni's mom. The door opens again and in she walks.

She spots her mom right away, and I notice as she mouths the word 'shit.'

Maria turns away from Alex and begins again. "Don't you think you should have told me my mother is in the hospital?"

"Not really." Toni's stance now matches Alex's. He comes to stand by her.

"Don't you get all high and mighty with me. You are no better than me just because you attend your fancy college. What room is she in?" Maria directs at Toni.

"Why should we tell you? What are you going to do? Help pay the bills. No. You are of no use here. Just go home. Guela can't give you anything. I know the only reason you are here is for another handout. That is the only reason you ever come around." The harsh staredown she is giving her mom would make a giant quiver.

"You realize I can just ask the nurse's station," her mom quips back.

"Then do that. Go work the problem out yourself, because we both know you are too lazy to do shit. Once you find out Guela is unresponsive right now and can't give you anything, you will leave and not come back." Toni looks like she wants to take a swing at her mom. "And don't think you can go pawn anything at Guela's house either. You have already sold anything worth any value of hers. Everything else is Alex's."

"Really, that's what you think I would do?" Her mom seems truly offended.

"No, Maria, we KNOW that's what you would do because you've done it before." Alex decides to jump in the conversation. "Don't go into the house. That shit is mine, and you will have me to deal with. I won't hesitate to turn your worthless ass in."

Their stances, ready to fight, begin to worry me, so I begin to make my way closer to Toni. I'm sure she can handle herself, as she has done so all her life, but now that I'm here, I want to do that for her.

"You two think you are so entitled, but she is my mom. Your dad and I will get the house. You can then move all your shit out."

"Like hell he will!" Toni blurts out as I watch her mom's hand come up to slap her. I catch it and hold her in place.

"Enough!" I grind out, not happy to get in the middle, worried I've overstepped.

"And you are?" Maria turns her attention to me.

I raise a brow in question at Toni for an answer.

"He's my boyfriend," she states flatly. Whether it's because she didn't want to share that information with her mom or she's that unenthused about me, it hits me in the gut. I let her wrist go.

"Well, well, and here I thought you would never settle down since you 'learned'"—she air quotes with her fingers—"from my mistakes."

"Don't talk about things you don't understand. Go see Guela if you can manage finding her or go home." She tries to get her mom to leave again.

She huffs as she turns around to walk back out the door she came through.

Unsettled with the situation, where I stand, and how she'll react, I stand frozen. She turns to face me as Alex walks out the door behind her mom.

"Thank you. It wouldn't be the first time she has slapped

me and probably won't be the last." She takes the step into me, her arms tucked between us and her cheek flush on my chest. I bring my arms around her, holding her tight, not wanting to let her go.

"Anytime. But I can promise you one thing, darlin', if I'm with you, no one is placing their hands on you." That I can guarantee.

I can hear her breaths as she calms the adrenaline flowing through her. After a few quiet moments, she asks, "Are you sure you want to be a part of this crazy? It's this bad all the time."

"I want to take you away from crazy. There is no reason why you should have to go through that."

"I can't ask that of you."

"You aren't asking; I'm telling you that's what I want to do if you'll let me." I kiss the top of her head, wishing she would let me protect her.

She pulls back, looking up at me. "I...I don't...don't know how to do this. I've never been here before. I've never trusted anyone to see this part of my life."

"There's nothing to do except let me be with you. Don't push me away. Don't shut me out. Can you do that?" The need to tell her how far I've fallen for her is sitting on my lips.

She nods. "I'll try."

"Darlin', I've fallen hard. You have my heart. Don't go crushin' it again." This is as close as I can come to telling her I love her. She may frighten with too much too soon.

She slides her hands up from my chest to rest on my shoulders, tip-toeing at the same time. I meet her halfway as our lips come together.

TONI

. . .

THIS KISS IS unlike any we've shared before. All our previous kisses have been solely physical. I never thought of them as a way of showing affection. Right now, in this moment, it's gentle and filled with hope for more. I may have his heart, but he has mine in return. As much as I am dreading the potential of mine being broken, I actually want to fall.

Trusting people other than my grandmother and cousins is something I have never done. My friends only know what I want them to know, never revealing too much so no one can have the upper hand on me. This is going to be difficult, but it may be nice not having to censor my life. Life can be exhausting, trying to remember which mask is needed. Hood life and never showing weakness, college life and trying to appear just like the others, or club life to make men spend more money are all facades I have had in place to crawl my way out of the place I call home.

Alex walks back in, announcing, "Your mom left as predicted." He plops himself in the closet chair next to us.

"Figures." I pull away slightly from Garrett, unsure how to be me with him.

"Have y'all figured your shit out yet?" He smirks in my direction, knowing how hard this is for me.

"Trying to." My eyes roll in exaggeration at him poking fun at us while squeezing Garrett to show I'm in this with him.

"Let the record show, I told her to tell you a LOOONG" —he drags the word out—"time ago. She was the one who was insistent you shouldn't know our crazy family shit."

"Oh my gawd. You were the one who gave me the idea to let him think I was dating someone else!" I exclaim dramatically. No need in getting us in our first fight five minutes after we get together.

I feel Garrett's chest vibrate with a soft chuckle as he

kisses my head again. "At least we're here now." He lets me go to sit in the chair across from Alex.

"How'd you learn Spanish, gringo?" Alex asks him. I'm actually curious about this myself.

"Most of our ranch hands speak Spanish, so I had to learn if I was going to work alongside them," he answers casually. I sit next to him, wondering how much of his life he'll share with Alex.

"Ranch hands?" Alex asks, raising his brows in confusion.

"Our family beef cattle company. We employ men to work on our ranch."

"Wow! Okay." I don't think Alex is following what this means. "If you have guys working for you, why do you need to work?"

"We always want to make sure we are raising the best cattle. Our name and reputation are in every one we sell—sell for slaughter. It's where your steaks and burgers come from." Garrett noticed Alex's confusion.

"Wait. You raise cattle to sell for slaughter?" His eyes widen.

"Don't tell me I've offended you too? Vegetarian?" Garrett jokes.

Alex laughs it off. "Nah, man. I just never think where my food comes from."

"Most people don't."

"The doctor wants to see us." Javie barges through the door. Alex and I stand immediately. "She will meet us in Guela's room."

As much as I didn't want him around before, all I can think is I don't want to hear whatever she is going to say alone. I turn back to Garrett and extend my hand to him.

He grabs it instantly, and I give him a small tug to follow me. He walks alongside me, holding my hand.

"I'm so sorry to have this conversation with you," the

doctor begins, and I know the news she will be sharing with us won't be good. "Your grandmother is not waking up, and the last EEG we did isn't looking good. Her brain activity has been slowing."

My legs feel as if they are about to give out. I can't process what she is saying. She will be fine. She HAS to be fine. His chest presses into my back as his arms come around my waist, holding me. How he knows I need this support I don't know, but I can't express enough gratitude that he caught me and didn't let me fall.

Words suddenly became foreign to me as the 'what-ifs' swirl around my mind. Processing a question to ask is too difficult. The boys always wait for me to take the lead on important or professional matters.

"What exactly does that mean?" Alex inquires, noticing my struggle.

"We will give it a couple more days to see if she improves. Does your grandmother have a health directive?" When no one answers her, she continues, "Do you know what her wishes are about staying on life support?"

"No. She has never mentioned it. Should we know?" Alex asks.

"Yes, but many family members are tasked with making the decision if the patient's wishes are unknown."

More information is shared and questions are asked, all while my brain cannot seem to follow. As soon as the doctor walks out, Javie falls to his knees by her bed, clutching the blankets, and I make my way to her side, crawling in her bed carefully. Closing my eyes, I just want to stay and protect her, give her any strength I can.

Garrett

· · ·

Toni is crushed with this news. Feeling like an intruder in such an intimate family moment, I debate walking out to give them their privacy, but I want to make sure she is okay. I move to the side of the bed Toni shares with her grandmother, ensuring she knows I am there. I am beginning to understand their family dynamics. Each of them has played a vital role in what she believes to be a dysfunctional family.

Alex stands at the foot of the bed, his features unchanged, watching Javie and Toni falling apart. He is the man in this family, protecting everyone he loves. It's his approval and trust I need to gain. A newfound respect begins for him having to take charge in the most difficult situations—a responsibility he has probably had since he was a child.

He pats Javie on the shoulder, and an unspoken communication takes place as I watch Javie stand up, composing himself. They watch Toni until she feels their stares. She slowly stands, leaning slightly into me. The three of them share a few looks before Alex nods his head once. Without even speaking, they have come to some decision.

Alex is the first to turn around, walking to the door. Toni grabs my hand, pulling me with her.

"I want to go to my guela's house tonight," Toni says as we walk down the many corridors of the hospital.

"Okay. Can I take you or are you going with your cousins?" As selfish as it sounds, I don't want to leave her since I just got her back.

"Will you go with me?" The quiver in her voice filled with uncertainty is new. She has always been so self-assured and decisive. I'm navigating new territory.

"Of course," I say, squeezing the hand she is clutching to remind her I am here—for all of it.

. . .

THIS SIDE of town should not be new to me as I drive past it each time I head to the ranch. I just never ventured off the freeway around here for any reason. Small, old houses that line the streets, small local businesses with burglar bars, and bus stops with many people waiting are eye opening. When you grow up with a certain amount of means, you never know the other side. I'm a visitor here, learning how polar opposite her and I have been raised. More so than I could have realized. Does it change the way I feel? Absolutely not. It's just a reality I have to be cognizant of.

I park on the street in front of a tiny but well-kept home. A clean yard and pretty plants decorating the front is the first impression of the pride her grandmother takes in her home.

"This is where I grew up." Toni is looking down at her hands. "There is still time for you to escape—if you want."

"Why would I need to escape?" I grab her chin softly, pulling her face up to look at me. "I'm here, Toni. I wanted to be here before, but you were scared. But I'll keep proving to you I'm here to stay."

A tear slides down her cheek. "I just...I'm scared. I'm losing my grandmother and what if...what if you decide this is too much bullshit? I think I'll break."

I open my door, walking around to her side. I open her door and help her down. I wrap her in my arms. "All I can do is continue showing you I'm here. Build your trust. Especially since you have never trusted anyone."

She takes a big breath, blowing it out slowly, then pulls away, looking up at me, and nods with a small smile. She motions with her head to follow her into the house.

A small living room is on the other side of the front door. Alex is sitting on a chair, his head laying back, eyes closed. Toni sits on the couch, curling into a corner, so I sit with her. Javie comes out of the kitchen, holding a coffee cup.

"I made coffee," he announces to the room. He sits on the chair opposite Alex. "What's our plan?"

Toni sits up from her curled position. "We can't lose the house. If my mom and your dad get the house, you know they will sell it and blow through the money in record time and come back with their hands out."

"Toni, I hate to do this to you, but you are the one with the connections now. You know regular people who know about shit like this. Can you find out what our options are?"

Knowing I'm the new one here, I take the chance and offer, "I'll call our lawyer and find out what options you have."

"You can't..." Toni begins as Alex says, "Thanks, man."

"We can't ask him to do that," Toni directs to Alex.

"He didn't ask, I offered," I remind her. "Besides, I have resources. I should use them."

"But we can't pay," she counters.

"I didn't ask you to. It's fine." I kiss her nose. "Now that is settled."

"How long are we keeping her on life support?" Javie says so quietly I barely hear him.

"You know we can't afford to keep her on too long. I don't even know what type of bills we are going to get for this so far," Alex states very matter of factly. I wonder when he gets his chance to break down.

"I know."

"We follow doctor's orders. She said they are waiting a couple of days, so we will too."

"Where is your dad?" Toni asks, changing the subject.

"Don't know. He has been gone a little over a week. Probably shacked up with whatever dumbass is buying his alcohol."

CHAPTER TWENTY-THREE

A NEW LIFE

Toni

THE NEXT COUPLE of days go by in a blur. Hospital visits and classes fill my days. I always have Lola or Garrett by my side. They are what I never knew I needed. They anticipate not only my needs but my cousins' as well, bringing snacks, meals, drinks, or an unexpected laugh when things are feeling too heavy.

The day comes when we have to make the decision, so we are all at my guela's house. As hard as it is, we know tomorrow our lives will forever be changed. We are worried about how we will manage paying for a funeral. We know it can't be anything fancy—what she deserves for saving us—but we want it to be nice. Alex felt weird going through the things in her bedroom to locate any information on the house or maybe even a small insurance policy, so he volun-told me.

Knowing I can't do it on my own, I ask Lola to help.

Another female in her room seems better than a male. We walk in, and her scent crashes into me. No one has been in her room since that day. Her bed is still unmade. I crawl in, wishing to surround myself in her. Lola sits next to me, rubbing my leg.

"I'm so sorry, friend." Tears fill her eyes. She didn't know my grandmother, but her pain is coming from caring for me.

I don't have a response. What do you say to that? People can be sorry all they want, but it doesn't change what is happening.

"Do you want me to start?" she hesitantly asks.

"Please." I was strong when I agreed, but I felt myself crumble as soon as I walked in.

"Where do I start?"

"Her closet, I guess. She has boxes in there, but I don't know what they have in them."

I close my eyes, letting my mind travel back to each happy memory I had in this house. This is my only safe place. Looking back, I remember not wanting to stay here, wanting the love my mom was supposed to give me, wanting desperately to stay with her and for her to put me first. As time went on, I didn't want to go with my mom. Even as a child, I knew I wasn't her priority.

The only sound in the room is Lola rummaging through my grandmother's things.

"Darlin', we are getting hungry. I'm going to pick up some food. Suggestions?" He only pokes his head in the door.

I sit up. "Whatever the boys want."

"They said for you to choose." He raises a brow for me to answer.

"I'm sure there are some great tacos on this side of town. Am I right?" Lola looks at me.

"Yes. Have Alex call in to Norteno," I tell Garrett.

Lola claps her hands in excitement. I've never seen a girl

get so excited for tacos before Lola. "Tell Alex I need a couple of asada tacos with avocado, please."

"And you?" he asks me.

"Get me the same thing."

I fall back into the bed, unsure if I will be able to leave, and listen to Lola still rifling through things.

"Look what I found!" Lola exclaims a few minutes later.

I sit up at her declaration, watching her get up from the floor, a floral box in hand. She places the box on the bed in front of me. It is filled with different items: a spiral with notes, memories, and lists in her writing fill the pages; a few bank statements which seem unnecessary since there is no money; pictures; a small jewelry box; and a manila envelope.

I open the manila envelope, sliding the contents on the bed. There are envelopes with each of our names, including my mom and uncle, and a notarized letter stating her wishes for the house. She has left the house to the three of us. A notebook page folded in half is also included.

Unfolding it, I see her handwriting. I fold it again, placing everything back, closing the box, and taking it to the living room.

Garrett is walking in with Javie, bags in hand.

"I think Lola found what we need."

"What?" Alex says behind me from the kitchen.

"I think all we need is in this box," I answer him.

"You know what's in there?" he presses.

"Not everything. I want to open it with y'all."

Javie comes close to me, lifting the box out of my hands and taking the lid off to view the scattered items.

"Let's eat first," Alex says. He may be procrastinating reading the documents because he knows it will be all too real when we finally see those things.

Lola is already in the kitchen, helping set everything out. She is placing plates for each of us, along with glasses and soda, on the table. I watch Alex sit first, his shoulders slumping. Each of us takes a chair as Lola is opening the foil-wrapped tacos and calling out what belongs to whom. It's silent around the table except the sound of chewing.

"Holy moly, that jalapeno is hot!" Lola exclaims, breaking the silence. Everyone looks up from their plates at her as she fans her mouth and gulps water.

A round of laughter fills the air. The two new people I have brought into our lives have brought light to our usual jaded lives.

"Try milk. It will work better." Alex gets up from his seat, pouring her a small glass.

She takes it from him, chugging it down before tossing the offending food on a napkin.

"I'm just dragging this out," Alex says, grabbing the box from the counter and placing it on the table. He lifts the lid, and I grab the manila envelope.

"We each have a letter in here from her, but this note isn't addressed to anyone." I pull that one out first.

"Read it," Javie says.

"Do y'all want some privacy?" Garrett asks as I unfold the letter.

"Nah. Stay here," Alex answers, sitting down again.

To Alejandro, Javier, and Antonia,

I loved having you in my life. I hope I did a better job the second time around. I'm sorry I couldn't give you more, but I did the best I could. I hope I made up for you not having your parents in your life. You will not need to worry when I die. The house belongs to you. Even though you weren't always good, you have made me proud. You didn't have to take care of me, but you did. Thank you. When I pass, go to Garcia's Mortuary. I made plans there.

All of my love,

Guela

THE LETTER IS WRITTEN in Spanish, but I read it in English for everyone.

"Here is a notarized letter stating her wishes for the house to go to us." I pull out the sheet I had seen earlier and hand it to Alex and Javie so they can read it.

"She planned this." Alex sounds surprised.

"I'm sure she knew she wouldn't live forever, so this was her way of continuing to take care of y'all," Lola speaks softly.

I hand each of them their letters and place my mom's and uncle's in the middle of the table.

"This is it," Javie whispers. I don't know if he meant for us to hear or was speaking to himself, but I had the same thought.

Nothing will ever be the same. Guela was our magnet, always bringing us together. I wonder, with her gone, if I will still have my cousins. Especially since Alex has been working so hard to keep me away. The letter she meant for me is clutched in my hands, a deep curiosity about what it says, but knowing when I do, it will be the end. Garrett's arm comes around my back and pulls me close.

I glance up, checking on my cousins, to find Lola hugging Javie from behind. Her head is laying at the top of his back as her arms are wrapped around his broad back. She's tiny compared to him. His head is down, face tucked carefully in his crossed arms on the table. Alex is stone-faced, as usual, staring at nothing. I've always wondered what goes through his mind.

Garrett

.   .   .

Toni is sleeping peacefully in my bed after the emotional rollercoaster she has been riding. I knew she needed to sleep, but she wanted to continue doing things. I coaxed her into taking a Tylenol PM so she could rest. All the worry lines between her brows she has been wearing for the past week have softened.

I step outside so that I do not disturb her while I call my mom. It rings several times before I hear her, "Hello, son."

"Hi, Mom. Hope I didn't disturb you."

"Of course not. I'm just sitting here, reading. Why do I get the pleasure of speaking to you?"

"Remember the girl I told you about the last time I was home? We got back together."

"I'm happy for you...but I'm confused why you're telling me. You don't normally share these things with me."

"Because she's the one. And I need help."

"You did not get that poor girl pregnant, did you?"

A laugh erupts that I can't control. After drowning in Toni's sadness, it feels good, even if it means my mom thinks I am in the wrong.

"Would you stop laughing and explain?" My mom now sounds exasperated.

"Sorry. I just can't believe that would be your first thought of me."

I proceed to tell my mom everything about her, even where she works, her family, and her grandmother. My mom listens intently and asks questions. I know her heart is breaking just like mine did when I found out everything she was hiding from me and the reason.

"So, they found a notarized letter from her grandmother, leaving them the house. I just don't know if that's enough for them to keep it from their parents."

"I'm not sure about that, Son, but I will call the lawyer in the morning."

"Thank you. Also, you are going to see a large charge for food on my card. I'm going to hire someone to cater after the funeral."

"I would expect nothing less. Have you thought about the floral spray?"

"The what?" What is she talking about?

"Never mind. Text me her grandmother's favorite flowers or colors. I'll handle that. Send me all the information. Your dad and I will be there."

"You don't have to. I don't think I want to introduce you to Toni on such a sad day."

"It's the sad days when people need community the most. We will be there, whether you choose to introduce us or not. Love you, Son. Don't forget the favorite flowers or colors." She hangs up, knowing I would try and argue with her some more.

My whole life, I never considered how easy my life had been. I never had to wonder if my parents would be there for me. It was a given they would be there to handle everything, cheer me on, support me, and guide me. I never considered others didn't have what I had.

WE ARRIVE at the funeral home early so that Alex, Javie, and Toni can have time alone before others show up. I sit on the bench behind them, Toni in between her cousins. As difficult as the days leading up to this were, this is going to be so much more emotional. This will be their goodbye. Toni is at the casket after Alex and Javie each take a turn. I can tell she is crying, her body betraying how quiet and strong she wants to appear. Alex turns around, looking at me and giving me a nod to go to her. I listen and bring her back to sit.

· · ·

Sitting in her grandmother's backyard, watching the people come and go, some talking to the kids, others talking to their parents. I wish Toni's mom would say something nice to her sometime during the day, but I haven't seen them speak at all. My mom had found a company to not only cater but to also supply tents, tables, and chairs so they could host at the house.

Looking around, I don't see Toni in the backyard, so I make my way inside to find her. As I walk through the living room, I see her hugging my mom. Toni's head is laying on my mom's shoulder, and her arms are wrapped around my mom's waist. An intimate hug you share with someone you trust. Watching them, I know we are going to be fine. Mom has brought her into the family.

EPILOGUE

Toni

GRADUATION IS something I had only dreamed of. I was working for it, but hidden in the back of my mind, I wasn't sure if it would really happen for someone like me. We worked so hard to get me to cross the stage. With Garrett's help, I've come to see I may not have had the 'normal' family, but I had all the support I needed. I didn't just get the support, but I gave it, too. We all worked in tandem to ensure we were taken care of. According to Garrett, this is exactly what family does: work together for the success of the whole.

A knock on the door breaks me out of my thoughts.

"We're here!" Mrs. Anders walks in with Mr. Anders behind her.

She comes straight for me, hugging me tightly. "I'm so proud of you," she whispers in my ear. Four simple words bring tears to my eyes. A woman I've only known for about six months has become one of my biggest cheerleaders. I have been able to share so much with her without judgment.

She has acted as more of a mom to me in this short time than my own mom has. I texted my mom the graduation date and time, but I have not heard back from her.

"Do I get a hug, too?" Garrett whines, coming out of his bedroom.

"You said when we started dating, you were sharing," I tease him back as I let his mom go so she can congratulate him also.

"Your mom insisted on stopping by before we head to the graduation. We are on our way. When are you all leaving?" Mr. Anders pipes in, trying to get us all to hurry.

"We are leaving now," Garrett answers.

Who knew crossing a stage could fill you with so much pride? I wonder if everyone who walks feels this way, too, or if it is just me because of where I came from. I want to skip all the way back to my seat, but think better of it and continue walking but did wave in the direction of where I can hear my name being yelled.

"I told you." Alex comes up to me after the ceremony, hugging me.

"You did." I hold onto him. "You are the main reason I'm here. Thank you."

"Nah. It was your brains." He pulls away, not wanting to accept my gratitude.

Whether he accepts he did so much for me or not, I will always be there for him saving us. He has never asked for anything in return for all he does to keep the family moving forward. He could have been lost in the barrage of drugs and gangs, but he stayed smart and dealt without being lost, always thinking about the end game of surviving, not building a fucking *Scarface* empire.

This is another thing I have to thank the Anders for. Mr.

Anders has encouraged Alex to get his GED. He is working on a couple of classes and will be testing this summer. Mr. Anders has even given him a job on the ranch. He is learning about being a ranch hand. It's not glamorous work, but it has made him happy—an honest dollar made and not having to worry about the cops knocking down your door to arrest you.

Javie is so good with his hands he found a paid apprentice job with a welder. Who knew welders were in such high demand and made a really comfortable living?

The Anders' ranch is not too far from Guela's house. They just jump on the freeway and, in about thirty minutes, they are there. Garrett told me he passed my neighborhood on the freeway all his life and never thought about what was concealed behind the rundown shopping centers. Maybe we can leave the hood. Maybe it doesn't have the hold I always thought it did. Maybe it's just wanting it bad enough and working for it. That's really it. Working for it. When things get rough, many quit, not weathering the storm.

"I need to get my ass in gear, too!" Lola comes up to me, hugging and kissing my cheek. Her immeasurable positivity is a fresh welcome to my life. My doomsday mentality can take a break with her around.

"You do. No more breaks to find yourself. I think the you you are is perfect." I hug her back. This friendship, one of trust and mutual respect, is something I will always treasure.

As Alex requested, I stayed away from the hood parties I was so inclined to join before. I would crawl back to the hood —the only place I thought I deserved. I never felt like I fit into this 'normal' life until Garrett and Lola forced me to re-evaluate it. I tried talking to Amelia on a few occasions to encourage her to finish her Associate's degree and to kick her piece-of-shit boyfriend out. She didn't take to kindly to my 'judgment' and stopped speaking to me.

You never know whether the moments that pass us by will

be a monumental part of our life. We go about our daily lives as always, never knowing how or when the people we meet or the experiences we have will shape us. Life is just one big experiment. A bunch of trials and errors, hoping they lead you to prosperity.

I wish my mom was here. To hear her say, just once, she is proud of me is all I ask but not something I will get. I'm not surprised she didn't show, but it still stings a bit. But even with this small hole, I am happy. This content feeling full of joy is strange but very welcome.

Garrett is talking quietly to his dad a few steps away from the group. I hope all is well, because I've learned they are the same and can clash at times. At that moment, they both turn to face me, smiling. That's a good sign.

Garrett comes to stand right in front of me. "I am so incredibly proud and happy for you." He places a small kiss on my lips then drops down on one knee. He holds out his hand, holding a beautiful solitaire engagement ring.

"I don't want to spend my life with anyone but you. Will you do me the honor of being my wife?"

Stunned at his request, I am speechless at first. This can really be my life. "Yes," I respond happily.

Garrett saved me. Not by being the knight in shining armor who whisked me off to the castle, but by opening up my heart. Showing me what true love, respect, and trust looks like.

AFTERWORD

I have included the first two chapters of Tragically Beautiful
for you. You can find it after About the Author.

ACKNOWLEDGMENTS

First of all I need to thank my family. To my husband who tolerates my face constantly focused on my computer screen, I love you and would not be chasing this big dream without your support. To my daughter who I want to model chasing dreams and working hard. I want her to know the world can be hers as long as she works for it. To my dad who continues to be proud even if he doesn't quite understand or enjoy the genre I write. To my mom who I miss everyday, who enjoyed reading just as much as I do.

Next I need to thank my alpha readers. Shirley, Adelina and Selena, THANK YOU! Without your kind words and critique I would have stayed stuck. I was so nervous turning it in to the editor. The story changed so much from when I first began, I doubted myself.

Thank you to the indie community. It has been a wonderful adventure filled with ups and downs, but through it all these amazing authors are there supporting, cheering, answering questions, etc...

But there are two indie authors I especially have to thank, Melanie A. Smith and Maria Ann Green. These two amazing ladies have helped me throughout this process. They have offered words of encouragement, helpful ideas, feedback, and actual hands on help. Go read their books! I promise, you won't be disappointed.

A huge THANK YOU and SHOUT OUT to Maria Ann Green! She jumped in and helped me complete my book cover when I was battling software and losing. I have her to thank for completing the amazing cover I began.

To all the readers, bookstagrammers, bloggers, reviewers THANK YOU. I am amazed with the time and energy everyone spends sharing the books they love. The books that transport them. The books they get lost in.

ABOUT THE AUTHOR

Tori Alvarez is an educator by day and an author by night. A daydreamer by heart, she finally began writing the stories that would play in her head.

Tori writes real, honest romance with a hint of steam. She is a sucker for happily ever afters, so you will always find them in her books too.

Tori is a Texas girl born and raised. She lives in South Central Texas with her husband, teen daughter, dog & cat.

You can follow her at:
Website & Newsletter Sign up:
http://www.torialvarez.com

facebook.com/tori.alvarez.3551

instagram.com/mstorialvarez

goodreads.com/torialvarez

pinterest.com/mstorialvarez

bookbub.com/profile/tori-alvarez

Tragically Beautiful

A Graffiti Hearts Book

ALEJANDRO

17 Years Ago

Listening and being quiet was the easiest way to find out the secrets our parents kept from us. They were always so focused on their discussion, they didn't pay attention to their surroundings. Things have never been easy, and I'm only ten. I listen because I like to know what struggle is coming my way so I can plan for it.

Like when my dad loses his job again. Or when mom stays out too late with her friends. Or when we don't have money to pay rent. I know this is when he gets drunk and mean. It is best for Javie and I to stay away. I've taken one too many beatings for being in the wrong place at the wrong time or jumping in for Javie, but he was too little to take it. It's my job as his big brother to protect him.

Javie and I are on the couch, watching TV as Dad walks into the apartment, stumbling around drunk. As soon as I see him, I tell Javie to go to our room and close the door. Mom isn't home, and that will set him off.

"Where's your bitch of a mother?" he yells after coming back into the living room from his bedroom.

I shake my head and raise my shoulders, not knowing where she went. Any words leaving my mouth will be used against me.

"She didn't have work today. Shouldn't she be taking care of her damn kids?" he spits out angrily.

I always wonder why he calls us "her" kids. Aren't we his kids too? I stand slowly to make myself scarce while he is looking in the fridge. Just as I enter our bedroom, the front door opens. I close the door quickly and crouch in the corner hidden out of their view to listen.

"Where the hell have you been? Out whoring?" Dad starts in right away.

"Out. Why the hell do you care anyway?" She responds casually.

I know this is going to get bad. I hope I can make it into the room quickly enough to hide Javie if he comes this way. I just can't move yet, I need to know what is going to happen. Güela will need to come pick us up if this was going to be one of their explosions.

"Because you're my fuckin' *vieja*. You should be home when I get home. Have a fuckin' meal ready and take care of the damn kids." He shouts.

"You can make yourself something to eat," she calmly states. Today is different. She usually gives it back just as hard as he dishes.

"What the fuck, puta." He goes straight to calling her bitch, the one name he knows sets her off.

"I'm leaving. Just thought I would let you know." Her voice is flat, uncaring. I want to peek around the corner to look at her, but I can't risk being seen.

"What do you mean you're leaving?" Her statement catches him off guard; he sounds confused.

"Leaving you. I'm done." I hear her take a deep breath. "I thought it would be different. You said it was going to be different. We were going to make things happen. But here we are, still stuck. Getting evicted every year. No money. Having to move in with your mom or my parents. Stuck with two kids."

Stuck with two kids? Did she not want us?

My dad is silent. All the fight he just had in him was let out with her words.

"I don't understand."

And he didn't. I don't know if they loved each other really. They got pregnant with me in high school. And like any good Mexican family in the hood, you kept the baby and got married. My parents dropped out of high school to start working.

"*No puedo.* It's too hard."

A few seconds later I hear the front door open and close. I crawl to our bedroom door and sneak in. I wasn't sure if his anger would show soon, so I put Javie in the closet, and I laid on the bed. Best he finds me, not him.

CHAPTER ONE
ALEJANDRO (ALEX)

NOVEMBER

Hospitals are foreign to me. I have never had to set foot in one until today. That's a strange thought. A twenty-seven-year-old man who has never been in a hospital must not be normal. But here I am. In an uncomfortable seat, waiting patiently for news about my grandmother. My cousin Antonia is leaning against me, and my brother Javier is on her other side. I don't know how long we've been sitting here like statues, waiting to hear anything. Inside me the panic is raging, but I will never show this to either of them. I promised myself a long time ago I would take care of them, and I have done just that.

The waiting room door opens, and I'm greeted by the most beautiful blue eyes. A girl followed by Garrett walks in looking directly at Antonia, but I'm sure she only knows her as Toni.

"How is she?" The girl, who I can only assume is a friend of Toni's from college, asks. There is a sadness in her eyes as she inquires.

Toni straightens up and grabs her hand, squeezing. "We still don't know much." She then walks into the arms of Garrett. In spite of Toni's efforts to push him away, he is here, worry written across his face.

Blue Eyes takes the seat Toni just vacated and extends her hand to me, "I'm Lola. And which cousin are you?"

I'm mesmerized by her. Her smile is soft and caring and her eyes welcoming. I need to stop staring and answer.

"Alex. And that is my brother, Javie, over there." I point to the corner of the room where he'd moved when they walked in. She turns to him, lifting her hand in a small wave.

"Have you heard anything?" She turns back to me asking.

"They are running tests, but they think it was a stroke. She still hasn't woken up." Toni answers before I have a chance to open my mouth.

"Can we get you anything?" Lola offers, her eyes full of worry.

"I'm good," Toni answers, "but I need a few minutes."

I watch as Toni walks out with Garrett in tow. She needs to try and make that relationship work. I know she doesn't want to trust him, but she needs people in her life who are not tethered to the hood.

Lola stays in the seat next to me. She's fiddling with her hands nervously. I'm probably not the type of guy she's accustomed to being around. I stand up to give her space. She looks up at me as I do. I force myself to turn away because it feels like I could get lost in her eyes.

"We're good here if you have to go," I tell her, giving her an out. She probably didn't plan on being in a room with a couple of thugs.

"I'm fine. I want to be here for Toni," she answers, her voice soft.

Silence surrounds us. Javie is pacing now, making circles around the room, and I have taken up residence in a corner.

After several long, tense minutes of trying to avoid looking in Lola's direction, I hear her ask, "Are y'all okay with me being here? I can wait for Toni out in the hall if you'd rather."

"It's fine. Sorry, am I making you nervous pacing?" Javie goes to sit by her.

Lola gives him a genuine smile that makes her eyes dance.

"You didn't make me nervous. Y'all were just so quiet, I wasn't sure if I was the reason."

A twinge of hate bubbles knowing he's close to her and I'm not. I shake my head. What the fuck? Caring whether Javie is by some chick I just met? I drop my head side to side, cracking my neck to let the frustration out. There's too much going on right now. That's all that is.

"My brother is not one for many words." There is a teasing to his voice. He's flirting with her.

"Oh."

"You'll get used to it." He shrugs his shoulders.

Why in the hell would she need to? I think to myself. It's not like she will be spending any time with us.

———

It's been a month since Güela passed away, and there has already been so much change. Charity is not a word or action I humbly accept. The whole concept makes me feel weak. Out of control. Incapable. Those are feelings I avoid at all cost. I take care of my family, end of story. Until I can't. While I'm grateful Garrett has accepted Toni and all she hid from him, including us and the hood life we were brought up in, I hate knowing he and his family took care of so many things when Güela passed. He has the monetary resources to jump in and resolve any and all of the obstacles we came across.

Güela's house is now ours, Toni's, Javie's, and mine, thanks to his lawyer. My alcoholic deadbeat dad and Toni's money-hungry mother were circling like vultures, ready to swoop in and sell. They would have blown through the money in record time.

I feel obligated to him now, and I hate owing people. You never know when they are going to cash in and what you will be expected to do. I like to be the one in power. I like to be the one owed.

This neighborhood has taught me how to survive. I may not have much money, but I sure do hold power status with the connections I have made. I listened and learned the ways. I never pushed for more, letting my work speak for itself. Too bad my dumbass dad ruined it for me and I had to give up the business. Asshole is probably going to prison for his last fuckup, getting busted for selling weed at a bar.

Now I don't know what I'm going to do. Toni is insistent I don't go back to selling. But if I don't sell, how in the hell is a high-school dropout supposed to make money?

The front door opens, interrupting my thoughts. Toni walks in with Lola close behind.

"Hey," Toni says casually, walking toward the hallway to the back room. She came home last Friday too. She goes into Güela's room with Lola, and they spend time in there. I haven't asked why, but I figure it's her way of coping.

Lola looks at me as her lips pull in a small smile. She lifts her hand up giving me a quick wave. I nod in return, acknowledging her. I have not really spoken to her. What's the point? I'm still mesmerized by her beauty, but that's all it is. Pure physical attraction, and I can get that anywhere.

Lola

The past few weeks have been hard on Toni. Her family dysfunction has surprised me a couple of times, but I think I was able to hide my reactions. I don't want my naivety to jeopardize our friendship. I'm glad she finally began to trust Garrett. He's been her rock and helped carry her burden. He has more knowledge in terms of what needed to be done.

"Pizza tonight?" Toni asks. We are laying in her grand-mother's bed. This has become our new normal for Friday nights. The grief of losing her grandmother still heavy, she copes by coming to her house on the southside to spend time with her cousins.

Meeting Toni's cousins was a shock. I don't know what I expected, but they were not it. It is not fair to have that much beauty in one family. She's gorgeous and the guys...wow. Speechless. It is strange how different they each are. Javie is unassuming and caring. He is easy to talk to and makes you feel welcome. Toni is strong-willed and speaks her mind freely and often. Alex...he's...breathtaking. Since meeting him, I have not seen him show any emotion. When he walks into the room, he owns it. During all the turmoil they have had to endure, I have not seen him cry once. Not lose his temper. Not break down. He is a rock.

"Sure," I answer her. I always want tacos from the taqueria down the street, but everyone told me last weekend they were done with Taco Fridays. "Is your boyfriend leaving for the ranch tomorrow?"

I love to call Garrett her boyfriend since she tried to avoid it for so long. It took a bit for her to adjust to his status. His family owns the biggest cattle ranch in Texas, so they are wealthy. It is hard for Toni to trust him because she feels less-than since she grew up in poverty. He keeps reminding her she is more than enough.

"Not this weekend. I have to go to his stupid fraternity party tomorrow." She also hates the fraternity parties.

"But I'll be there." I prop myself up to look down at her. She's still laying on her back, staring at the ceiling. The usual when we arrive, she spends several quiet minutes becoming extremely acquainted with the ceiling. I know she's letting herself drown in grief since I was there a few years ago when my mother passed. I just lend my silent presence. She always asks about dinner when she's ready to move on.

She rolls her eyes, sits up, and makes her way out of bed, so I follow her.

"Pizza night," she announces to the room, where Alex, Javie, and Garrett are watching TV.

"Really?" Javie questions.

"Yes," I answer moodily. "I'll give up one Friday since it seems everyone voted behind my back." I couldn't hold the smile back.

It's strange, but this tiny home has quickly become my favorite place to be. But it's not really the home; it's the people inside that make it a safe space.

"I'll call it in. What do y'all want?" Garrett says.

"Nah. I'll go get it," Alex announces.

Once Alex makes a decision, no one ever questions it. He rarely lets anyone take the lead. I saw how hard it was for him to accept all the help Garrett and his parents gave. He wanted to be able to handle everything that came at them after his grandmother's passing. But all of it required money. Money that they didn't have. His posture changed around Garrett when he was having to accept money. His presence wasn't quite as large. It was a miniscule change, but watching him constantly, I've picked up on a few things.

Now that things have settled and the three of them own their grandmother's house, I have watched him step up more. His demeanor stronger, more powerful.

"Make sure you add jalapenos to it," Toni chimes in.

I go into the kitchen for a water as Alex walks in behind me. He begins rummaging through a drawer filled with junk.

"What are you looking for?" I ask as I watch him taking all kinds of papers out.

He doesn't answer, so I take the couple of steps to him and look up at his face. "Need help finding something?"

"I'm fine. You can go to the living room with everyone." He seems to always dismiss me. I can't remember a time that we were in the same room alone.

"You look frazzled. If you tell me what you are looking for, I can help. You know girls are better finders than guys are, right?" My mom said that often. My dad would complain about a lost item, and my mom would find it in seconds.

He finally looks down at me, glaring. "I've got it."

"Fine." I spin around, mad that he has dismissed me again.

As much as I want to get close to him, he keeps me at a distance. I walk back out into the living room and take a seat on the couch by Javie. Unlike his brother, Javie has welcomed me with open arms. I thought he was flirting with me when we first met, but it has quickly turned into a comfortable platonic relationship. He's easy to talk to.

"Are you going to the fraternity party Toni's been complaining about?" Javie asks me.

"Yup. Wanna go?" I ask him. I'm part of Greek life, but I'm not happy in that environment. I go through the motions because that's what's expected, I guess.

"To a fraternity party?" Javie releases a booming laugh. "Nah. I don't think I would be welcome there." His smile is kind.

I don't know why I invited him. He would probably stick out, but not as much as his brother. They are both ruggedly good-looking, but Javie's personality is friendly. Alex somehow announces sex and danger. And as much as his body language silently yells to stay away, I just want to get closer.

"I don't know about 'not welcome,' but most of them are a bunch of conceited a-holes," I agree.

Alex walks out of the kitchen to the front door, announcing, "I'll be back."

I wonder if he's this cold all the time or only in front of me.

CHAPTER TWO
ALEX

FEBRUARY

I'm crawling out of a bed I shouldn't be in to make my way home. I refuse to spend the night with any girl because I don't want anyone to get false hope for a potential relationship. I've never been in an exclusive relationship. No one has ever excited me enough to want to be.

I sit on the bed, sliding on my boots on, when Cara walks out of the bathroom and stands in front of me. She pushes my knees open to slide herself closer to me. My gaze travels up her nude body.

"Where are you going?" She is trying to act nonchalant, but I can clearly hear the hurt. Fuck.

"I gotta get home." I grab her hips and pull her closer letting my face fall between her round, large breasts, kissing softly. Her head falls back as she relishes the attention.

"Stay here," she says, in a slightly whiny voice.

"Not today. Maybe next time." I try and soften the blow. I nibble up to her mouth.

Her arms wrap tightly around my neck. She's trying her

best to keep me here. I grab the backs of her thighs, picking her up, and she wraps her legs around my waist. I can't deny she is hot. Her kisses move down to my neck, and I feel the sucking. She is trying to mark me to keep others away.

Hickeys. The mark of the neighborhood. If someone has one, they are taken. The last one I gave and received was before I dropped out of high school. I haven't been interested in anyone enough to give one, and I sure as hell won't get one. I turn around, quickly laying her down so I can separate us.

I place one last kiss on her lips picking my shirt up off the bed to slide it on.

"Fine." She quickly pulls the sheet to cover her naked body.

"I'll see you later." If I would have known she was going to stick so quickly, I would have avoided her like the damn plague. I have no time for this shit in my life.

The drive home is quick. A small neighborhood tucked away, hidden from the rest of the city. A dirty secret never to be revealed. Burglar bars, graffiti, frequent bus stops, run-down buildings—that's my life. What has always been my life and what will always be my life.

I park on the street in front of a small, old house. The only home that has provided stability in this shit place.

I fall into bed, my head spinning from the alcohol as a memory of Güela hits. I know I can't keep this shit up indefinitely; I just don't have a way out.

"Who were you with last night?" Toni asks.

"No one important." Which is the truth.

"Who is no one?" She will continue until I answer. She may be my cousin, but after growing up together she is more like a baby sister. Güela took us all in when our piece-of-shit parents didn't grow up and threw us on her doorstep.

"Does it matter?" I take the seat across the table from her.

She finally looks up from her laptop, the one I bought her so she would have her own for college, closes it, and stares at me. She is the only one who will bust my balls on my life decisions.

Javie and I have been living with Güela since I was ten and he was eight. Toni's mom had already left her at Güela's. So it's been us three with a grandmother since then.

"Yes."

"April. New to the hood." I lean back waiting for her to start.

"April..." She lets the name hang. "So what is April like, and when can I meet her?"

Since I won't be seeing her again, I answer, "You won't be meeting her."

"Why not?"

"Because I'm not dating her."

"But you'll have sex with her? What does she need to do to keep your attention?" She shakes her head in disapproval.

"Why not?" I shrug not in the mood for this conversation. "And as for my attention...I guess no one is interesting enough to keep it..."

"No tienes verguenza?" Güela turns on me, disappointed in my lack of shame.

"Si ellas la van a dar, la tomaré. (If they are going to give it, I'll take it.)" I answer Güela.

In return she slaps the back of my head with her hand. "Y cuando te vengan embarazadas? Qué vas a hacer? (And when they come to you pregnant? What are you going to do?)" she questions. I know she worries. We shouldn't be having this conversation now.

"Condoms. Always use condoms." There is no other answer I have for her.

Toni and Javie bust out laughing at the bluntness I just displayed. Güela, not so much, because she gives my head another slap with a dish towel this time.

"But for real, Toni. I don't know what will keep my attention. I just know no one has."

I don't know what I was thinking, but having sex with Cara did not erase Lola from my thoughts like I thought it would. She has become a permanent fixture around the house the past few months, and the more she's around, the harder it's getting to control thinking about her and keep her at a distance. It seems like she wants to get close, but I can't let her. She deserves a man who can take care of her, and I have nothing to offer. Life isn't passing out options in my direction.

Lola

Toni, Javie, and Alex have finally decided to clean out their grandmother's room. With Toni staying at the house more often, they thought it was time. Their home is located between the university and Garrett's ranch. It makes it easier for Garrett when he's coming back into town from ranch. Toni is going to take over her grandmother's room, so we are going through her closet and drawers to separate things the family will keep or donate.

I am watching her as she looks at every item she holds. Her eyes close, and I can imagine a memory flooding her mind. She is incredibly strong. It took a couple of years for me to build the courage and go through my mother's belongings. My dad had everything boxed up until we were ready to sit together.

Toni and I are alone in the room. The guys wanted to give Toni some time alone. They said they had each already come in and had their moment. I wonder how Alex handled his time. Did he finally let himself break down? I wish I could see behind his tough exterior. He is always cool and collected; life never seems to rattle him.

Toni and Javie follow his lead in all matters. They work together, but nothing is done until Alex gives the final approval. He is head of this household. Envy has creeped up on me a couple of times watching how Garrett fawns over Toni and Alex is her protector. But I want Alex as so much more than my protector.

"OMG," Toni exclaims happily. "Maybe Alex did act like a kid once upon a time."

She hands me an old photo of a young Alex jumping on a couch laughing while their grandmother watched him from a distance. My eyes are glued to his young, happy, carefree face. I know life wasn't easy for them, but I wonder why he feels he can show no one his true self. This mask of a man can't be the whole person.

She snatches the picture out of my hands and stands up before leaving the room. I follow her to see what she's going to do. Alex is in the kitchen, drinking a cup of black coffee, something I will never understand, and reading something on his phone.

"I found something that proves you can smile," she teases.

"And what is that?" He responds back, sounding bored and not looking in her direction.

She places the picture in front of his phone.

He glances at it. "Huh." Grabs it from her hands and tosses it on the table, going back to whatever was on his phone.

"That's it?" She's confused.

"I was a kid." He shrugs his shoulders.

Toni shakes her head, turning around walking out. I don't think he realizes I am close enough to see and hear their conversation or lack thereof. I stay frozen in my spot right outside the kitchen, watching him. He waits a couple of seconds then picks the picture up again, staring at it. I wish I could see his face, but I notice his shoulders slump just a fraction. I don't know what prompts me, but I walk up behind him and wrap my arms around him. I feel him stiffen.

A couple of seconds pass, then he pats my hand on his chest. I let him go as he stands up and turns to me. His lip pulls up on one side, a peace offering I suppose, and he walks away, leaving his coffee and the picture on the table.

It is in this moment I realize my feelings for him are growing. I knew I was physically attracted to him. My body hummed when I watched him. I was attracted to how protective he was over those he cared for. Toni and Javie had his devotion. But now I know he feels things; he just doesn't allow others to see that part of him.

Manufactured by Amazon.ca
Bolton, ON